Who can resist

Name: Steele

Codename: Azrael—"Angel of Death"—because he goes places where even angels fear to tread

Specialty: One shot, one kill

Weaknesses: Women in high heels, freedom under siege, and eBay

Profile: Prefers to work alone—except in the bedroom

Mission: Kill the bad guy, save the world, and hopefully end up with the girl

BAD ATTITUDE
A Novel

Coming September 2005 from Pocket Books

ALSO BY SHERRILYN KENYON

Tie Me Up, Tie Me Down
With Melanie George and Jaid Black

Big Guns Out of Uniform
With Liz Carlyle and Nicole Camden

SHERRILYN KENYON

BORN TO BE *BAD*

POCKET BOOKS

New York   London   Toronto   Sydney

This book is a work of fiction. Names, characters, places and incidents are products of the author's imagination or are used fictitiously. Any resemblance to actual events or locales or persons, living or dead, is entirely coincidental.

An *Original* Publication of POCKET BOOKS

POCKET BOOKS, a division of Simon & Schuster, Inc.
1230 Avenue of the Americas, New York, NY 10020

"One BAD Night" copyright © 2005 by Sherrilyn Kenyon
"'Captivated' by You" copyright © 2005 by Sherrilyn Kenyon
"BAD to the Bone" copyright © 2003 by Sherrilyn Kenyon

All rights reserved, including the right to reproduce this book or portions thereof in any form whatsoever. For information address Pocket Books, 1230 Avenue of the Americas, New York, NY 10020

ISBN-13: 978-1-4165-0750-5
ISBN-10: 1-4165-0750-7

First Pocket Books printing September 2005

10 9 8 7 6 5 4 3 2 1

POCKET and colophon are registered trademarks of Simon & Schuster, Inc.

Front cover image by Franco Accornero

Manufactured in the United States of America

For information regarding special discounts for bulk purchases, please contact Simon & Schuster Special Sales at 1-800-456-6798 or business@simonandschuster.com.

"'Captivated' by You" was originally published in *Tie Me Up, Tie Me Down* in 2005 and "BAD to the Bone" was originally published in *Big Guns Out of Uniform* in 2003 by Pocket Books.

CONTENTS

ONE BAD NIGHT

CHAPTER 1

If sin had a proper name, it would be Jason Banks. He was what Samantha Winslow's mother would call sex-on-a-stick, and as much as she hated to admit it, Sam wouldn't mind taking a bite out of him.

In more ways than one.

But then she wasn't the only woman who felt like that. He was what her mother often referred to as a man-slut. Ever on the make, he went through women faster than Sam went through panty hose. And considering that she seldom put a pair on without running them, that said it all.

He had that boyish kind of charm that could get him out of most any fix with anything female. Incredible good looks that didn't belong on a mere mortal man, and enough intelligence to get him into all manner of trouble.

And at the moment, he was in the kind of trouble that none of the above could bail him out of. The kind of trouble that was always fatal.

Sighing, Sam stared at the picture of him in her

hand, taken by their surveillance team last week as he left his flat in London for a rendezvous with a group of known European terrorists.

He wore a pair of dark designer sunglasses that hid his devilishly green, taunting eyes. His dark brown hair was tousled around his head, but then he always wore it a bit shaggy. She was one of the few people who knew that he paid a small fortune for that supposedly lackadaisical cut that fell perfectly around his sculpted face.

The black leather jacket and turtleneck he wore only added to the air of dangerousness that enveloped him. A dangerousness that was belied by his charming smile.

He was gorgeous. No doubt about it. What a waste that something so hot was about to be extinguished.

She jumped as her cell phone rang from the black leather car seat beside her.

Picking it up, Samantha flipped it open and answered it.

"Have you seen him yet?"

She let out a small growl at the sound of Retter's dispassionate voice as she scanned the empty dark street where she was parked. "I'm waiting for him to show now."

"C'mon, Sam. Don't get cold feet on me. If you can't finish this, tell me now so I can do it for you.

We have to make sure, no matter what, that our target is neutralized."

"Don't worry. I know what my mission is, and I understand why I have to do it. The Road Runner is through this time. I told you I'd take care of it, and I will."

"Good." The line went dead.

Samantha sighed as she tucked her phone into her pocket and glanced wistfully at Jason's picture. He was about to become one seriously unhappy double agent.

But she had a job to do, and that was her top priority. Jason knew their code, and he knew the rules.

So did she.

Return with your shield or upon it. If you betrayed the Bureau, the Bureau would exact full retribution.

After all, they weren't called BAD without reason. Originally the acronym had stood solely for Bureau of American Defense, but since their inception, they had taken BAD to heart and it had become a way of life for all of them.

You screwed BAD, and BAD screwed you. The entire lot of them were renegades who lived solely for their missions. This wasn't a job to them; it was a way of life and a code of honor they held dearly.

And Jason had betrayed them.

Now it was time to make him pay.

After laying the picture aside, Samantha screwed

the silencer onto her weapon and held it in her lap while she waited for Jason to enter the street. She was outside his favorite club in Berlin, a known terrorist hangout where all sorts of riffraff from all over the world liked to gather and sell their secrets.

It was here that Jason had given over the name of one of their BAD operatives: Hunter Wesley Thornton-Payne. A name that truly suited the self-centered, proselytizing prick. But prick or not, Hunter was one of them.

That had been the week before Jason had blown Hunter's car into pieces to show the terrorists that he was on their side.

It had been a stupid thing to do.

The door to the club opened.

Samantha froze as she saw Jason coming out. She curled her lip at the sight of him draped around two of the sleaziest-looking women she'd ever seen and given the fact she'd been raised among strippers, that said a lot.

She studied his lips as he talked to them so that she could understand what was going on.

"So we're going back to your place, huh?" he asked the artificial redhead on his right in German. "Are you sure your daddy won't come home and disturb us?"

"Oh, no, he's gone until Monday."

Jason smiled wickedly.

Just keep smiling, asshole. Samantha aimed the infrared at his chest.

Jason froze as he saw the red dot suddenly appear on his black sweater, then quickly shoved the women away from him. He reached for his weapon, which was concealed at the small of his back.

Samantha squeezed off two rounds before he could even draw it and watched as they hit him dead in his heart. She was, after all, the best shot in her class. It was why Joe had recruited her from the FBI to work for BAD.

That and the fact that she was a workaholic who didn't let anything like ethics, laws, or morals stand in the way of doing her job.

Jason staggered back as a dark red stain spread over his chest. His eyes large, he fell to the sidewalk. The women with him screamed and ran back toward the club.

Samantha whipped her car around and sped toward him. Parking it next to where he'd fallen, she hopped out and opened the passenger door.

She moved to stand over Jason.

"Sam?" he gasped in disbelief as he struggled to breathe.

She grabbed him by his sweater and hauled him to his feet. "Get in the car, Jason. Now!"

They were running out of time.

He staggered a few steps before she shoved him

roughly into the seat, slammed the door shut, then ran to get in as a group of bouncers came running from the club.

Gunning the engine, she whipped her rented car through a back alleyway, far away from the scene. Sirens rent the air. Hopefully no one had caught a good look at her or her car before they notified the authorities.

If they had, she was screwed.

Jason lay in the seat beside her, panting in pain.

"Keep breathing, you lousy bastard," she said to him. "I want you to suffer before you die."

Jason was trying to make sense of words that seemed to come to him out of a hazy fog. He felt so strange. So weird. He'd been shot before, but it hadn't felt like this.

His body didn't respond to anything, and his breathing seemed to have a ten-second delay.

All he could focus on was Sam's angry face. Of course she would be angry. She didn't know the truth, and he couldn't afford to let her learn it.

"Sam?"

"Shut up, asshole. I don't want to hear anything from you right now."

He licked his lips, which were suddenly chapped from dryness. Streetlights streaked across Sam's angry face as she whipped them through the Berlin streets.

There was an air of calmness to her that belied the

anger in her tone and the tight grip she had on the steering wheel. She wasn't classically beautiful, but there had always been something about her that had appealed to him.

But not at the moment. At the moment, he wanted to kill her for this.

"Where are we going, Sam?" he tried again.

She cast a glare at him that was bone-chilling. "Just shut up and die."

Jason closed his eyes as a wave of nausea consumed him. Fine. They were enemies, then; it was her choice, not his.

Unable to fight the darkness that wanted to drag him under, he surrendered himself to it and let it take him.

Samantha breathed a sigh of relief as they reached the warehouse apartment she had rented under an unknown alias. They would be safe here, at least long enough for her to interrogate Mr. Banks and find out the truth about Hunter's "death."

She woke him up enough so that he could assist her in getting him into the building, but not so much that he could fight her. Jason was a large man who could snap her neck and leave her dead faster than she could say "Boo."

That was if she gave him the chance.

Samantha wasn't a fool.

They staggered toward the elevators that took her upstairs to her apartment. It wasn't easy directing him, since he kept trying to fall down, but after a few minutes she had him inside the small apartment.

She led him to the full-sized bed and allowed him to collapse onto it. He fell right back into his drug-induced sleep. Good. That would give her time to make a few preparations for when he came to.

Samantha wasted no time in removing his leather jacket, sweater, and T-shirt, then handcuffing his arms to the wrought-iron headboard. She used his shirt to mop up the red gel from his chest that had exploded when she'd shot him with the tranquilizers. It was designed to look like blood in case he was under surveillance by their enemies at the time she shot him. They had to make it look as real as possible.

The last thing either of them needed was for someone to know he wasn't dead . . . yet.

Sam hesitated as she reached for his fly. It was suddenly disconcerting to undress an unconscious man. Really, it should be easy, but it wasn't. It was like she was invading his privacy or something.

You've got no choice.

She had to strip him down for both their sakes. He could have a bug hidden in anything. All of his clothing had to be destroyed before the bad guys found them.

Biting her lip, she forced her hands to unbutton his jeans. It wasn't as if she were a virgin, or she hadn't done this with other guys.

Still, it felt odd. Bizarre.

Especially once she had his pants pulled off.

"Whoa." She breathed in awe as she ran her gaze over his long, lean, muscular body, covered with deep, tawny skin. His shoulders were wide and sculpted like a gymnast. Even while unconscious, he had a well-defined eight-pack of abs she could do laundry on.

She'd never really looked at a guy's legs before, but Jason's were remarkable. Well muscled and athletic and dappled with dark hairs, they were quite a pleasing sight.

Who was she fooling? They were more than pleasing, they damn near begged her to fondle him.

Honestly, she'd expected him to go commando. He seemed the type of guy who wouldn't wear any kind of underwear. But in total contradiction to his "rules and decency be damned" attitude, he wore a pair of white-and-blue-striped cotton boxers. There was something strangely old-fashioned about his choice, and that was completely at odds with what she knew about this man.

God, you are scrumptious, she thought as she took in

the sight of him lying on the bed. His darkly tanned flesh was smooth and dimpled over the muscles she knew he worked hard to perfect.

There wasn't an ounce of extra fat anywhere on him. He was the perfect specimen of male flesh, and it was all she could do not to scale all six feet of him and lay herself over him like a blanket.

That image hovered in her mind, making her whole being burn. Every female hormone in her body begged her to rub herself against him. To taste those lips that were parted ever so slightly while he breathed.

To dip her hand through the small slit of his boxers, through his short, crisp hairs, to see if he really was as large as he appeared, and to stroke him until he was hard and begging her to take him.

What would he taste like?

Feel like?

Sam shook her head.

Get a grip! What the hell is wrong with you? Yes, he looked good, but she had a job to do, and if she didn't get it done, they could both die. Not to mention the small fact that he was a traitor who had come way too close to killing Hunter. But for Hunter's lazy habit of starting his car by remote, the agent would be dead now.

And Jason would have been the one who killed him.

Growling from her wayward lust, Samantha forced herself to strip those boxers off and cover him with a blanket. This wasn't the time to get personal with Jason.

It was time to get serious. And seriousness dictated that she keep herself calm and cool toward a man she fully intended to kill.

CHAPTER 2

Jason was dreaming of a luscious, naked nymph with long brown hair that she whipped over his body to torment him. Each lash of the silken strands against his bare skin made his body jerk with painful need. She had deep chocolate brown eyes that pierced him with anger and with a potent desire he'd never expected.

She ran her long, manicured nails over him, scraping his skin in a bittersweet pleasure that caused him to arch his back, aching for more of her touch. He wanted her to kiss him, but every time she came close to his lips, she would veer off with a teasing laugh.

His nipples hardened as her breath fell against them.

"Sam," he said under his breath, wanting her to sate the lust she'd stoked.

Instead of easing him, she pulled back with a sadistic laugh and vanished into a cloud of cold, dark smoke.

Jason came awake to a fierce pounding ache in his skull. His arms were sore, and his chest throbbed. The tendrils of his dream hung on the fringes of his memory, but the pain in his body caused it to flee entirely. It was a full minute before he remembered what had actually happened to him outside the club.

Someone had shot him in cold blood.

Confused anger gripped him as he recalled Sam shoving him into the car and then her rude behavior toward him as he tried to explain to her what had happened. Why he'd betrayed them.

She'd refused to listen.

As he tried to move, he realized someone had handcuffed him. Frowning, he twisted his body to find himself stripped completely bare on a full-sized wrought-iron bed in a room he'd never seen before.

It was cold and uninviting, with a minimal amount of furnishings that said it was only a temporary place and not someone's home. One lone lightbulb shone brightly over his head, casting weird shadows on the faded yellow wallpaper. He could hear the faint sound of a television set with a program in German seeping through the walls, along with misplaced male laughter. The air was damp and musty, as if the room needed to be aired out.

Whose place was he in? How had he gotten here?

He could recall a few hazy images—stairs that made him stagger . . . a red door. But none of it made sense, and he damned sure didn't remember a bed or bedroom.

Had Sam brought him here?

Or had someone else cuffed him?

He wasn't sure if he should be scared or pissed. Deciding on the latter, he tried to pull himself free.

He still wasn't one hundred percent sure if Sam had been the one who shot him or not. Maybe she'd saved him after someone else had opened fire on him.

Granted, that wasn't likely, but who knew? Everything had happened so fast that he still wasn't sure about anything other than leaving the club with the two women who were going to take him into the lion's den. He'd been so close to finding his target and arresting him . . .

But after seeing the red sights on his chest and feeling the impact of a bullet, he couldn't really remember the rest of the details clearly. Things had happened too rapidly.

For that matter, he wasn't sure how long he'd been unconscious.

As he looked at his chest and saw the remnants of red dye on his skin, he decided that it must have been Sam who shot him after all. Who else would have gone that far for a charade?

For some reason, the shooting had been a ruse. One that seriously ticked him off, since it had interfered with his case. Damn it!

Then again, given what he'd done in London to

Hunter, he was lucky one of the BAD agents hadn't killed him tonight. But he had trusted Retter, his European BAD contact, to understand what he'd been doing.

If he hadn't . . .

Well, he'd be lucky to be in one piece come dawn.

Jason tightened his hands around the cuffs that were secured to the iron and tried again to pull himself free of the headboard.

Damn, it held.

"So, you're finally awake."

He paused at the sound of the silken voice that went over his body like a lover's caress. What was it about Sam's southern drawl that set him on fire? It always had, even though she herself wasn't the kind of woman he normally found appealing. Stern and somber, she took everything way too seriously.

Most times, she kept that accent under wraps, but whenever he heard it peeping through . . .

He burned.

"At your beck and call," he said in a light tone that contradicted his serious mood and situation. "You know, Sam, when women handcuff me naked to the bed, they usually make sure I'm awake for the pleasure of it."

Her eyes narrowed ever so slightly as her cheeks pinkened. He had to give her credit, she was beautiful like that.

He grinned at her. "You didn't have to go to all this trouble, love. If you wanted my body, all you had to do was ask."

Samantha glared at him. "You and that arrogance . . ."

He wiggled his brows at her. "Yeah, but it makes you want me even more, doesn't it?"

Her tense expression didn't waver. "Want you dead, you mean."

He scoffed at her. "You wouldn't really kill me."

Before he could blink, she pulled her weapon out from the holster at the small of her back and angled it at his temple. "There you're wrong, Mr. Banks," she said from between clenched teeth.

Jason sobered as her sweet breath fell against his cheek. Gambling and women were two things he knew extremely well, and gambling on women and their motivations had never failed him.

He'd never lost at a game of chance or bluff.

"Am I?" he asked, arching his brow at her. "If you wanted me dead, I have a feeling I'd be in my grave now, not tied naked to your bed."

Her brown eyes sparked fire an instant before she pulled back and dropped her weapon back in its holster. "Is there no limit to your arrogance? Why are you not afraid of me?"

He shrugged. "I know people. I understand them."

"You don't know *me*."

"Sure I do," Jason said, raking a slow, penetrating glance over her body. He'd known her from the moment Joe had first introduced them. Sam had been completely uptight and overly serious, yet he'd seen through her veneer.

Intrigued by her lack of humor, he'd done some checking on her background and found out exactly why she was so hard-nosed.

"You were the studious daughter who was appalled by your mother's wild ways as she sought one more good time. While she went out at night with another 'uncle,' you stayed home, convinced that your education would buy you out of your run-down apartment and save you from being another pregnant sixteen-year-old destined for minimum-wage jobs and revolving husbands. You could only afford college through scholarships and the GI Bill, so you wrapped yourself up in textbooks while playing weekend warrior until you were recruited by the FBI." He paused to rake a meaningful look over her. "Did you ever once go out drinking in college with your friends?"

Samantha stiffened at his eerily correct recitation of her life. It bothered her a lot more than she cared for. "Shut up, Jason."

"Why?"

Because he was telling the truth, and she hated him for it. Why was he able to see what she'd hidden from everyone else? No wonder he was cocky. He really could see straight into people's souls.

"You know," she said coldly, "I think killing you might be enjoyable after all."

Even through her anger, Jason could tell he'd struck a nerve with her. A painful one. It was a curse he'd inherited from his Romanian mother, his ability to sum up people with an unerring accuracy. His mother had blamed it on her Romany blood. Maybe some of that was true, but Jason had never really believed in any hokum.

But in his professional life, the ability to sum people up quickly was a godsend.

In his personal life, it sucked.

"Sorry, Sam," he said quietly.

She didn't respond.

"So why do you want me dead?" he asked, trying to change the subject back to why she'd dragged him here.

"Oh, let me count the ways. Would you like them alphabetically or placed in the order of their significance?"

He snorted at that. "Alphabetical works for me. If I hum a few bars, would you sing it?"

She rolled her eyes at him.

"C'mon," he said, almost playfully. "Why am I here, chained naked to your bed? Really?"

"Because I'm going to kill you. Really."

There was no misreading her tone or her body language. She meant that.

He gave her a sincere stare. "I didn't betray BAD, Sam. If I'd wanted Hunter killed, I wouldn't have rigged his car. I'd have gone for him one-on-one."

She shrugged nonchalantly. "It makes no never mind to the ones in charge. You've compromised yourself. There's nothing to be done to salvage it."

Was she telling the truth? "Then why did you tranq me and not kill me?"

She gave him a nasty glare. "I couldn't leave you dead on the street. We don't make those kinds of mistakes. You're only alive until Retter gets here, and then we'll dispose of you properly."

Jason clenched his hands. "I didn't try to kill him, Sam. You have to believe me."

"I don't have to do a damn thing."

Why couldn't he make them see reason? "C'mon, you know me. When have I ever gone at someone's back?"

"London."

"Sam!"

Every expression on her face told him he was talking to the wall.

Her cell phone rang. While she answered it, Jason twisted his hands, trying to find some-way to break free of the cuffs. As a kid, he used to be able to bend his thumb in and escape . . .

Unfortunately, he'd lost that talent.

"Really?" Sam said as she narrowed her gaze on him. "Uh-huh. And you're sure about this?"

He truly hoped she wasn't talking about his death.

"There's no doubt? No chance for error?"

Jason strained, trying to make out the words that were coming from the phone in a tone reminiscent of Charlie Brown's teacher.

"All right, then. I'll do it." She hung up the phone.

"Do what?"

She didn't answer as she drew closer to the bed. "You really went too far this time, didn't you? Selling us out. Slumming with the enemy . . ." She clucked her tongue at him. "Tell me what I should do with you."

"Let me go so that I can finish my assignment and prove to all of you that I'm innocent."

"Yeah."

Jason threw his head back and let out a disgusted sigh. What was he going to do?

Sam left the room for a few seconds, then came back with her weapon drawn.

Jason tensed as he realized she'd screwed the silencer onto it. For the first time in his career, he was really scared. There was no way to fight back. No way out of this one.

"Don't, Sam. You're only going to hate yourself when you find out the truth."

She snorted at his words. "I assure you, Banks, that'll never happen."

Her eyes cold and empty, she aimed the gun at him. Jason refused to flinch. He'd never been a coward. If she was going to do this, then she was going to kill him with him looking her dead in the eyes.

She didn't even blink before she squeezed the trigger. Jason sucked his breath in, waiting to feel the bite of a bullet tearing through his body.

He didn't.

Instead, a slow smile spread across her face. "Did you wet yourself, Banks?"

Jason cocked his head in disbelief as her words rang in his mind. "What the fuck is this?"

She pulled the mag clip from her back pocket and slid it into the gun. "Basically, I'm harassing you for the near fatal heart attack you gave poor Hunter in London . . . and for all the other pranks you have perpetrated on the unsuspecting members of our group. Including me."

His anger melted under a look of disgust. "Dammit, Sam! Do you know what you've done? What you interrupted tonight? I was going—"

"To get killed," she said simply, interrupting his tantrum. "Not just by me, apparently. That was Retter on the phone a second ago. He said he'd just left one of his informants in a club, and the man had given him some interesting news. He said you were busted by your target, Banks. Big-time. Ariston found out from a plant of his in the MI-5 that you blew up a pig in Hunter's car to make it look like Hunter was dead."

"I told you I was innocent."

She rolled her eyes. "Retter said that you must have figured on Hunter being such a coward that he'd immediately jump the next plane home—which he did, but not before Ariston's people got a hold of his flight information. Ariston knew you hadn't betrayed the agency, and those two heifers you were leaving the club with tonight were about to take you down to his house, where they were going to fillet you into itty-bitty Jason pieces."

Jason felt the color leave his face as he went completely still. "Are you sure?"

Sam nodded gravely. "Retter had no doubt. If he had, he'd have told me to go ahead with my assignment." She sighed as if the thought of not killing him was more than she could bear. "Luckily you're not the only agent we have in Ariston's group. Now my mission is to hold you here until Monday, at which time Retter will construct a very real-looking death for you so that I can smuggle you out of the country."

He shook his head in disbelief. "I can't believe I let them fool me. I'm never fooled. Not like that."

Sam almost felt sorry for him. It hurt to be misled, especially on something that could turn out fatal. "It happens to the best of us."

His face spoke plainly . . . *Not to me.* "Fine, let me go."

Sam knew that she should, but as she looked down at him, completely helpless and at her mercy, the devil crawled inside her. This was a once-in-a-lifetime opportunity to pay him back for that little spy job he'd done on her. God love him, but this man had caused her endless hours of humiliation.

Now vengeance was hers, and this little booger was going to pay, . . .

"Why should I? Retter said to keep you in place until Monday. Well, you're in place. What better way to make sure you don't do something stupid."

"I'm lying here naked, Sam. I would like to get up and get dressed."

She didn't answer. Instead, she gave him a saucy smirk as she trailed one fingernail down his perfectly tanned, bare chest. Chills sprang up in the wake of her caress, and to her dismay, she wasn't entirely immune to the steely feel of that body. "I don't know, but you're awfully cute lying there all nice and nekkid." She skimmed the length of that hard, six-foot-tall body with her gaze.

In spite of herself, her mouth watered for a taste.

He gave her a droll stare. "You know, if I did this to you, you'd have me up on sexual harassment charges."

"Double standards are such a bitch, aren't they?"

He didn't comment on that. "So are you going to leave me here naked for the entire weekend?"

She shrugged again. "Why not? At least I know you can't get into any more trouble this way."

He glowered at her, but even so she saw the underlying amusement. "You are an evil woman."

Jason wasn't sure what to think. He really didn't like the idea of his cover blown, but spending the weekend with Sam wasn't the worst thing to ever happen to him.

That is, if she'd let him get up and get dressed.

"Evil to the core of my backwoods Mississippi self." She dropped a mischievous gaze down to his body and to the small lump that he wished wasn't so prominent. "You know, my mother has a theory about men . . ."

Before he could even react, she grabbed the blanket just over his erection and snatched it free from him and the bed.

"Sam!" he snapped as he and his obvious erection from her hand on his chest were completely bared to her gaze. "What are you doing?"

She draped the blanket over her shoulder as she took her time perusing every inch of his naked body . . . and he meant *every* inch. Her gaze was slow and hot as she seemed to savor staring at him. As much as he hated to admit it, there was something oddly erotic about this.

"I'm paying you back," she said with a wicked grin.

Jason had never felt so exposed to a woman in his life. "For what?"

"I overheard you talking to Retter eight months ago in our offices in Nashville. Do you remember?"

He frowned even more as he tried to recall which conversation she was referring to. "I talk to him all the—" Jason hesitated as he suddenly remembered *that* talk. It was back when he'd flown to Nashville for a few days to rest and debrief. It'd been an entire week of freedom and while he'd been there, he'd seen . . .

Oh, jeez. Had she really overheard them talking about *that?*

"Yes," she said pointedly. "I know you were spying on me in the locker room while I showered."

And it had been a most beautiful sight too. One that had haunted him ever since and had led to his dreams of her appearing to him as a water nymph out to seduce him. Though she wasn't a skinny woman or very busty, there had been something about the water sliding over the length of her tanned, athletic body that had scorched him. Even now he could see the water dripping from her breasts, see it sliding from her navel to get caught in the dark triangle between her slightly parted thighs.

He'd dreamed of nothing since then except of

parting those thighs more and seeking out the sweet-est part of her body with his tongue . . .

Oh, yeah, that moment had certainly been worth this little bit of embarrassment.

Her eyes burned him with fury. "Have you any idea how embarrassing it is to know that you and Retter have discussed my attributes? I can't even look the man in the eyes now. Any more than I can show him my backside for fear he's thinking of me in the shower. Thank you so much, asshole."

"That was an accident," he said, trying to placate her. "Joe had sent me in there to fix the light that the maintenance department kept missing."

He could tell by her face that she didn't buy it.

"Why didn't you tell me you were in there when you heard me enter?" she asked.

"I was going to, but you whipped your shirt and bra off so fast I didn't have the chance, and I knew if I said something then you'd be pissed, so I—"

"Spied on me."

He offered her a boyish grin. "I had my eyes closed the whole time."

She put her hands on her hips and narrowed those brown eyes on him. "Really? I believe you told Ret-ter that I had one of the best asses you'd ever seen."

Well, okay, so he hadn't closed his eyes even to blink . . . and she did truly have one of the best asses he'd ever seen on any woman.

"You should be flattered." He tried again to charm her. "At least I complimented you."

That flew over her about as well as a chicken headed south for the winter. Instead of easing her temper, it only seemed to worsen it.

"Who else have you told? Huh?"

"No one, I swear."

She shook her head. "And I'm supposed to believe a man who lies for a living. Yeah, right."

He gave her his sweetest smile. "I promise, Sam. I didn't say a word to anyone else."

Still he saw the doubt plainly etched in her face. "You are so unrepentant, aren't you? You can't even say you're sorry for being a peeping Tom. For invading my privacy!"

Jason crossed his legs, trying to hide his erection from her. "If I said yes, would you give me my pants back now?"

"No." She turned around and left the room.

"Hey!" Jason snapped as he realized he was hanging out to breeze in his entirety with no way to cover himself at all. God help him if someone came into the room unannounced.

Over and over his mind played a news clip, "American Agent Found Nude in Apartment." Laughter at eleven.

This wasn't funny!

"Sam! Get back in here."

"Why?" Her voice was faint, as if she were heading out of the apartment.

"Sam! I swear if you don't give me my clothes back, I'm going to make you pay!"

She returned not with his clothes but with a Polaroid camera. Jason went cold in fear. The last thing he wanted was to see his Longfellow stuck on some Web site somewhere.

Or worse . . . the office bulletin board.

"What are you doing?"

She answered by snapping a picture of him lying bare-ass naked on the bed.

"Sam, I swear—"

"Don't swear, it's not nice." She took another picture, and another.

Jason bent his leg up, hoping to block himself from her lens.

Looking completely satisfied, Sam pulled the pictures out and set the camera aside while she held the pictures in one hand, waiting for them to develop. She took a look at the first one, then smiled coyly at him. "Bet you're wondering what I intend to do with these, huh?"

He glared menacingly at her. "You better burn them."

She arched a taunting brow at that. "Why? I'm thinking they'd make a wonderful addition to this gay male revue Web site I know. Besides, it's not like most of Europe hasn't already seen you naked. I hear tell you make more time than a Swiss clock factory."

Jason growled as he tried to pull himself free.

She drew her breath in sharply between her teeth, as if she appreciated the way his muscles were bulging. "You keep doing that, baby, and I might have to take some more."

He growled even louder. "What is this? You know if I did this to you, you'd report me."

Samantha decided she had tormented him enough. He really was starting to get angry, and that was the last thing she wanted.

Besides, she fully intended to hand the pictures over to him . . . eventually.

Maybe in a year or two.

"Calm down, Banks," she said as she slid the pictures into her back pocket. "Believe me, I wouldn't report you. I'd just hire some thugs to beat you senseless. Or shoot you myself one night when you least expected it."

Jason cursed under his breath as she vacated the room again. Dammit!

And then he heard a door open and close.

Surely she hadn't left . . .

He was just beginning to get really nervous when she returned a few minutes later with a pair of sweatpants and a T-shirt. She dropped them over his groin before she pulled out a set of keys to unlock his handcuffs.

He frowned at the clothing that didn't belong to him. "Where are my clothes?"

She unlocked the cuffs. "I drove them miles away from here and dumped them in an incinerator."

He was aghast at that. He'd loved his leather jacket that he'd bought a few months back in Italy. No one had bugged his stuff. He was always careful to check for such things. "Good God, you're paranoid."

She arched a brow at him. "Like you wouldn't be? For all I knew, one of Ariston's thugs was following me to try and help you before I could shoot you for real."

Jason rolled his eyes at her as she turned around to give him her back while he dressed. "Aw, c'mon, babe, admit it. You really do love me. It killed you to think of me being dead."

With her back to him, she scoffed. "What I love is the sight of your butt as it's walking away from me."

Jason got off the bed. He moved toward her silently. Grabbing her, he started to spin her around, but before he could, she kicked his feet out from under him and had him on the floor, flat on his back.

"Ow!" he said, looking up at her as she placed her small foot in the center of his chest to hold him there. "I bet you're hell on a date."

Glaring at him, she removed her foot and moved away. "You'll never know."

No, but he wanted to. He pushed himself to his feet and gave her a hot once-over. "So what are we going to do for the next couple of days to pass the time?"

"I've got Parcheesi in the other room."

"Really?" he said, giving her a playful half smile. "Ever play Strip Parcheesi?"

She made a disgusted sound in the back of her throat. "You're such a pig."

"Yeah, but have you ever had a pig in the blanket? They're mouthwateringly yummy."

She wrinkled her nose at him, and for some reason he couldn't fathom, that look turned him on. "Yeah, I had one in college. It made me sick to my stomach."

He closed the distance between them, stopping close enough to her that he could smell her sweet perfume. "Maybe that pig didn't know what he was doing. But this pig . . . he knows how to curl a woman's toes."

"I'll give you that one," she quipped. "My toes always curl away from the floor anytime I see something disgusting."

Jason laughed. She was quick. He admired that in a woman. "So do you have a steady boyfriend, Agent Winslow?"

"Not since I shot him for snoring. Do you snore, Agent Banks?"

He ached to pull her into his arms, but knowing

her, she'd have him back on the floor—which, if she'd join him, wouldn't be a bad thing at all. "Guess I won't be getting any sleep tonight, huh?"

"Yeah, and not for the reason you think."

Jason had to shake his head at that. It wasn't often anyone got the better of him, but this feisty little woman from the Deep South had his number.

"Well then, I guess I'll just limp over this way and pout for a while."

"Yeah" she said, "you do that."

As he started to move, Jason heard something strange outside. It sounded like someone coming up the stairs.

Sam cocked her head.

"You hear that?" he whispered.

She nodded. She pulled a gun from an ankle holster and handed it to him before she drew the weapon from the small of her back.

"No one knows we're here," she whispered back.

"Maybe it's another tenant coming home." But even he knew that was bullshit. It sounded like at least two people, maybe more, and they were coming up the stairs in a way that sounded like someone trying to be quiet. Stealthy. More than that it sounded like someone who knew exactly where they were going, and that place was their door.

Sam bounded away from him, to crouch to the side of the bedroom door frame as Jason made his way over toward the window that led to the balcony outside.

He'd just reached it when something hit the front door. Hard. Two seconds later, gunshots exploded as the people outside fired into the door.

"Sam!" he shouted.

She was already darting toward him as the people in the hallway outside kicked the front door open.

Infrared sights danced eerily through the dim light, seeking a target.

"Kill them!" a tall blond shouted in German. "Leave no survivors!"

This was about to get ugly.

CHAPTER 3

Sam was less than happy as she saw the men rushing forward to kill them. And who could blame her? Being shot dead would ruin even the best of days.

Jason flung open the window as he opened fire on the men. She ducked shrapnel and flying bullets. He grabbed her from behind and pushed her toward the iron balcony and fire escape. Not one to argue with sound thinking, she squeezed off a couple of rounds before jumping outside.

As she headed for the roof, Jason grabbed her from behind. "Down, woman, not up. There's no place to go that way."

"They'll be waiting for us on the street."

"Trust me, they'll be waiting for us on the roof."

Before she could argue, he jumped on the fire escape ladder and took the express ride to hell as it rattled, then slammed onto the pavement below. How he managed to keep his grip and not jar his bones, she couldn't imagine.

Bullets ricocheted past her.

So much for her plan of running to the roof. Gripping her weapon, she started down the ladder after him. She heard more gunfire on the street below.

By the time she reached Jason, there were three bodies on the ground, and he was checking the clip on a much larger weapon than the one she'd handed him. It was obvious he'd stolen it from one of the dead bad guys.

"No offense," he said, slamming the clip back into the handle of the new gun, "your backup weapon is for Girl Scouts. But this"—he slid a bullet into the chamber—"is the weapon of champions. Now I can do some serious damage."

Before she could respond, bullets exploded around them. She turned and fired a round that caught a man on the fire escape. He groaned before he flipped over and fell to the alley not far away from them.

"Into the car," Jason said before he skidded over the hood to the driver's side.

"I don't have keys."

"Don't need no keys." He shot through the glass, then opened the door and got into the car. She gasped in protest, but it was too late. He'd already killed her little smart roadster rental. He leaned over to unlock her side.

By the time Sam was in, he'd already hot-wired the car. "I don't think I want to know how you came by that talent, especially when it concerns a European make."

"No, you don't," he said as he started forward under a barrage of gunfire.

The bullets sparked off the hood, but luckily missed shattering the windshield.

Sam ducked low as they went flying down the dark streets with no lights on.

"Damn," Jason said in a low tone as he shifted gears.

"What?"

"They're chasing us, and I have a feeling that their car is faster than this one. I swear I had a faster go-cart when I was ten." He snatched the wheel, making a drastic right-hand turn. "Don't you people have homes?"

Sam pulled herself upright to see the black Mercedes chasing them. She lowered her window to fire at them, hoping she could hit their radiator.

It didn't work.

And Jason was right. They were closing in.

"Do they have to build reliable cars?" she said from between clenched teeth as she ejected her empty mag. She glanced over at Jason. "You didn't happen to grab any spare ammo, did you?"

He handed her his gun.

Sam started to use it, then thought better of it. "Better to save this in case they catch us."

"Good point."

He turned around another corner so fast that she swore the car was on two wheels. She twisted in the seat and grabbed the seat belt. "Where did you learn to drive? The state fair?"

"Yeah. I love bumper cars. They taught me everything I need to know about New York City and Rome driving. Best of all, it taught me how to survive it."

Sam held her hands up over her face as they went crashing through a street vendor's cart. "That's real nice, Indiana Jones. Hope he didn't need that to feed his family or anything."

"Excuse me," Jason snapped at her. "I'm in the middle of a car chase here. Can you leave the sarcasm for later?"

Maybe, but sarcasm was how she coped.

Sam frowned as she heard the other car open fire on them. She braced herself, half expecting to feel a bullet in her back at any second.

"That's what I wanted . . ." Jason's voice was filled with dark glee.

She looked to see a v-e-r-y narrow arched tunnel in front of them. Her eyes widened as she took in the size of their car versus the size of the tunnel. "We won't fit."

"We'll fit."

"We. Won't. Fit!" she screamed as he flew into it.

Her heart pounded in terror as she prepared for impact.

It didn't come.

They did lose the side-view mirror, but other than that, they came through unscathed. Sam crossed herself, even though she wasn't Catholic.

The sound of twisting metal filled the air. Sam turned to see the car that was chasing them get lodged fully in the narrow arch. Luckily it had trapped them, so they couldn't even open the car doors to shoot.

"Wa-hoo!" she shouted, punching the roof of their little smart roadster. "You know, Jace, I could actually kiss you for that."

He flashed a wicked grin at her. "Hang on to that thought, and I'll collect later. Right now, we need to find someplace safe to hide."

She couldn't agree more. They also needed someplace where they could rearm themselves, which in Germany wasn't exactly easy. "There's a little two-bedroom inn on the outskirts of the city, toward Wedding. We should be safe there."

"You sure?"

"Yeah. The owner is related to Retter. I've stayed there a couple of times in the past."

Jason slowed down as he headed toward the northwest of Berlin, away from their "friends." "What I want to know is how the hell they found us."

Sam nodded. "That makes two of us. I took your clothes halfway to Poland before I burned them. Maybe they backtracked to the apartment after finding them, since the clothes had paused there."

He scoffed at her reasoning. "Trust me, they're not that smart."

"Then how do you explain it?"

"I don't know. Maybe we have a leak."

It was possible. "Speaking of leaks, Mr. Double Agent, that was really mean, what you did to Hunter in London. He won't even leave his Brentwood house now for fear of another car exploding on him."

Jason made a noise of complete disgust. "Please. I only picked him to target for my attack because I knew Mr. Prep-School-High-Brow has that damned remote that starts the car to warm it while he's still inside, drinking his coffee. God forbid, Hunter ever have a cold ass. He's the only agent I knew for sure wouldn't get caught in the blast."

Sam had to force herself not to laugh at his description of Hunter. The man did love to lord his superior breeding over all of them, and Jason was right—there was no way Hunter would manually start his own car. "Maybe, but you had Joe riled about it."

Jason shrugged. "He'll get over it . . . especially if I end up killed."

"That's not funny."

"No," Jason agreed as his handsome face sobered, "it isn't. The object isn't to die for your country, it's to make the other poor slob die for his."

There was a quote she hadn't heard in a long time. "Thank you, General Patton."

He arched a brow at her words as if they impressed him. "You know the good general?"

"My mother's favorite movie. I've watched it a billion times as a kid. I swear I've seen George C. Scott more than I have my own father."

Grinning at her, Jason slowed as they passed a German police car. Sam watched them cautiously until they were out of sight. Even though they worked with several German groups, she had to be careful. BAD wasn't officially sanctioned by the American government. They worked outside the parameters that guided the other agencies.

If they were caught, they were on their own. There was no diplomatic immunity or leniency to be had for them. Essentially, mother America would turn her back on them and leave them to rot. It was a risk they all understood, and one they each agreed to. None of them would have it any other way.

She looked at Jason as he navigated the streets like a pro. The streetlights cut interesting shadows across his handsome face. His jaw was set, and she could see the skill and determination in his eyes.

It was just the two of them now.

"I think we need to call Retter," she said, "and let him know we're on the move. I wouldn't want him to turn up at the apartment and get blitzed or shot or something."

He nodded before he turned down a street that led in the opposite direction from the one they were headed, just in case the bad guys were looking for them. For all they knew, the men after them could have Retter's cell phone tapped.

Jason scanned the street. "I'll look for a hotel with a lobby. We can catch a pay phone there."

He was right. She couldn't use her cell phone either. If the ones after them had a GPS trace, they could pinpoint them in a heartbeat.

It was strange; she'd never given Jason much credit for sense. Around the office he'd always been a jokester who was constantly playing pranks on the others.

But in the field . . .

He was truly capable. Frighteningly so. No wonder Joe had recruited him from the Marines.

"You know," she said slowly, "it's weird seeing you with your game face on."

That familiar grin curved his lips, and she had to admit, he could be incredibly gorgeous like that. There was just something about him that was so delectable she could eat him with a spoon. "Didn't think I could manage one, did you?"

"Not really."

He laughed. "Yeah, I know. It's part of my camouflage. You lure the enemy into dismissing you as a crackpot, then they don't watch you so closely. It makes taking them by surprise a whole lot easier."

She definitely had to give him credit there. "I never thought about it like that."

Jason whipped the tiny car in between two others in front of a small hotel. He checked behind them to make sure no one was following them before he got out.

Sam joined him on the street, then followed him into the lobby. They found the pay phones across from the front desk. Jason stood with his back to her, to guard their position.

Out of habit she reached for her credit card, only to remember that if the bad guys knew who they were, they'd be able to trace it to the hotel.

Grimacing, she shoved it back into her pocket and pulled out a few euros. "I need change."

He took the money from her. "I'll get it."

She waited while Jason went to the desk to exchange it. His German was flawless as he charmed the older woman working the desk. The woman absolutely preened before him.

"*Danke, Schatz,*" he said, winking at the clerk before he headed back toward Sam.

Not sure if she should be offended by his flirting

or not, Sam shook her head at him. He was hopeless. How could she ever take him seriously? He was always on the make.

She took the change from him and dialed Retter's cell.

He picked up on the third ring.

"Hola, mi amigo," she said, using a phrase they had set up in advance to let the person on the other end know they were in trouble and they might be bugged.

"Hi, Bella," he said in that deep, even tone of his, using one of her aliases. "Did the hunters find their quarry?"

"Ran them right out of the hole."

"Damn," Retter growled. "Did both rabbits make it?"

"Yeah. At least for the moment. But you know how bolt-holes go . . ."

"No place like family, huh?"

She had to smile at his intuitiveness. There were times when she swore that man was psychic. "Exactly."

"Okay. I've got some stuff here to work on. You see to the rabbit and make sure it doesn't die on us."

"You got it. *Hasta la vista.*"

"Buenas noches."

Sam hung up the phone and turned around. "All right," she said to Jason. "He knows where we're going."

"Good." Jason reached out and brushed a stray

strand of hair back from her face. His green eyes were sizzling as they scorched her with heat. "By the way, do you know how sexy you sound when you speak Spanish?"

There he went again. The man really couldn't help himself. "Oh, please."

He actually managed to look slightly offended. "No, I'm serious. It really turns me on . . ."

"Yeah, right. Please tell me what *doesn't* turn you on. I think I need it by the bucketful."

Jason stood back as Sam led the way out of the hotel. What she didn't suspect was that he was deadly serious. He didn't know what it was about her, but she lured him like Parthenope lured Odysseus—now there was an obscure metaphor left from one too many days spent in college.

It wasn't easy to think straight while he was this hard for her. Of course it would help if she didn't smell so damn good. He didn't know what perfume she wore, but if the military bottled it and sprayed it over the male troops, it could be a potent distraction.

It was all he could do not to pull her to him and just take a deep breath in her hair. Oh, yeah, he was losing it for a woman who would rather shoot him than look at him.

What was wrong with him?

Shaking his head to clear it, he headed to the driver's side of the car as she got in.

"We're going to need to ditch the car," she said as he joined her inside.

"I know, but we should be safe for a short while in it. Our friends don't strike me as the kind to call the cops to report it stolen."

"It's not their car," she said. "It was my rental. But if they found our safe house, they probably know about this car too."

"Oh." He headed back toward Wedding. "Good point."

All of a sudden, and for no apparent reason, Sam started laughing.

"What?" Jason asked, completely confused by what she found humorous in their current situation.

Had the woman snapped a wheel?

"Nothing," she said, trying to sober. "It's really stupid."

"Most things in life are, but if it's worth laughing at, I'd like to hear it. God knows I could use a laugh after the night I've had."

She drew a deep breath. "Yeah, I guess you could. It's not often you get shot, drugged, photographed, skinned of your clothing, and then chased, is it?"

"Well, now that you put it that way . . ." He winked at her.

She rolled her eyes before she answered his earlier questions. "I was just thinking of this stupid thing my mother used to say whenever things went wrong."

"And that is?"

"Where *are* we going and tell why am I in this handbasket again?"

Jason laughed at the polite twist on the old saying. "I think I like your mom."

"Yeah, and she would love you. My mom has a thing for good-looking guys."

His heart skipped a beat at her disclosure. Could it be that she might actually find him attractive? "You think I'm good-looking?"

Her face turned to stone. "Only when I see you in pictures . . ." But she couldn't hold that look. It melted under a devilish smile that melted him. "And naked, humiliated, and handcuffed to my bed."

Jason cringed at the reminder, even though a part of him liked this teasing side of her. Around the office she was always so stern and serious. He'd never guessed that she had a fun side to her. "You know, they say turnabout is fair play."

She gave him a daring stare. "And I say try it and die."

He gave her a hot once-over before he wagged his eyebrows at her. "I think you'd be worth a little death and dismemberment."

Sam had to force herself not to react to that deliberate baiting—at least not outwardly. Inwardly she was a lot more affected than she liked.

If only she could take him seriously—but Jason

wasn't the type of guy to have a monogamous relationship. In fact, she hadn't even known him to date. He was the classic guy who didn't want anyone or anything to tie him down. And she wasn't the kind of woman who dated casually. Too many years watching her mother flit from man to man had left her jaded. She wanted more from a relationship than naked, sweaty sex.

Not that anything was particularly wrong with naked, sweaty sex, but unlike her mother, she wanted a guy who would be there for the long haul. One who wouldn't head for the door at the first sign of daylight or trouble.

"Those are famous last words, Agent Banks. Shall I pull out the knife and test the theory of whether you're willing to die or not?"

He shook his head at her. "You don't let any guy next to you, do you?"

"Sure I do. I keep my gun under my pillow and cuddle him every night."

"Wouldn't you rather cuddle something that could hold you back?"

Jason waited for a smart-ass comeback, but for once he didn't get one. He glanced to the left to see Sam staring out at the road as if she were lost in thought.

There was a sad air around her that let him know he'd gone too far again. Damn. Why was it he kept putting his foot in his mouth where she was concerned?

"I'm sorry, Sam," he said quickly. "I didn't mean to strike another nerve."

She gave him a sideways look. "I didn't think men could be so perceptive."

"Considering I live and die by subtle signs, I learned to read body language a long time ago." Jason reached over and squeezed her hand. "Thanks, by the way."

"For what?"

"Saving my ass. I'm really attached to it."

The timid smile she gave him made his groin jerk. "No problem." She pulled her hand out from under his and folded her arms across her chest, letting him know that she wanted some time to herself.

He could respect that.

They didn't speak much as they rode through the dark German streets until they reached the cottage. It looked like one of those places out of some Grimm Brothers story. It was so picture-perfect that it had to have evil buried deep within it.

He frowned as he parked the car out of sight of the road. "Is it just me, or is this, like, Stepford perfect?"

Sam gave him a droll stare. "I love this place. It's very peaceful."

He disagreed. "So was Motel Hell. Remember

that movie? 'It takes all kinds of critters to make Farmer Vincent's fritters.' They had people buried in the backyard like vegetables in a garden. You snatched the bag off the ground expecting to find a cabbage, and instead it was someone's head. And Norman, he appeared normal too, didn't he? Right up until the point he stabbed poor Janet in the shower."

She gave him a droll stare. "How can someone this suspicious have been on his way to get killed earlier?"

Jason paused before he answered. " 'Cause they lured me into thinking they were stupid bimbos. They used my own trick against me. See what happens when you trust people? You end up planted in their backyard with a bag over your head."

Sam decided to ignore his paranoia as she led the way to the door and knocked on it.

The door opened a few minutes later to show her a tall, willowy blond woman. In her mid-fifties, she was plain in the face, but her rosy cheeks made her pale blue eyes shine with warmth and friendship.

"Samantha!" she exclaimed in a heavy German accent as she pushed open the screen door. "It's been too long since last you came. *Willkommen.* Come in, come in. You brought a friend this time. *Das ist gut, ja?*"

"Some days it is," Sam said with a smile. "This is Jason. Jason, Renate Fiebig."

She held a hand out to him. "Good to meet you, Jason."

"You, too," Jason said as he shook her hand.

Renate stepped back to let them pass, then scanned the street behind them before she shut and locked the door.

Renate bent her head close to Sam's and whispered loudly. "Are we hiding again, *meine schatzi*?"

Sam nodded.

Renate's blue eyes literally glistened with excitement. "*Das gut.* I love the intrigue. Rupert, he tells me nothing. 'You don't need to know about it,' Nate. Is for your own good that you know nothing.' But I want to know. Is thrilling, *ja*?"

"Rupert?" Jason asked.

"Retter," Sam explained. She'd learned the first time Retter had introduced her to his cousin that most of his family called him Rupert or, to his complete and utter horror, Ruppie. Neither of which were suited to the take-no-crap agent who could kill in cold blood without flinching.

Jason laughed. "Oh, jeez, don't tell me his real name is Rupert Retter? No wonder he never tells anyone his given name. And I thought Tee's name sucked . . ."

Renate stiffened as if his words greatly offended her. "That is not his name. It is Theobald Walter Rupert George Mark Retter Brahmar-Winsley. His maternal grandfather was Theobald, Walter is his father, George is our grandfather, and Mark was his uncle who died, therefore we call him Rupert so as to not confuse each other when we speak of him."

By his face, she could tell Jason was already confused.

"I'm impressed," he said with a light laugh, "and I want to know how he fits all that on his driver's license. Not to mention, how do you remember the correct order of all those names?"

Renate shrugged. "He could not remember it as a child, so we all learned it to help him until he learned the proper order."

Sam smacked him playfully on the stomach. "If you want to live through this, I would suggest you not tease Retter about it. He doesn't have much in the way of a sense of humor when it comes to his moniker."

"Who could blame him for that? But does Hunter know we have an agent with more names than he has? He's going to be dreadfully unhappy when he finds out. Next thing you know, he'll go add one just for spite."

Sam actually groaned at that. The sad thing was, he was probably right.

She looked back at the German woman. "We're sorry to impose, Renate. Do you have a vacancy where you can put us up for a couple of nights?"

"Of course, *schatzi*. But I only have the one room right now. The other is being repaired from a leak from the last storm that came through."

Jason inclined his head before she could protest. "That'll work. Thank you."

Renate nodded. "Have you need of food?"

Sam shook her head. "I'm fine. Jason?"

"I'm all right, but is there any chance you might have a change of clothes?"

"*Ja.* I always keep some things, just in case. You never know what can happen. Rupert came in two years ago completely naked." She frowned at the memory. "He never did tell me what happened. But with Rupert . . . one never knows."

That was certainly true enough.

"Do you need anything else?" she asked.

"Ammo," Sam added. "A couple of clips if you have them for my gun."

She nodded. Renate always tried to keep extra ammo for all the agents she knew. "Do you need some as well?"

"You got a forty-five mag clip?"

"Same as Rupert's?"

"Yes."

"*Ja.* Just a moment while I gather it."

Sam and Jason waited in the small, ornate living room, with hundreds of Hummel figurines tucked into every corner and shelf, while Renate left them alone. They could hear the wind whistling through the eaves of the house.

Sam kept her head cocked, listening for the sound of car engines, but so far everything was quiet. Peaceful. It appeared they had given the bad guys the slip.

"No one knows about this place," she told Jason. "We should be completely safe."

"Good. I could use a nice, non-drug-induced sleep," he teased her.

Sam grimaced at the reminder of what she'd done to him. "I knew I should have shot you for real."

It didn't take long for Renate to rejoin them. She led them up the stairs in the back to her loft, where she kept the two rooms she rented out. She opened the door on the left, revealing a small Hansel and Gretel–type room. Little German dolls in authentic clothing filled all the shelves.

Renate pulled down the window shades before they entered. "There are spare pillows in the chest, as well as more blankets."

She put three boxes of ammo down on a heavily carved cherry-wood dresser before she tucked the clothing in a top drawer. "The bathroom is downstairs," she told Jason. "Samantha can show you where. I shall turn in shortly, but the kitchen is well stocked. Please make yourselves at home."

"Thanks, Renate," Sam said, grateful for the woman's kindness. "As usual, I owe you."

"You can make it up to me tomorrow by telling me great stories of adventure. I shall make you blood sausage and potatoes for breakfast, and we will talk long, *ja?*"

"You got it."

Beaming at them, Renate left the room and closed the door.

Jason's gaze darted around the tiny area. "Not much space, is there?"

Sam glanced wistfully at the small bed. "Why don't we flip for it?"

"Ah, c'mon, Sam. We're both grown-ups. We can share. I won't grope you if you don't grope me."

A nervous jitter went through her, along with an unfounded wave of excitement. "I don't know. It's mighty tight quarters."

"Why are you hesitating? It's not like we haven't seen each other naked already."

She cringed at the reminder. Two could play his game. "Fine. You don't scare me."

And he didn't. It was the untoward hunger she felt for him that terrified her. Maybe there was more of her mother in her than she knew. For the first time in her life, the thought of a one-night stand didn't completely repulse her.

It would actually be kind of nice . . .

Trying to distract herself from that thought, Sam headed for the ammo and reloaded her gun. The last thing she needed was to hook up with a man like Jason. He was the epitome of why she'd sworn off men.

"Why are you an agent, anyway?" she asked him.

He shrugged nonchalantly as he pulled out an extra pillow from the chest by the bed. "I live for danger, and I wanted to do something with my life other than just pull a paycheck, you know? What about you?"

"I fell in love with the TV movie *Johnnie Mae Gibson: FBI* when I was in high school. I was absolutely fascinated by the Bureau. My mother thought I was nuts, but the more I looked into it, the more I wanted to be an agent. I thought it was the best way to make the world a better place for people."

"Then why did you leave?"

She laughed wistfully at the memory of how many times she'd gotten into trouble for not following policy. "I got fed up with the protocols. Every time I turned around, they were writing me up. Sometimes it seemed like there was no justice for the victim. Like our laws were only designed to protect the guilty. So when Joe came to me and told me about BAD, I jumped at the chance to be able to use my training the way it was meant to be used."

He drew close to her as she spoke. "Heroes to the end."

She nodded as she looked up at the light playing

across his sinfully handsome face. His lips were so inviting. His eyes dark and warming.

He lifted his hand up to cup her face.

Pull back . . .

But she couldn't. She was paralyzed by those green eyes that beckoned her toward him.

Her heart pounding, she knew he was going to kiss her.

Sure enough, he dipped his head down and parted her lips with his own.

CHAPTER 4

At first Sam tensed and started to pull back, but as she tasted the decadence that was Jason, her resistance faltered. It'd been way too long since she'd kissed any man. Way too long since she'd had sex. She'd almost forgotten what it felt like to have a man touch her.

And those lips of his . . . they were both firm and soft. Demanding and scorching.

As much as she hated to admit it, he was a choice piece of cheese. She ran her hand over the T-shirt and felt the rippling of hard, developed muscles of a man in the prime of his life. At the height of his prowess.

Her body thrummed with unexpected need as his tongue swept against hers with masterful strokes that left her breathless and hungry for more.

Much more.

The man seriously knew how to give a kiss.

And it made her wonder if he was as competent in other areas as well . . .

Jason growled as he finally got to taste that saucy

little mouth that lived to taunt him. The sweetness of her breath on his face, of her soft curves pressed up against his body . . . It was enough to drive a man wild. His fantasies of her naked and in his bed played through his mind, driving his lust to a furious level.

He wanted this woman with a desperation that made no sense whatsoever.

His cock throbbed as he cupped her bottom in his hands and pressed her hips closer to his. But it wasn't enough to even begin to sate the hunger inside him.

He lifted her up and rested her on the dresser. Deepening his kiss, he used his hips to separate her thighs so that she had her legs wrapped around his waist. He ran his hands over her back as he slowly slid his hard erection against the center of her body, needing to feel closer to her.

He wanted inside her so badly that he could taste it, feel it. The need was born of desperate longing and one too many wet dreams of her underneath him.

Sam couldn't think straight as she felt Jason's erection through their clothes as he pressed it against the part of her that was craving him with an unreasoning madness.

This is insane . . .

But she didn't listen to the voice in her head. All she could think of was Jason lying naked on the bed.

He'll never have a relationship with you.

And that was probably a good thing. She didn't

have time for a boyfriend anyway. She didn't need the distraction of a significant other any more than Jason did. Two drastically different people, they would never be right for each other.

Still, her body craved him, and she didn't even understand why.

You don't have a condom.

That finally succeeded in calming her down. She pulled back from his lips and pushed him away. "We don't have protection, Jason."

His lips were swollen from her kisses, his green eyes smoldering as he looked at her like a starving man glimpsing the last steak on the planet. "Then let me taste you, Sam," he breathed raggedly. "I want to hear you scream out my name as I make you come for me."

Part of her was offended, and another part was thrilled. No man had ever been so selfless with her.

He returned to her lips. She had to admit he knew how to lick and tease. That mouth of his was golden.

Should she?

You'll be just like your mother . . .

No, she was still an entirely different person. Jason wasn't the out-of-work lampreys her mother dragged home. She wasn't expecting him to save her from anything or to move in. They were just two grown adults wanting a few hours of physical connection. No promises. No broken hearts.

Jason nipped the corner of her mouth as he struggled for control. Half afraid she'd turn him away, he reached for the hem of her dark brown turtleneck. He moved it up her body slowly, giving her time to stop him if she changed her mind.

To his relief, she didn't. He pulled the shirt off, leaving her bare except for the tan bra.

She whisked his T-shirt over his head, then drew him back to her so that she could tease his neck with her tongue while her hands explored his back. Jason smiled at her as he reached around her back to unhook her bra. He ground his teeth in pleasure as her breasts sprang free into his waiting palm. It felt so good just to touch her. He ran his palm gently over the creamy mounds, delighting in the way her nipples hardened against his callused fingers.

He dipped his head down so that he could draw that puckered tip into his mouth.

Sam moaned as pleasure tore through her. Her stomach jerked with every lush stroke of Jason's tongue on her nipple. His touch made her so wet, so hot for a man who shouldn't even be on her menu.

Yet here she was, virtually naked with him, and she wasn't even sure why.

He left her breast, then picked her up from the dresser to carry her to the bed. He laid her back against the lumpy mattress and stared down at her with an unwarranted tenderness as he removed her holster and weapon. He dropped it on the night-stand.

"I hope this thing doesn't squeak," he said teasingly as he bounced against the mattress to test it.

"That makes two of us." She scooted up on the bed as he reached for her shoes.

Sam watched as he slowly removed her shoes and socks, then massaged her feet. His touch was strong and sure, yet gentle and soothing. She trembled as he reached for her fly. His eyes were locked on hers as he slowly undid the button, then slid the zipper down.

The expectation of his touching her was excruciating.

He dipped his head down to lightly lave her navel before he lifted her hips and slid her jeans and panties off in one fall swoop.

Absolutely on fire, she licked her lips before she grabbed him and pulled him close for a hot kiss.

Jason was thrilled by her eagerness as he slowly explored her mouth. She had the sweetest little tongue he'd ever known. As they kissed, she wrapped her body completely around his, and he had to admit there was nothing better than the sensation of her small breasts pressed up against his chest. His swollen cock burning, he reached between their bodies to trail his hand down her stomach to the short, crisp hairs.

He moved his hand lower, wanting to touch the part of her that was still alien to him. The part of her that he craved most to touch and stroke.

He separated the tender folds so that he could feel just how wet she already was. He smiled in satisfaction as he ran his hand over her, letting her wetness coat his fingers before he slid one deep inside her.

Sam shivered at the sensation of his long, rough finger stroking her, and when he slid in two, she gave a cry of satisfied pleasure.

"That's it, baby," he said against her cheek as she moved her hips against those wonderfully pleasing fingers. "Show me what you like."

Arching her back, she cupped his head to her as he trailed a path of scorching kisses over her. It was so strange to be so open with him, so bare.

She didn't really understand why she was doing this, and yet she felt no shame or regret.

She wanted him to touch her like this.

Jason paused to thoroughly explore her breasts. He rubbed his cheek against the right one, savoring the softness of her flesh on his roughened skin. Her fingers lightly stroked his scalp before she scraped her long, manicured nails over the skin of his back, raising chills the whole way.

Her skin tasted like heaven, but it still didn't sate him. He wanted something more from her than this . . .

He moved farther down her body, over her stomach, to her silky thighs. Jason couldn't remember the last time he'd been with a woman like her. One who wasn't on the make or out to land a guy with a steady paycheck.

Like him, Sam was addicted to her job. She understood the necessity for what they did. The necessity that they stay unfettered.

Even so, she wasn't a cheap lay he'd picked up in a bar. She was a decent woman. The kind of woman he could leave alone with a friend and not have to worry about finding them in bed together when he returned.

She was the kind of woman a guy took home to meet his family. The kind of woman a guy proposed to . . .

Sam bit her lip as Jason spread her thighs. He paused to look at her as he gently blew a hot breath over her cleft. She shivered in pleasure.

Smiling at her, he dipped his head and took her into his mouth. She threw her head back as exquisite pleasure tore through her. The sensation of his tongue on her body . . . It was unbelievable.

It'd been so long since she last slept with a man that she had all but forgotten what this felt like.

His tongue swirled and teased her as he sank his fingers back inside her body.

Sam was breathless as she buried her hand in his

hair and held him to her. It was as if he were living just for the ability to taste her. As if he enjoyed giving her this pleasure even more than she enjoyed receiving it.

She lost all track of time and reason as she felt wave after wave of ecstasy course through her, and when she came, she did cry out his name.

Jason smiled wickedly as he felt her climax. But it wasn't enough for him. He refused to leave her until he had wrung every last shiver from her body.

"Please!" she gasped as he continued to tease her. "I can't take it anymore."

Jason laughed as he wiped his face against her silken thigh, then gently nipped the tender skin with his teeth. Still he kept one finger inside her, wishing it was his cock buried there instead.

He brushed his fingers over her as he kissed her hip, her stomach. Stretching out beside her, he gathered her into his arms to hold her close.

Sam lay quietly as her body slowly drifted back from heaven. She drew a ragged breath as she felt completely cocooned by his strength and tenderness.

"That was incredible," she breathed as she snuggled against him. It couldn't have been more intimate had he been inside her.

She frowned as she realized just how much pain he must be in. He'd given her release, but there had been none for him. None.

Jason lay there quietly as his body burned. He

hissed when he felt Sam's hand cupping him through his sweatpants. The sensation of her hand against him set fire to his very soul. He'd dreamed about having her for so long . . . he'd never thought the reality would be this hot.

Pulling back, he looked down to find her staring up at him.

"I think turnabout is fair play, don't you?"

At first he didn't trust his hearing. Could she really be serious?

But as she slowly slid the sweatpants down his legs, he realized that she was.

Jason was speechless as she bared him to her hot, hungry gaze. In all honesty, he hadn't expected this. He'd hoped, but he hadn't really allowed himself to think that she would . . .

He growled as she nipped his thigh with her teeth.

"Tell me what you like, Jason," she drawled as she wrapped her hand around his cock and gently ran her fingertip over the tip of him.

"Slow and easy," he said, amazed that she'd asked. He'd never thought a woman like her would be like this in bed.

It was incredible.

He watched her with half-hooded eyes as she cupped his sac carefully in her hand before she lowered her head to him.

He ground his teeth in pure bliss the instant her

tongue swept against his cock. She circled him slowly, carefully, before she took him all the way into her mouth. Jason shook at the sensation of her caressing him.

Good girls weren't supposed to know how to do this . . .

But he was damned glad that she did.

Sam closed her eyes and savored the scent and taste of Jason. She could feel his body jerk with every flick of her tongue, and she enjoyed the sensation of it. She felt powerful and uninhibited. In the past, she'd always been slightly embarrassed with such intimacy, but there was none of that now, and she didn't understand why.

She wanted to please him in a way she'd never wanted to please any guy.

She looked up to see him watching her with an open smile that warmed her even more than his touch. He cupped her cheek in his palm and stroked it with his fingers.

It was such a tender gesture that it tore through her. He was surprisingly gentle and tender. She'd never suspected that Mr. Cocky could be so giving.

She felt his body tense an instant before he came.

Jason swore he saw stars as his orgasm claimed him. To his delight, she didn't pull away. She continued to stroke and caress him until he was completely weak and spent.

This was without a doubt the sweetest moment of his life. He opened his eyes to find her crawling up his naked body to lay herself down over him.

And for the first time, he wondered what it would be like to have a steady girlfriend. What it would be like to come home every day and experience something like this.

Someone like her.

"Thanks, Sam," he whispered. "I really needed that."

She nipped his chin with her teeth. "My pleasure." She brushed her hand over a vicious scar only a few millimeters away from his heart. "Oh, this looks like it must have really hurt."

"Yeah, when I was younger, I was in this really—"

"It's me, Jason," she said, interrupting him. "I know you got it two years ago when you and Kyle were in the Middle East, and you got impaled by a piece of shrapnel that barely missed your heart."

He lay there for several seconds, unable to speak. God, he'd told that lie about being in a car wreck so much that even he had started to believe it. For years now, he'd been living undercover. Hiding who and what he was from everyone. Even something as simple as a scar had to be explained with lies.

But with Sam, he didn't have to lie. That felt even better than the sex had—well, not really, but it was a damn good second.

For the first time in years, he was with a woman he could be honest with. One who knew him. One who understood the world he lived in. She wouldn't think twice about seeing his weapon on the counter. His need to keep it close by at all times wouldn't even cause her to blink. She'd told him that she slept with her gun too.

She was just like him in so many ways.

Not even his family knew what his real job was, or even where he lived. They sent stuff to him in Nashville and called him on a 615 area code, never knowing it was all being forwarded to another country. Likewise, he'd have to send stuff to the BAD offices to have their director forward it on to his sister and mother.

But this . . . this was wonderful, and it brought a wave of relief to him. It'd been too long since he'd just been himself with someone. He liked not having the stress of guarding every word out of his mouth. Of being able to go to sleep without the fear that she might slide a knife through his ribs. He hadn't spent a night with a woman since the minute he'd become an agent for that very reason.

A lax undercover agent was a dead one. He'd taken those words to heart a long time ago.

Sam was different. He was just another man to her, doing the same job and taking the same risks that she herself faced.

He cradled Sam with his body and held her close, savoring her soft curves pressed against the length of him. He buried his face against her hair and inhaled the sweet fragrance that was uniquely Sam.

"I don't usually do this," she whispered.

He smiled at her hesitant words. "I know, and that's why it means so much to me."

She tucked her head beneath his chin while he kept his hand buried in her hair, playing with it. It was so strange. Something inside him seemed to shatter. He felt for her in a way he'd never felt for another woman. It was so sudden. He didn't even know how to explain it.

It was a warm tenderness that seemed to seep into every molecule of his body. It wasn't the kind of emotion, he'd ever felt before. It was more like a girly emotion, and yet he had to admit that it made his heart sing, and it made him want to hold on to her for a long time to come.

Closing his eyes, he held her close and savored the feel of her breath on his skin.

"Do you ever date, Sam?"

She stiffened as if the question offended her. "Like that's any of *your* business. My personal life is just that . . . personal." She pulled back to look at him.

Smiling at her prickliness, he tapped her playfully on the end of her nose. "You know, I think I'd like to take you out when we get back. If you don't mind."

She scoffed. "Yeah, right. Me and you, couple of the year . . . puh-lease."

He rolled his eyes at her. "C'mon, Sam, don't blow me off. At least think about it. One date. That's it. It won't kill you, will it?"

Sam cocked her head as she studied the sincerity in his green eyes. There was something odd in his gaze, and she wasn't sure what it was.

It'd been a long time since she'd lain in bed naked with a guy. In truth, she missed having moments like this. She missed having someone to care about. Someone who cared about her.

It was against her code to date someone in the office. And since those were the only guys she was ever around, that had seriously curtailed her social life.

"C'mon," he said, wrinkling his nose into an adorable expression. "One movie. If I piss you off, you can shoot me afterward."

She smiled in spite of herself. "Okay," she said. "One movie, and I will shoot you if you piss me off. For real."

His eyes warmed her. He'd started to pull her lips to his when they both heard a car door slam outside.

They both went ramrod stiff.

Sam pulled back from him, then followed him to the window so that they could look out to the driveway below. There was a black Mercedes parked there, not unlike the one they had trapped in the tunnel.

There was total silence in the darkness that was only illuminated by the full moon overhead.

Through the large, overgrown trees, they watched the black car carefully, waiting for the doors to open. When they did, four men dressed in black, looking mean, were getting out and heading very purposefully toward the front porch.

By the way those guys surveyed the yard and surroundings, it was obvious they were professionals, not tourists looking for a place to stay.

Completely naked, Jason pulled back from the window. "I think we better get dressed. Fast."

Sam was already reaching for her clothes. She tossed Jason the black pants, which he caught in one fist.

She fastened her pants and strapped her holster to her waist, then glanced back out the window to see the men coming closer.

All of a sudden, she saw the glint of moonlight on a weapon as one of the men drew it out from under his coat.

"We need to warn Renate," Sam said. She'd barely taken a step forward when the door to their room swung open to show her the older German lady.

Gone was the friendly, sweet face that Sam knew so well, and in its place was an expression of grim determination. It was the game face of a seasoned agent who knew what was going on. More than that, Renate's blond hair was pulled back into a ponytail, and she was armed to the teeth.

Good grief, the woman looked like Rambo! Complete with ammo belts and a long black coat.

"Get dressed, *meine liebs.*" She tossed a wad of black clothes in their direction. "It appears playtime is over, and now is time to riddle them with holes."

Jason pulled a black turtleneck over his head fast as he saw Renate move to the window with a grenade in hand.

"Careful," he warned her. "They might shoot you through the window."

"Bah," Renate scoffed as she slid the sash up just a bit. "That would be possible if not for the bullet-proofing of my glass. Only a missile or rocket could penetrate this window."

He cast a knowing look at Sam. "See, I told you this place was too picture-perfect, huh? Believe me now?"

Before she could respond, Renate tossed the grenade and slammed the window shut. A few heart-beats later, it exploded, flashing light and resounding thunder through the room.

Renate urged them into her closet, where she showed them a trapdoor that opened onto a narrow ladder that led straight down into total darkness. She started down first to lead the way.

Sam went next, followed by Jason.

"Afraid of nuclear invasion?" Jason asked Renate as they descended in the pitch blackness.

"Nein, the nuclear shelter is out back with a full stock of supplies. This is just the escape tunnel so we can get away from them. But have no fear. They will not find the tunnels. Come. Follow. I will lead you out of here to safety in town."

"The shelter is out back," he repeated sarcastically to Sam over his shoulder. "Along with Mother, no doubt. Want to shower at Bates Motel now?"

Sam bit back her laughter lest she offend Renate. "Shut up, Jason, and be grateful we have her."

"Believe me, I am," he said sincerely. "But could someone please tell me how these assholes found us?"

Sam had wondered about that too. "That's a really good question."

"Bugs," Renate said as they reached the bottom rung. The older woman stood back as they joined her in the subterranean dampness.

It was obvious they were underneath the house now, in a narrow tunnel that appeared to lead in only one direction, north. Renate moved to a wall on their right and flipped a switch. The ladder drew back up and sealed itself shut, pinning them in total nothingness.

It was almost scary. They could hear Renate, but they couldn't see her.

Instinctively, Sam reached for Jason's hand, needing something solid to ground herself with.

"We're not bugged," Sam said quietly. "I made sure of it."

It sounded like Renate was opening a box of some sort. "Then your car is."

Two seconds later, something snapped, then their tunnel was illuminated by eerie green light as Renate shook her glow stick.

Jason ground his teeth as he looked at Sam. "I knew we should have ditched it."

"Well, what is done is done," Renate said charitably. "Come, *Kinder*. I will see you out of here."

"Yeah, but where will that leave you?" Jason asked.

She smiled wickedly. "Trust me. They will not harm me, and if they do . . . I will show them what it is I did before I retired."

Sam exchanged a curious look with Jason before she asked, "And what exactly was that?"

Renate had that look on her face of a trained agent reciting her latest spiel on who and what she was. It was the overly practiced vacant and "honest" look only another agent would be able to pick up on. "This and that. Now, follow."

Jason cast a cocky smile at Sam. "I think Renate has a past."

Renate harrumphed, but didn't speak as they went farther into the dingy, damp tunnel. Single-file, they moved silently and quickly through the winding passageway, which was wide enough for two of them to walk side by side.

Sam hesitated as she heard something faint behind them . . .

Two seconds later, Renate froze, then tossed the glow stick back the way they had come.

There was no mistaking the sound of people moving out of the way. Renate threw back the side of her coat to reveal an XM8 lightweight assault rifle. "How did they find us?" she asked.

"Yeah," Sam breathed as Renate seized the weapon like a pro and readied it. "She definitely has a past."

"Run, *Kinder.*" Renate said, indicating the passageway ahead of them. "You get to safety. I shall take care of these pigs. Follow the tunnel, and I will join you shortly."

Jason hesitated. "I don't know . . ."

Sam grabbed his arm and pulled at him. "My mission is to get you back to Nashville, Jason. Your cover is blown, but you still have a lot of inside information about Ariston and his friends that we need."

Renate opened fire. The sound of the spray of bullets was deafening.

"Go!" Renate snapped. *"Schnell!"*

Jason didn't argue further. He personally didn't care what happened to him, but he didn't want Sam to be hurt. Taking Sam's hand, he ran with her for what seemed like miles into the darkness.

The sound of gunfire and German curses echoed around them. It sounded like a war zone behind them as Renate whooped and goaded as if she were enjoying every minute of it.

"Come to Mama, you swine-dogs!" Renate shouted in German before she shot again.

Reminding himself not to make that woman mad in the future, Jason kept his grip on Sam.

They continued to run blindly ahead.

After a few minutes, and two loud, echoing screams, everything turned quiet.

The silence was even more deafening than the noise had been, and it made Jason's ears ring.

It wasn't until he could hear their breaths echoing in front of them that he realized they were drawing near the end of the tunnel. Slowing down, he held his hand out in front of them until he felt the end.

He let go of Sam to search the wall with both hands.

Damn. Where was the ladder out of this place?

In the darkness behind him, he could hear someone running after them.

Both he and Sam angled their weapons on the sound.

"Don't shoot!"

They relaxed as they recognized Renate's voice.

"Are you alone?" Jason asked.

"*Ja.*" Renate drew up beside them.

Jason could hear her moving, but he couldn't see her. After a few heartbeats, he heard the sound of a motor whirring.

"Step back," Renate warned as a trapdoor opened above them and a steel ladder extended from the top down to where they waited.

With the exception of Sam lying naked at his feet as she tasted him earlier, that had to be the best damned sight Jason had ever seen.

Jason let the women climb up first before he joined them. They were in the woods just outside a small German town. Renate moved to a switch that was hidden in an ancient tree, then pressed it to cover their tracks.

She cast a harsh look at them. "You are the extractor in this, *ja*?" she asked Sam.

Sam nodded.

Renate's gaze hardened. "Then they must have been suspicious and bugged him."

Jason snorted at the mere idea.

"It's not possible," Sam said. Her defense warmed him. At least she knew better than to think for one minute that he'd be so stupid as to get bugged. "They must have found the tunnel from the house."

"*Nein.* Believe me, I know what it is I do. They must have bugged him sometime earlier. Whatever device he has transmitted out tunnel location to him. It is the only way they could follow."

Sam shook her head. "I destroyed all of his clothes. Nothing, and I mean *nothing*, was left on him."

That didn't daunt the German lady in the least. "Then it must be subdermal."

Jason scoffed. "Yeah, right. No one's injected anything into this body—" He froze an instant before he cursed.

"What?" Sam asked.

"That fucking flu shot."

She was completely baffled by his anger. "What flu shot?"

"The one Ariston demanded I have if I were to meet with him months ago. He requires it of every associate. He gives you the name of his doctor, you go in, get the shot, and once the doctor calls him, he sets up a meeting. That lousy bastard."

Renate gave him an I-told-you-so look. "It is always so. Never let anyone inject you."

"It was supposed to be a flu shot," Jason snapped.

Sam shook her head. It had been a good ruse. She wasn't even sure if she wouldn't have fallen for it. "So what do we do now? Obviously, they're going to be after us." She looked at Renate. "You wouldn't happen to know of someplace that has the equipment we need to dig it out?"

"And a doctor to do it," Jason said defensively. "I

don't want just anyone poking around my body for a subdermal transmitter."

"Have no fear," Renate said. She led them from the woods toward a small cottage in the town. A sign outside proclaimed it a veterinary clinic.

There were no lights on, but a small dark blue car was parked in the driveway beside it.

Renate led them onto a small porch behind the house.

"What are we doing here?" Sam asked in a low tone as Renate let herself in by way of the backdoor.

"We're helping Jason," she whispered as she pulled them into the clinic, then closed the door.

"By breaking and entering?" Jason asked.

She waved his words away. "Geller and I go way back. Trust me, he won't think anything of our being in here."

Jason exchanged a puzzled look with Sam as Renate went to a cabinet and pulled out an RFID reader pen. RFIDs, microchips implanted under the skin, were currently used to tag pets so that they could be returned to their owners should they run away from home.

"I'm not a lost dog, Renate."

"*Nein,* you are a man with a subdermal tracer bug. Trust me. I know all about these things." She ran the pen over him.

Jason cursed again as he saw the pen blink green

when she passed it over his right butt cheek. "Yep, that's where the bastard injected me."

"*Ja,*" Renate said. "They have you tagged, *schatz.*"

Sam felt for him as Renate went to the office phone and called the good doctor who owned the clinic, asking him to come and extract it.

Sam almost felt sorry for poor Jason. She couldn't imagine having something like that injected into her body and not knowing it.

"I'm not letting a vet cut into my butt," Jason said as soon as Renate hung up.

"Either him or me," Renate said in a tough tone that brooked no argument. "I figure Geller is less likely to leave a scar on that beautiful gluteus maximus. But if you'd rather I handle it . . ." She picked up a scalpel from a tray on the counter.

Jason visibly cringed. "It's all right. I'll wait for the doctor and the local."

Sam laughed as she heard the doctor climbing down the stairs outside the clinic.

A few seconds later, the clinic door opened. Since Renate didn't spear the newcomer to the wall, Sam took that to mean he was the doctor she'd called.

Geller turned on the lights and frowned at the three of them standing in his clinic, dressed like armed burglars. If he thought it particularly odd that two strangers had broken into his office and home in the middle of the night along with a woman armed to her teeth and carrying an assault rifle, he kept it to himself.

He was dressed in a wrinkled sweatshirt and jeans that looked like he must have had them wadded up by his bed. His short white hair was tousled as if he'd been sleeping. Yawning, he pushed his thick glasses back up on his patrician nose and moved stiffly toward them.

"Is he the patient?" he asked Renate, indicating Jason.

"Ja."

Sam looked at Jason, whose face told her that this moment was just as surreal to him as it was to her.

Renate crossed the room and handed the reader to the doctor. "Sam and I shall wait outside in case more of our *friends* should come by while you extract it from him."

"Danke."

Jason passed an almost fearful look at Sam, who felt guilty for leaving him there.

"It'll be okay," she assured him. "Can I get you anything?"

"Ice cream . . . I'm going to want to sit in at least a gallon of it when this is over."

She forced herself not to laugh at his request. "I'll see what I can do."

Renate led her to the small porch out front. Exhausted by all that had happened in such a short period of time, Sam looked up at the bright full moon. How could the weather and town be so peaceful after such an eventful night?

She'd shot Jason, handcuffed him naked to a bed. Photographed him. Had mind-blowing sex without actual intercourse, and twice narrowly escaped gun-wielding loons.

Yeah, just another day in the life . . .

"What time is it?" she asked Renate.

"Almost four A.M."

Sam sighed. "Man, it's been a long night."

"Ja," Renate agreed. "I remember nights like this when I was your age, and I worked for the Stasi. Everything seemed so important. Every mission vital for the well-being of others and for my country. I lived my life solely for my work, but after time my body slowed down against my will. My eyesight wasn't so good . . . I couldn't shoot quite so far. My reflexes slowed year by year, and then finally the Wall came down, and there was no need for us anymore. It's why I retired." She sighed wearily. "But you know, I learned something too late."

"And that is?"

"That the world had gotten along long before I had come into it, and it will continue on long after I am dead." Renate's blue eyes pierced her with sincerity. "Take my word for this, *Schatzi*. Retirement is miserable when you spend it alone. All the years I spent trying to protect the futures of others, I forgot to plan for my own."

Renate sighed heavily. "If I could have one wish, it would be to have had a child of my own. But what is done is done. It is too late for me to go back and change the decisions I so foolishly made, thinking my work was more important than my life." She glanced back toward the door to the clinic where they had left the men. "You have a nice-looking man there, *schatzi*. Do you love him?"

Sam hesitated. Did she? "I don't know. I'm just getting to know him, really."

"Well, take it from one old retired agent to another. The years, they pass by way too fast. Take a few minutes and get to know your man a little better. Don't send him off because work is more important than living. Trust me, they are both equally vital to the heart. Maybe what the two of you have will work, maybe it won't. But at least you'll have something to look back on and say 'I at least tried,' *ja*?"

Sam nodded. She'd never really thought about it that way before. Always focused on the job and her missions, she really hadn't given any thought to what would happen the day she left the agency.

It was a sobering thought.

"I hear you, Renate."

The door opened to show Geller leaving the clinic to join them on the narrow porch. He spoke to

Renate in a thick German dialect that Sam couldn't quite translate. It sounded like he was saying the bug was state-of-the-art.

"What is all that?" she asked Renate.

"He says the bug is a work of art. Pure genius. It has a small digital broadcaster that he burned out after he removed it. So you will be safe now. No more unexpected visitors. But Geller would like to keep the bug and dissect it, if that's all right with you and Jason. He has friends in Europol who will be very interested in this latest technology."

"Sure. Any chance we could get a copy of that report?"

Renate nodded. "I always make sure that Rupert knows about such things."

No wonder Retter stayed on top of so much.

Glancing at her, Geller said something in German that made Renate burst out laughing.

Sam didn't understand it. *"Frühspritzer?"* she asked Renate, wondering what that one word meant. She'd never heard it before. "What is he saying?"

Renate sobered before she answered. "Whoever designed the bug, they had it labeled. It appears they must have many of them that they are using, and so it was coded with an individual signal to help identify it. It had one word that it kept transmitting . . . *Frühspritzer.*"

"And that is?"

Renate laughed again before she explained. "It means premature ejaculator."

Horrified and yet strangely amused, Sam laughed. She looked at Geller. "Did you happen to tell this to Jason?" she asked in English.

The doctor shook his head. "There are some things a man doesn't need to hear about himself."

No doubt. That would most likely disturb poor Jason, and he had been through enough for one night.

"Do you need a ride back to your house?" Geller asked Renate.

"*Nein,* but if you will loan me your auto, I shall take the two of them back to Berlin."

The doctor looked skeptically at her. "Do you feel up to the drive? You look tired. Not that you look bad, you never look bad, but I can tell you haven't slept much."

Renate actually blushed. "*Ja,* I am tired."

"Then I shall be honored to drive you," Geller offered. "After all, I wouldn't want you to fall asleep driving."

Sam pressed her lips to keep from smiling at the look that passed between them. Maybe Renate wouldn't be alone for very much longer.

"I'll go get Jason." She took a step, then paused. "*Danke,* Geller. I really appreciate your help."

"My pleasure."

Sam left them to return to the clinic, where she

found Jason looking less than pleased. But even so, she was struck by the image of him there. He was all man, and yet there was something incredibly endearing about him as he stood with the right side of his pants pulled down, holding an ice pack to his bared cheek.

He gave her a sullen look as she neared him. "I swear I'm going to find the doctor who did this and kill him."

She really felt for him. "You can't do that, Jason."

"Bet me money."

Sam smiled as she closed the distance between them. She reached out and touched the hand that held the ice pack. "Ahh, poor baby. Want someone to kiss it and make it better?"

Jason arched a brow at her offer and at the heat that seeped through him at the mere thought of it. "Yes."

To his amazement, she actually bent over, pulled his hand and the pack away, and placed her lips to the swollen area. He had to admit the feeling of her lips on his skin went a long way in soothing the ache there, though it caused a whole new one somewhere else.

She smoothed the single stitch with her finger as she looked up at him. "Should I inspect your entire body, just in case there might be more hidden bugs?"

He grinned at her teasing tone. "Geller already

double-checked, but if you feel the need to do some independent hands-on inspection later, that could be arranged."

Sam walked into his arms. "Promise?"

"Hell, yeah," he breathed before he lowered his lips to hers, kissed her, and dropped the ice pack as he pulled her closer for some serious necking.

He was really getting into it when he heard someone clear their throat.

"Should we come back later?" Renate asked.

He broke away from Sam's lips to find Geller and Renate standing in the doorway. He cast a wistful look at Sam. What he wanted to say was yes, but that wasn't the correct answer, and he knew it. "Nope. We're good."

He felt Sam pull up the right side of his pants in a gesture that was sweet and endearing. It was something a girlfriend might do to look after her boyfriend.

The thought made his heart beat faster with a hope the likes of which he hadn't felt in a really long time.

He draped his arm over Sam's shoulders as they headed for the doctor. "So what's the game plan?" he asked Sam.

"Renate and Geller are taking us back to Berlin. I vote we find us a nice, quiet hotel somewhere on the outskirts and spend the rest of the day in bed."

Jason laughed. "I like the sound of that."

"Sleeping, Jason," Sam said hurriedly as her cheeks pinkened. "Unlike you, I need to rest."

"Good," he whispered in her ear so that the other two couldn't hear him. "I want you to rest. You're going to need all your stamina later."

Sam sighed at his incorrigibility. But in truth, she was starting to find even that charming.

Renate led them out of the clinic, toward Geller's car, while the doctor locked up. Sam got into the back seat first, then slid over to make room for Jason.

As soon as he was in, he pulled her head to rest in his lap.

Sam smiled at his consideration as she felt his hand toying with her hair. "How's your butt doing?" she asked.

He groaned at her question. "Let's just say I'm not looking forward to this trip."

Sam yawned as Geller got in and started the engine. Truthfully, she was exhausted. By the time they pulled out of the driveway, she was sound asleep.

Jason smiled to himself as he listened to Geller and Renate make chitchat in the front seat while Sam slept in his lap. How had he ever thought that she wasn't the most beautiful woman in the world?

Looking at her now, he couldn't imagine why he hadn't asked her out long before this.

He lightly stroked her cheek, marveling at the incredible softness of it. He'd known Sam for years, but until tonight he'd had no idea of how much strength and courage she possessed.

Glancing up, he caught Renate staring at him.

"She is beautiful, *ja?*"

"Like Aphrodite."

Renate smiled approvingly. "You should probably get some rest too. I am sure this night has been just as long for you."

Jason couldn't agree more. Leaning his head back, he closed his eyes and let images of Sam play through his mind. He fell asleep with the sound of her musical laughter teasing him.

—

Jason jerked awake at the sensation of someone gently shaking his shoulder. Blinking open his eyes, he found Renate, sans her ammo and weapon, standing at the open car door.

"Forgive me, Jason," she said in a low tone. "We arc at the hotel in Berlin."

He rubbed his eyes and yawned as he tried to clear his head. Dawn was already breaking over the city. "We don't have passports for check-in."

"Don't worry. The owner and I go way back. I have explained things to him, and he will make sure that no one knows who or where you are."

He was truly grateful to her. "Thanks, Renate."

"No problem."

He didn't want to wake Sam, but the minute he tried to pick her up, she bolted upright.

"It's okay," he said quickly. "We're at the hotel."

Nodding, she yawned and followed them inside. Without a word, they crossed the lobby and got into the elevator.

Renate led the way to their room and opened the door for them. Once they were inside, she handed him the key to the room while Sam headed straight for the bed.

"I can't thank you enough for all you've done for us," Jason said.

"It's all right, *schatz*. Friends of Rupert's are family to me. You go on now and sleep."

He didn't need to be told that twice. After showing her out and bolting the door, he headed for bed himself.

Jason pulled his weapon out from its hidden holster at his back and tucked it under his pillow. A slow smile spread across his face as he realized Sam had done the same.

Completely exhausted, he joined her on the bed and pulled her into his arms. She felt so good there . . . too good.

Snuggling close, he closed his eyes and returned to sleep.

Sam came awake with a start as she felt something heavy draped over her. She was so used to sleeping alone, it took her a full ten seconds to realize that it was Jason's arm.

And as she lay there, trying to remember where they were, she realized that he did, in fact, snore.

She laughed in spite of herself.

Still, he slept.

Smiling, she stretched in the bed until her hand made contact with something solid under her pillow. She pulled it out to find Jason's gun there.

Tickled by him, she left the bed quietly and sneaked off to shower and take care of a few very necessary things.

CHAPTER 5

Jason woke up to the sensation of someone gently stroking his hard cock underneath the blanket. Soft, gentle fingers brushed down the length of him, toying with the tip. He thought he was still dreaming until he opened his eyes to find Sam stretched out beside him.

"You snore," she said accusingly.

"No, I don't."

"Yes, you do. Like a buzz saw."

In spite of her dire tone, he smiled. "Do I really?"

"Yes."

"Then I guess you're just going to have to shoot me, huh?"

"Guess so," she said as she cupped him under the covers. Her warm hand felt like heaven as her fingers massaged his sac, making him even harder. "But what a shame to see something so fine terminated, huh?"

He closed his eyes as she continued stroking him. He'd never had a woman wake him up like this before. A man could definitely get used to it.

Sam nipped his hip with her teeth before she pulled away. Jason whimpered at her action. "Don't leave."

"I'll be right back."

Disappointment filled him—at least, until she returned to the room wearing absolutely nothing but a smile.

She rejoined him on the bed and rolled him flat on his back. Jason frowned until he saw her lift the small foil package up to her lips.

"Where'd you get that?"

"I went shopping this morning. There's a drugstore just around the corner."

He grinned at her. "A woman after my own heart."

Jason cupped her breast in his hand as she unrolled the condom down the length of his cock. Not even the cold lubricant could dampen the heat he felt at her touch.

Sam nipped the salty flesh of Jason's knee. She'd been dreaming about this all morning. For the first time, she understood her mother's obsession with the male species. They did have their moments of worthiness. Jason was not only the hottest things on two legs, but he'd been extremely considerate to her. Even thoughtful.

Most of all, though, she liked the feeling of waking up in his arms. And all she wanted was to feel Jason deep inside her.

Unable to stand it anymore, she climbed up his body to straddle him. A shiver swept through her at the sensation of his hard muscled body nestled between her spread thighs.

"Hi, beautiful," he said as he guided her hips back with his hands so that he could impale her.

She hissed as he filled her to capacity. Surely there was nothing better than his thick fullness deep inside her body.

Jason raised his hips to drive himself in even deeper as she rode him. He cupped her breast in his hands as he watched her taking her pleasure from his body.

He loved the feeling of her body wrapped around his, of her milking him ever so sweetly. Unable to stand her slow rhythm, he rolled with her until he had her pinned below him. He captured her lips as he sank himself back inside her warm heat.

Sam groaned at the taste of Jason as his tongue matched the thrusts of his hips against hers.

There was nothing slow or easy about the way they made love now. It was fast and frenzied as they each sought their own piece of heaven.

For some reason she didn't understand, Jason pulled out of her.

"I want to go deep inside you, Sam," he said raggedly in her ear. He propped the pillows up and draped her facedown over them.

Sam spread her legs wide, waiting impatiently for him to return to her.

Jason sucked his breath in at the sight of her spread out for him. Grinding his teeth, he separated the folds of her body until he could see the most private part of her. She shivered as he gently fingered her.

Growling deep in his throat, he ran his tongue along the edge so that he could taste her before he rose up and entered her body again.

They cried out in unison.

Sam reached out and clutched the headboard as Jason returned to thrusting against her. Each stroke seemed to go even deeper than the last. And when he moved his hand to stroke her while he thrust, she moaned so deeply that it left her hoarse.

The pleasure of him behind and inside her was more than she could stand. Her body burst apart into ribbons of ecstasy.

Jason smiled as he felt her come for him. He moved faster until as his own climax built, and when he exploded, he could swear he saw stars.

Sated to an unbelievable level, he kissed her gently on the shoulder before he collapsed by her side.

Sam snuggled up so that she could rest her head against his chest. "That was nice."

"Nice?" he asked with a laugh. "I personally don't think it gets much better."

Honestly, neither did she.

But before she could pursue that, the phone started ringing. She frowned at Jason.

"You expecting anyone?" he asked.

"Maybe it's the hotel staff." She reached for the phone and answered it.

"What the hell happened last night?"

Her scowl deepened at Retter's angry tone. "What are you talking about?"

"What am I talking about? Renate called me a few minutes ago to say that you two were no longer staying with her and that she laid waste to four men early this morning who had entered her home with murder on their minds."

Sam detected a note of amusement under his anger. No doubt Renate had told him exactly how much she'd enjoyed their little midnight adventure. "Oh, yeah, you missed the fireworks. But we're all okay, including Renate. She's something else, by the way."

"You have no idea. Are the two of you still breathing?"

"Since I'm talking, I would have to say yes. Hard to talk without it."

"Good. I have a chartered car headed your way with all the paperwork you two need to jump the country. I want you both on a plane out of here within the hour. You got it?"

"Aye, aye, Captain."

He hung up.

"What was all that?" Jason asked as she set her phone back on the hook.

"We're heading home."

His frown matched her earlier one. "When?"

"Now. Retter has a car on the way."

She saw the deep reluctance in his green eyes. "What about Ariston?"

"I'm going to assume that Retter has it covered. Besides, that's not my mission. Getting you home is."

Jason looked like he wanted to argue.

Sam brushed the hair back from his face. "I know it sucks to have to leave an assignment unfinished. But there's nothing we can do. Sometimes it just happens."

"Yeah, but it's never happened to me before."

She kissed his forehead. "C'mon, baby. We need to shower and get dressed."

Jason nodded, but as he got out of bed and he felt the tug of the stitch on his ass, a thought occurred to him.

"Holy shit," he breathed as his mind whirled with a whole new thought.

"What?"

"Ariston . . . How many other people has he tagged besides me?"

She shrugged. "No telling. Why?"

Jason darted past her to the bathroom. "C'mon. We have something to do before we leave."

Sam and Jason showered, then dressed quickly. By the time they reached the lobby, their car was already there, waiting on them.

She frowned as Jason refused to leave. Instead, he headed to the front desk, where a large black-haired woman stood wearing a black suit. "Is there a computer here for guest use?"

"*Ja,* there is a business office just over there." She pointed to a small room next to the door.

Jason headed for it.

Sam followed after him, confused by his odd actions. "What are you doing, Jason?"

"I'm finishing business," he said in a low tone. "Didn't you use to do a lot of hacking in the FBI?"

"It wasn't hacking," she said defensively. "It was all done with court orders. Why?"

"Because I want you to hack into Dr. Berg's files and get a list of everyone he's given flu shots to in the last year."

A slow smile spread across her face as she suddenly understood what he wanted done. "You want to see who else he tagged, huh?"

He nodded.

Her blood rushed through her veins as she followed him into the office. If he was right, this would be a great way to find out who Ariston dealt with . . . and where they were.

Luckily, there was no one else using the room; there

wasn't even a staff member present. Sam grabbed the closest computer and started searching for the doctor's office.

Jason tapped his thumb against his thigh as he watched Sam navigate through the German medical files. Luckily they had a unified system that allowed her access to all of Berg's clients, along with their addresses and names.

"There are several Bergs listed here."

"Franz-Josef Berg, with a hyphen."

"Got him."

Jason leaned over her shoulder as she pulled up the records. He pointed to a line in their billing system that didn't make sense to him. "What's that?"

"Gold," she breathed as she matched the strange billing code against the key in Berg's system. She pulled up Jason's chart under his alias to show him. "Here," she said, pointing to the line. "See where your account was charged. There's another code that you didn't see that was billed to Herr Ariston."

"Yeah. For what?"

"A colonoscopy."

Jason gaped. "I beg your pardon? No one stuck nothing near my rear entry. That is sacred."

She shook her head at him. "Since he's a general practitioner, I figured as much. Apparently our doctor has a sense of humor. My guess is he's disguising the implant charge as that one."

" 'Cause he was shafting me."

"Yup."

Jason gave a short laugh. "Who else did he shaft?"

She pulled up a quick list of names. "A short enough list that it shouldn't take us too long to run them all down."

Jason kissed her. "I knew you were brilliant."

"Not me, baby. You're the one who thought of it."

"Yeah, but I couldn't have hacked the system without you."

Sam loved the fact that he wasn't trying to take all the credit. She printed out the list and quickly backed out of the system. Once they had it, she took a few minutes to call Retter with the news.

"I'll meet you guys at the airport. You can hand it to me then, and I'll get started on the colonoscopy retrievals."

"You got it."

She hung up the pay phone, then made her way out to the car with Jason.

Jason kept his attention solely focused on Sam as they rode to the airport. He was still amazed at how everything had turned out—at least, until he remembered something.

"Ah, no."

"What?" Sam asked.

"I just remembered that everything I own is in London."

"Don't worry. We'll get someone to pack it up for you. I'm sure Hunter would be glad to personally take charge of seeing it all packed up and returned to the U.S."

He snorted at that. "Why don't I find that knowledge comforting?"

She laughed. "Probably because he wants you dead for scaring him."

Jason shook his head. Unlike her, he didn't find that amusing, but he had other things to think about than Hunter and his vendetta. "So what happens to me now? I've been in Europe so long, it'll be hard getting used to a new place . . . a new person."

Sam felt for him. That was the hardest part about being an undercover agent. You were constantly responsible for reinventing yourself. She reached over and squeezed his hand.

They remained silent until they reached the airport, where their chartered flight was waiting. They found Retter in one of the seats on board the plane.

Tall and well muscled, he had long black hair and was dressed in a tan sweater, black coat, and jeans. He had at least three days' growth of whiskers, and his piercing eyes were covered by a pair of dark sunglasses.

"Bonnie and Clyde," he drawled. "Nice of you to make it."

"Shut up, Rupert," Jason said.

Retter went completely still before he spoke. "The only people who call me that are all female. Now unless you want me to make you one of them, I suggest you revert to my more tolerated name."

Jason held his hands up in mock surrender. "Fine."

"Here's the list," Sam said as she handed it to Retter, then took a seat beside Jason.

Retter's face was grim as he skimmed the names. "This is a nice tidbit. Thanks." He got up and headed for the exit. But before he left the plane, he turned around to look at them. "You two do know that Joe will shit when you get back to Nashville, right?"

Sam frowned. "What do you mean?"

"Well, he sent Dagmar and Dieter out together and they got married. Then there was Rhea and Ace. If one more set of agents hooks up, I'm sure we'll all get a memo about it."

"Who said we were hooking up?" Sam asked.

Retter's gaze dropped to where her hand was resting on Jason's knee.

Sam immediately pulled it away.

Jason put it back.

"Yeah," Retter said. "Thanks for clogging my in-box with more Joe hysteria." He ducked out to the plane and left them alone.

Sam gave Jason a withering stare. "What was that about?"

"I was just claiming my woman."

"Claiming your woman? What century is this?"

"The twenty-first."

"Then why—"

He broke her words off with a kiss. Sam sighed at the taste of him. When he pulled back, his eyes warmed her. "I'm not asking you to marry me . . . yet. I'm just asking you for a chance to see where this relationship might take us. So what do you say, Sam?"

She smiled at him. "I say, let's see about making Joe a little bit crazier."

EPILOGUE

Jason sat in Joe's office while his boss debriefed him. It'd been a long flight in, and frankly, he was looking forward to just sleeping for about ten to twelve hours.

"Jason?"

He blinked at Joe's sharp tone. "Yeah?"

Joe rolled his eyes. "Go on, get the hell out of here before I shoot you."

Stifling a yawn, Jason got up and passed Tee in the doorway. He paused as she entered the office with Joe. "Tee?" he asked, holding the door open. "Where did you make my reservations?"

The tiny Vietnamese-American agent stared blankly at him. "What reservations?"

His stomach sank. "For me to crash?"

She snorted at him. "You don't need reservations."

Jason gaped at her. Granted, Tee could be unforgiving and downright cruel at times, but damn, he hadn't done anything to his knowledge to piss her off. "Where am I supposed to sleep?"

Someone cleared their throat.

Jason turned to find Sam standing a few feet away, looking about as tired as he felt—though it looked a lot better on her than him. He was stunned that she'd hung around while Joe gave him the third degree and threatened sanctions against him for blowing up Hunter's car.

She unfolded her arms to show him a pair of handcuffs. "I'm taking you into custody," she said with a playful wink.

Jason smiled as his heart pounded. He definitely liked the sound of that. "I thought you went home."

"I was waiting for you."

Crossing the distance between them, he draped his arm over her shoulders and kissed her lightly on the head.

Joe stood in the doorway beside Tee as he watched the two of them leaving with their arms wrapped around each other. He made a disgusted sound in the back of his throat.

"Oh, knock it off, Joe," Tee said as she pushed him back into the office.

"Knock it off? C'mon, Tee. You and I both know that love and work never cohabitate well."

She said something to him in Vietnamese.

He grimaced at her as she put a folder on her desk. "I hate it when you do that. What did you just call me?"

"Fuddy-duddy."

It sounded better in Vietnamese. "Fuddy-duddy I may be, but how the hell are we supposed to guard national security when I can't even keep my agents' pants on?"

Tee glared at him. "Relax, Joe. It's nine o'clock at night. Go home."

He was tired, but she didn't look like she was anywhere near leaving. "What about you?"

Tee sat at her desk. "The bad guys never sleep—"

"So why should I," he said, finishing her favorite line. He knew Tee was more than capable of handling herself in any given situation, but he wasn't about to leave her up here alone. Anything could happen. Not to mention, the office was really lonely when you were by yourself.

"It's okay. I've got some work I need to do too."

Joe returned to his desk and sat down to review the list that Jason had given to Retter. He'd assigned a new agent the job of surveying two men on the list they knew were aligned with extremist groups. If they were lucky, the RFID chips could be used for the good side as well.

But as he started to pull up the files on the computer for the men, his gaze caught a glimpse of Tee as she bent over to retrieve a fallen pen from the floor. Her butt came off her chair, gifting him with a perfect view of her attributes. He hardened instantly.

Grinding his teeth, he looked away before she caught him ogling her. There were things in the world that were a lot more important than his rampant lust for his co-director. Although at that moment he was having a difficult time remembering what they were exactly.

"You hungry?" Tee asked as she straightened up.

"Always."

She shook her head. "I knew you'd say that. Want to eat Off the Grill tonight?"

"Sure."

"Your usual?"

"Yeah."

Tee looked up the number on her PDA, then dialed it. "Hi Dave, this is Tee again. I'd like to get the rib eye steak medium rare with a baked potato and cheese, no butter or sour cream . . ."

Joe forced himself not to smile as Tee ordered his food to perfection. She really did know him.

Except she didn't know the most important thing where he was concerned, and that was just how much she meant to him.

It was the one thing he could never let her know.

⚓

"So did Joe chew your entire butt off?" Sam asked as she drove him from their office in the Bell South tower from downtown Nashville toward her apartment in Franklin.

"I don't know—I think someone needs to check and see."

Sam slid a sideways look at him. She had to admit that even exhausted, he was acute and able with a comeback. "You do know that I'm not used to having a boyfriend, right?"

"It's okay, I'm not either."

Sam groaned at his joke. "I'm trying to be serious here, Jason."

"I know, Sam. It's, uh . . . it's going to be interesting. Most agents who try to have a relationship end up hating each other."

"True."

"But since you started out hating me, hopefully we've put that behind us." He winked at her.

Sam smiled at him. He was right. When she'd headed off to Germany, her intent had been to kill him, not bring him home to her apartment. Her mother always said that life was big on surprises.

Nothing had surprised her more than finding Jason so delightful or enticing.

"Don't look so fretful, Sam. I can find my own place to live tomorrow, and I won't impose myself on your life until you're ready for it."

And that was what she liked most about him. He really was perceptive. As she drove down I-65, she felt something she'd never felt before . . . a sense of excitement about having someone to come home to.

"You know, if it takes you a little while to find that place to live, I'm okay with it."

He reached over to brush her hair back from her cheek. "Good. But if I start to wear out my welcome—"

"I'll shoot you."

BAD TO THE BONE

For my mother,
who has given me my overactive imagination,
my husband,
who doesn't mind it,
and my friends and family,
who support me.
God bless all of you!

PROLOGUE

Marianne Webernec was completely average at age thirty, but what she desperately wanted to be was extraordinary.

Exceptional. Spectacular.

For once in her life she wanted to be the heroine in one of the Rachel Fire novels that she gobbled up as soon as they were published. To be tall, thin, and devastatingly beautiful. The kind of woman that men everywhere lusted for. The kind of woman who walked into a room, and men fought each other just for her smile.

But what she was, even after her makeover, was a mere five-feet-four-inch size-ten woman with medium brown hair that was pinned back from her round face to fall just below her shoulders. She had eyes that were flat brown, not amber, not flecked with anything un-usual or worth noticing. Her breasts were too small, her hips were too wide, and her feet were pinched by the narrow tips of her high-heeled shoes.

She was . . .

Average.

Painfully, woefully average.

"I think you're stunning."

Only if she had a stun gun in her hand.

Marianne looked over her shoulder to see Aislinn Zimmerman staring at her. Aislinn was what she wanted to be. Rich, model thin, with long, curly red hair, perfectly manicured nails, and big bright green eyes that seemed to glow. Aislinn was every bit as beautiful as her namesake from Aislinn's mother's favorite romance novel, *The Wolf and the Dove*.

Marianne had spent her entire life hating women who looked like Aislinn. They were everywhere. On television, in magazines, and on the pages of the books that Marianne loved to read. Books where the gorgeous, drop-dead heroine nailed the gorgeous, drop-dead hero.

They were ever an unnecessary reminder that at the end of the day, Marianne Webernec would never be one of them.

She would always be average. White noise in the background of a world that went on oblivious to her presence no matter how much she longed for it to be otherwise.

"Thanks," Marianne said to her lamely, knowing the truth in her heart. But that was okay.

Because in the next few minutes she was going to

walk through the door behind Aislinn and become the one thing she'd always wanted to be . . .

A covert CIA agent pursued by the evil archvillain who would turn out to be a good guy trying to uncover the man who had killed his brother.

Okay, the plot was a bit clichéd, even a little trite. But Marianne loved Rachel Fire's book *Danger in the Night*. She had read it so many times that her copy at home was in pieces barely held together by tape.

For the last four years that book and its hero, Brad Ramsey, had lived in her heart and in her mind. He was the man she dreamed of seducing every night when she closed her eyes.

She had licked every inch of his divinely masculine body from head to foot, and had made him beg her for mercy. They had made love everywhere from Caribbean beaches to the snowdrifts of Moscow.

In her mind she had ridden him hard and furiously, and made him hers.

Oh, to really be the book's heroine, Ren Winterbourne. The sultry, sophisticated agent, woman of the world, who knew every way possible to make a man beg for her touch. Ren never doubted herself. She always knew exactly what she wanted and how to get it.

Marianne was still searching for her place in the world. And when it came to men, she would never understand them. They were completely alien beasties.

She sighed wistfully. Her entire life was a study in what could have been. If only she'd been smarter, taller, prettier . . .

But she wasn't.

Her mother had once told her that life was about acceptance. That she needed to be content with what was dealt her and be grateful it wasn't worse.

Starting this instant, Marianne was going to take her mother's advice.

Mostly.

She was going to walk out that door and . . .

Stumble, knowing her.

"Do I have to wear the heels?" she asked Aislinn, holding her foot out toward the beautiful redhead as she flexed her ankle.

Some things were best done with level feet. Especially when the last thing Marianne wanted was to be embarrassed. "I'm really not a high-heel kind of person. I'm more the I'll-stumble-and-twist-my-ankle kind of woman."

Aislinn laughed. "Sure. What would you like?"

"Got anything flat and black?"

Aislinn flipped open her stylish silver cell phone and pressed a button. "Hi, Gwen, Ms. Webernec would like a selection of flat black shoes to go with her rust-colored miniskirt dress. She's a size eight medium. . . . Thanks." Aislinn closed the phone. "Give her ten minutes, and she'll bring us a new boxload of them."

It was good to be queen.

At least for the day, or in this case, a whole month. Marianne smiled at the thought.

One full month of being catered to and pampered. Having her every want met without complaint.

Oh, yeah, forget Julia Roberts in *Pretty Woman*. This reality was *so* much better.

After all, Marianne Webernec, average Jane high school teacher, was about to head off to Sex Camp.

CHAPTER ONE

Kyle Foster lay behind a short clump of bushes, scoping out the large compound that lay sheltered in the sand—his latest target.

It was fifteen hundred hours, and all the explosives were rigged. Their timers set. The beach was silent, with a mild northwesterly wind that would carry the shrapnel and debris a minimal distance, toward the empty lagoon.

He was watching the countdown on his watch, waiting for something that would alleviate his extreme boredom.

He'd thought it would be the well-placed, perfectly executed explosion.

It wasn't.

At fifteen seconds and counting, disaster struck as an unknown, unexpected civilian popped out of the small wooded area near the compound.

Kyle cursed. There was no way to stop the explosives, and he didn't dare shout at her.

Damn civilians never took orders well. Instead of

doing as they were told, they invariably assumed the position of a deer in the headlights and asked, "What?" Which would be followed by the ever aggravating, "Why?"

By then it would be too late.

If he said, "Bomb," she'd scream and probably run straight for the explosion. Murphy's Law.

He was out of time.

Combat trained and ever ready to fight, Kyle launched himself from his covert position to intercept her before she drew any closer.

He mentally continued the countdown in his head as he ran full speed toward her. . . .

Marianne saw nothing but a blur from the corner of her eye. One second she was heading toward the small sand castle that looked as if someone had constructed it with careful, minute detail. The next some large something had scooped her up into its arms and run off with her.

Breathless from shock and the feel of two extremely strong arms carrying her while the man ran across the beach, she didn't even have time to protest as the two of them flew in the opposite direction from the castle.

Just as they reached the pathway she'd been following, she heard a sharp *click*.

The man holding her threw the two of them to the ground and rolled them under some bushes as a massive explosion rent the air. The earth beneath them shook.

Her breath was knocked out of her from their fall, and panic welled inside her.

A sleek wall of muscle covered her body again as something began to rain down on the sand around them. She was overwhelmed by the combined scent of Brut, warm masculine skin, and Finesse shampoo.

Marianne instinctively covered her face until the "rain" stopped.

"What in the world just happened?" she asked, her heart pounding as she dared peek from between her fingers.

The man lying on top of her lifted himself up to look down at her.

Marianne gaped.

In all her life she'd never seen anything like him. His eyes were bright and blue. Electrifying and filled with mirthful mischief. They reminded her of the boys in her classes whenever they were planning some youthful prank.

Only there was nothing boyish about the man on top of her. He was obviously in his mid-thirties, his face ruggedly handsome, with sharp cheekbones and at least a full day's worth of stubble on his cheeks and chin.

He was even more handsome than the actor they had playing Brad Ramsey.

And the feel of his long, hard body covering hers . . .

It was heaven. Pure heaven.

He swept a heated gaze over her face and body before giving her a devilish grin that should belong to the worst sort of Regency rake. Not to mention the fact that his waist was lying between her legs, and she felt a sudden swell pressing against her intimately. One that let her know this was no small man. Nor was he completely uninterested in her.

It was all she could do not to moan in pleasure.

"Hi." The deepness of his voice was as startling as their meeting.

"Hi," she answered back rather lamely.

Kyle tried to remember what the woman had asked him a second ago, but all he could really think of was the peekaboo dimple she had in her left cheek. It flashed at him as she frowned.

Not to mention the fact that she felt damn good underneath him.

Her white tank top had fallen off one shoulder, leaving it bare where it beckoned him to touch and kiss the smooth skin it revealed.

Her dark brown eyes were warm and friendly with a healthy dose of suspicion in them. She had sleek brown hair that fell around her head, onto the sand. It was the kind of hair a man dreamed of running his hands through. The kind of hair a man liked to feel whipping his chest while the woman who had it sat on top of him, grinding her body against his until they both came.

It took every ounce of control he possessed not to rub his swollen, aching groin against her and dream of sinking himself deep inside her hot, wet body.

Oh, yeah, he so wanted a piece of this woman. One small taste of her lush, soft, feminine curves.

"You . . . uh . . . you want to get off me now?" she asked, her voice sounding a bit peeved.

"Not really," he answered honestly. "I kind of like it here." More than he dared admit even to himself.

And he found himself suddenly fixated by the bared skin of her shoulder, which didn't seem to betray a bra strap.

Was she naked under there?

His cock tightened even more at the thought of her naked, unrestrained breasts being only a tiny push of fabric away. Of taking one of them into his mouth and suckling its tip while she buried her long, graceful fingers into his hair.

Marianne arched a brow at the man's unexpected response and tilted her head as she watched him. She wasn't sure if this was part of her whole fantasy package or not. What with the explosion and all, it was possible he was one of the actors who had been playing out her novel.

But Rachel Fire hadn't written a scene about a sand castle being blown up.

Then again, there was a scene in a few more days where they blew up a cabin, so maybe the man had been practicing.

At any rate, he was a cutie-pie. Gorgeous, in fact. His darkly tanned body held the muscular definition of an athlete. One that begged a woman to run her hands over it.

"You always sweep a woman off her feet like this and throw her on the ground?"

He laughed at that, a warm, rich sound that made her actually tingle. "No, I have to say this is a first. But given how it seems to be turning out, I might make it a habit." He winked at her, then pulled back from her slowly and held his hand out to her as if to shake hers.

"Kyle Foster," he said.

Hmm, not one of the names in the book. Maybe he was one of the extras they had hired to play commando with.

"Marianne Webernec," she said automatically as she shook his large, callused hand and did her best not to think about what it would feel like to have it cup her breast or have those long, masculine fingers sunk deep inside her body.

He had beautiful hands. Powerful hands. Strong and manly, they appealed to her in the best sort of way.

"Oh, wait," she said, trying to distract herself from

those thoughts. "I'm supposed to be Ren Winter-bourne. Sorry, I keep forgetting."

He scowled at her words. "What are you? A federal agent or something?"

"Something, definitely something." She started to push herself to her feet.

Kyle helped her up with an effortlessness that overcharged her hormones and made her yearn to lean into the strength of his body until she swooned from delight.

What was it about this man that made her want to do him right here on the beach? She'd never been sexually flagrant before, but something about Kyle Foster made her long desperately to rip that tight white T-shirt off and have her way with him whether he wanted it or not.

"You must be from the other side of the island," he said in that innately masculine voice.

He released her all too soon, and she ached from the loss of his body heat being so close. It had warmed her more than the overhead sun.

"Uh-oh. Did I really come all that way? They told me I wasn't supposed to go too far away. Did I end up on the private side of things?"

"Yeah, but it's okay. I'm the only one staying here right now." He glanced around the vacant beach. "It's been boring as hell up until now."

"Tell me about it. For a fantasy vacation, it's been

rather meek compared to what I was expecting."

Interest sparked deep in those electric blue eyes. "What were you expecting?"

Marianne squelched a smile. She'd been expecting something along the lines of studly fine Kyle Foster to come into her life and ravish her day and night until she couldn't move, never mind walk.

Marianne bit her bottom lip at the thought and lowered her gaze to the snowy sand to keep him from seeing just how embarrassed she was.

"I don't know," she said with a small shrug. "Some handsome man to throw me down on the ground and save me from an unexpected explosion?"

Kyle laughed again. He didn't know why. Normally, he was about as serious as they came. His sometimes partner, Retter, had often commented on the fact that Kyle's face would freeze if he ever cracked more than a half grin.

But something about this woman made him feel . . .

Well . . .

Kind of giddy. There was no other word for it. And he really hated that girly-sounding word. *Giddy* and *Kyle Foster* went together about like a cobra and a mongoose.

He must have been even more bored than he suspected. She wasn't ravishing or even beautiful. She reminded him of the woman next door.

A woman who shouldn't draw his notice at all, and yet he found himself staring at her and the way her tiny, light freckles kissed the skin across the bridge of her nose.

Even more startling was the desire he had to taste every one of those freckles with his tongue. To kiss and tease each one and see how many more she might have in other, more provocative areas of her body.

Like those creamy thighs that were virtually hidden by her drab tan walking shorts. Thighs that would look much better naked and wrapped around his neck . . .

Marianne felt suddenly awkward as she realized the T-shirt Kyle wore displayed more of his muscled chest than it concealed. Of course, built the way he was, it would take several layers of sweaters and a heavy overcoat to disguise that body.

He reminded her of a linebacker. One with a very tight end.

He was gorgeous all over. From the top of his sun-kissed dark brown hair to the toes of his scuffed black leather biker boots.

She frowned as she noticed that.

"Who wears boots on the beach?" she asked unexpectedly.

He glanced down at his feet. "I didn't even think about it. Guess it's not normal, huh?"

She smiled up at him. "Says to me you don't spend a lot of time on the beach."

"Not really. I'm here under extreme protest. What about you?"

"I'm this month's winner."

He frowned as if he had no idea what she was talking about.

"You know," she said, "the Hideaway Heroine Sweepstakes winner? I'm the one they chose this time."

"Ah," he said, nodding. "So how's it going?"

Twirling a small section of her hair, she shrugged. "It's going, I guess. South more than north, but I suppose nothing's perfect."

"Now, why would you say that?" He indicated the vibrant blue sky with his thumb. "Just look at that sky. It's perfect. Great day. You got the beach to run around on, the surf sliding up. Hell, you can even hear birds chirping."

"Which is why you were blowing up a sand castle?"

He gave her a guilty smile that made her knees weak. "Well, okay, nothing's perfect."

Marianne licked her lips as she watched him hitch his thumbs into the front pockets of his jeans. He had such a manly stance. One of power, like some sinuous beast just prowling the beach waiting for a morsel to gobble.

How she wished she were that morsel.

"So," she said, stretching the word out, "do you do that a lot? Blow up sand castles?"

"Only if they deserve it." He glanced back to the hole in the beach where his sand castle had been. "That one, unfortunately, had gone bad. Real bad."

She covered her face as she laughed again. "I guess I better stay on the straight and narrow then, huh?"

"Marianne?"

She cringed as she heard the voice of "Brad" coming through the trees from the opposite direction of her uncovered pathway. The actor was extremely handsome, but he was pale and rather feminine compared to the man in front of her.

"I guess I need to be going," she said reluctantly.

She started away from Kyle, but he caught her hand in his. The feel of that steely grip on her skin made her entire body burn.

Before she realized what he was doing, he'd pulled her against the hard, lean strength of his body and lowered his mouth onto hers.

Marianne sighed at the taste of his lips as his tongue explored her mouth, flicking masterfully in and out. It made her breathless and weak. She held on to those broad, muscled shoulders as she felt the heat pounding between her legs. Heat that made her wet and desperate for this man.

His muscles flexed beneath her hand, whetting her

appetite all the more. How she wished she were touching his tanned skin, sinking her teeth into all that lush, fabulous maleness.

Kyle growled at how good she tasted. But then he'd known instinctively that she would.

His cock hardened to the point of pain as he imagined what it would feel like to lay her down on the beach and spend the next few hours watching her come for him over and over again while he slid himself in and out of her sleek wet heat.

There were few things in life he liked more than the sight of a woman caught in the middle of an orgasm. The sound of her delighted cries as he nibbled and teased the last tremor from her body.

And this was a woman he could savor from now until the end of time. . . .

"Marianne!"

He didn't want to let her go, but then, he'd never been the kind of guy to perform before an audience, nor did she strike him as the kind of woman who would appreciate him trying to broaden their horizons in that respect.

Reluctantly he released her.

Damn. Kyle didn't say anything as he watched the klutz—who tripped over the sand castle's crater as he crossed the sand—take off with his woman.

He glanced at the blackened hole on the beach.

Target number one had been destroyed.

Target number two . . .

She would have to be conquered.

For the first time in a month he felt the familiar adrenaline rush surging.

At last he had a mission.

Marianne Webernec and her sweet little mouth that had tasted like honey.

One taste, and he'd been hooked. And he wasn't the kind of man to leave well enough alone once his curiosity was aroused.

Curiosity, hell, his whole body was aroused, and he wouldn't be sated until he'd tasted a whole lot more than her lips.

No way. Before he was through with her, he would know every minute part of her body and every way to make her scream out in pleasure.

Kyle smiled at the lecherous thought.

This was one challenge he was going to savor well.

Chapter Two

"Hey, Sam," Kyle said to the surly man behind the concierge desk as he entered the lobby of the small luxury hotel where he'd been staying literally against his will.

Since Kyle had been shot in the line of duty (about six times, they assumed—five bullets had been dug out, and there was some debate on what had caused the sixth wound), his boss had decided Kyle needed a vacation at the hotel his agency owned on a remote, private island out in the middle of the Atlantic.

Kyle thought the six-week "vacation" was completely unnecessary, but Joe had insisted, and anyone who had ever tried to argue with Joe Q. Public soon found out they would have a better time moving a mountain than budging Joe even an inch.

So here he was, a highly trained special ops agent, bored, healed, and raring to go, only to find Joe laughing at him every time he called and begged for a plane ride off this godforsaken island.

At least until twenty minutes ago, when fate had finally shone on him again.

Suddenly the thought of the next week looked promising.

Kyle stopped at the desk where Sam sat holding a long-neck beer propped on his knee while watching a Lakers game on ESPN. In his mid-fifties, Sam looked like the picture-perfect image of a stout Scotsman. He had a ruddy complexion and a wide, serious face that was topped by a thick unruly mane of stark white hair. He wore black-rimmed glasses that continually slid down his broad nose and that he constantly pushed back up.

But the most interesting thing about him was his companion Roscoe. An old basset hound, Roscoe had about as much attitude as any dog Kyle had ever met. And in a strange way, Kyle liked that old dog as much as he liked Sam.

Kyle paused at the counter and respectfully waited for a commercial before he interrupted the hotel's manager. "Tell me something, Sam. What's on the other side of this island, and why am I not supposed to go over there?"

Sam shrugged as he looked up from the small television. He took a quick swig of beer before he answered. "That's them weirdos from that publisher, Rose Books. You'd have to ask Joe for more details. He's the one who rents this part of the island from them so we can do some covert training, or in your case emergency R and R. I think he knows the owner of the publishing house or something."

"Do you know what goes on over there?"

"Yeah, and it's spooky as all get-out."

"Spooky how?"

"It's Sex Camp."

Kyle choked at the unexpected answer. "What?"

"Sex Camp," Sam repeated simply, as if there were nothing unusual about the title. "They have these women what read those romance books, and every few months or so one of them wins a trip out here to live out their fantasy novel, and they put on this whole grand show with the winner."

Sam pushed his glasses up. "Makes you want to know what's in them romance novels women read. I've been reading Tom Clancy for years, and all I get is submarines and war stories." He snorted. "I ain't never had the itch to run into the woods with a bunch of sailors and try to throw them on the ground. You know what I mean?"

Not really. Sam had a bad habit of not always making sense. "Beg pardon?" Kyle asked.

"Listen," Sam continued as he idly stroked Roscoe's head. "A word to the wise, son, you got to be real careful walking around after dark whenever one of them fantasies is going on. They don't call it Sex Camp for nothing. I've seen them do things on the beach that'll make you go blind. Hell, some of it I didn't even know was humanly possible."

Kyle couldn't keep his mouth from hanging open as he thought about Marianne being the latest winner. There was no way his sweet little visitor would do something like that.

Was there?

And if there was, then she'd better damn well be doing it with *him*.

"Are you yanking my chain?" he asked Sam.

"Nah, why would I?" Sam gave him an intense stare over the top rims of his glasses. "You think they're normal women when they come off the plane, but they're really raving nymphomaniacs cleverly disguised."

"Bullshit."

"Nah, boy, it's true. They come off the plane looking all nice and normal, and within twenty-four hours they turn into Debbie Does Dallas or Richard or whoever she can find. It's horrifying what happens to these women." He pointed to his dog. "See Roscoe here? He's only two years old. He went into the woods one night, and now look at him. Their antics done aged him twenty years overnight. And don't get me started on them men they got. I don't know where they find them. But something about them ain't right, neither. So I stay on my side of the island as far away from all of them loons as I can get."

"I don't believe you."

Sam shrugged and turned back toward the television as the game resumed. "You don't got to believe it. Truth is truth. You should be here whenever they're doing one of those historical reenactments. They make us run around in costume in case we accidentally bump into one of their winners. It's a big pain. We have to say things like 'my lady' and shit. I feel like a blooming idiot. Can you just imagine my fat ass in a tutu or tights or whatever those godawful things are called?" He blew out a disgusted breath. "I got too-too much for those things, and their director, Aislinn Zimmerman, once tried to borrow Roscoe for scenery."

Roscoe whined at that.

"That's right, boy. Don't worry. Old Sam would never let them abuse you." He glanced back at Kyle. "That's why I keep Roscoe hidden. The last thing I need is my poor dog going blind, too."

Kyle stood there stunned by Sam's disclosures. He just couldn't see the woman he'd met doing something like that. She'd seemed so pure. Innocent.

No, he didn't believe it. But this whole scenario would require more research.

Heading for the elevators, he decided it was time to get down to business and do what he did best.

Research, infiltrate, and take whatever action necessary to achieve his objective.

Three hours later Kyle sat back in his office chair, reviewing his reconnaissance data.

Marianne Webernec was a high school teacher from a small town outside Peoria, Illinois, whose only claim to fame was once winning the statewide spelling bee in junior high school. She hadn't even been homecoming queen.

She'd graduated with good grades, not exceptional ones. Done college in five years, then went back to her hometown to teach German and French at the local high school.

She'd never even had a speeding or parking ticket. Not even in college.

There wasn't much here to say she was anything out of the ordinary.

Nothing except for the way his body had reacted the moment he had held her in his arms. The way her hard, puckered nipples had looked underneath the cotton of her tank top.

The way her warm, welcoming mouth had tasted . . .

Someone knocked on his door.

Instinctively Kyle reached for his weapon, only to roll his eyes at the reflex. Some habits died hard. It was why Joe had sent him here to the island. There was no chance in hell any of his enemies would ever find him. In all the world, this was the only "safe" place any of the BAD agents had.

He pulled his hand back from the holster.

"Come in."

The door opened to show Sam with Roscoe at his feet. "Hey, you busy?"

Kyle swiveled his desk chair around. "Not really. What'cha need?"

"Well, after you left, Roscoe got me to thinking. . . ."

Kyle arched a brow at that. The older man had a strange relationship with his pooch.

Sam came in and handed him a small paperback. "I sent Lee over to the other side of the island to find out what was going on over there for you, and he came back with that book. It's what they're reenacting at the moment, so I thought you might want to read it for a good laugh or something. I know you're not used to inaction, so I thought it might give you something to do."

Kyle inclined his head to him. "Obliged."

Sam nodded, then turned and left with Roscoe in tow.

Alone again, Kyle stared at the white cover with the title *Danger in the Night* and the author's name, Rachel Fire, emblazoned over it. On the spine was a single red rose logo from Rose Books. He turned the book over and scanned the back. The first thing that caught his attention was the name of the heroine, Ren Winterbourne, which was what Marianne had called herself.

The next one was the plot synopsis.

Undercover agents.

Kyle laughed out loud. This was perfect. His little schoolteacher was dreaming of . . .

Well, him.

Oh, yeah, this was the best. Leaning back in his chair, Kyle began to read the first page of the book, which was a small form and an invitation to the readers:

What's Your Fantasy?
Do you ever dream of getting away from it all? Just for a week or two?

Have you ever read a romance novel and thought . . .

What if?

Have you ever, just once, wanted to be the heroine in a book and to have the man of your dreams come in and rock your world?

Your dreams could come true. Enter the Hideaway Heroine Sweepstakes, and you, too, could be headed off to be the heroine in your favorite romance novel. Just send in your name, address, and phone number, the title and author of your favorite book, and the reason(s) why you need a break from your everyday life.

One lucky winner will be selected every two months. No purchase necessary. Enter as many times as you like.

For more information, please visit RachelFire.com.

Good luck!

Kyle turned the page, and the hot sex scene on the first page was enough to shock him to his core and make his cock so stiff, he couldn't even sit comfortably.

Holy shit, this was what Marianne read for pleasure?

Just what else did his simple little teacher do for fun?

Marianne sighed as "Brad" pulled his gun out from under his coat. Of course, it got tangled in the hem and he almost dropped it, but once he finally wrestled it free, he pointed it at the others.

"Back off," he snarled, and yet it sounded somehow less than convincing even to her.

The other men around them made snarling noises and animal-like gestures that reminded her of an old campy *Batman* episode from TV. She half expected Olga and her Cossacks to come barreling out at any moment, followed by Vincent Price playing Egghead.

It was all she could do not to laugh.

Strange how the idea of this hadn't seemed ludicrous when she'd told Aislinn Zimmerman that she wanted to be Ren Winterbourne, but for some reason the reality of it left her feeling like a fool.

"Come on, Ren," Brad said, taking her by the arm. "I'll get you out of this."

How she wished he could.

Unfortunately all of this would continue for at least another week until her fantasy life was over and she could return back home to Illinois.

Who would have ever thought *that* would be appealing?

Someone please save her from Brad, the bad actor, and the poor souls who were being paid to act like clean-cut criminals.

She half ran out of the building with Brad towing her along by her hand. This was the part where Brad in the book was supposed to pin Ren up against the wall and kiss her senseless.

Instead, Brad ran with her down the beach toward the hotel where they were staying.

"Are they behind us?" he asked.

"No," she said without looking. In her fantasy vacation package, unlike the book, the bad guys never really came after them. It was as if they were afraid of hurting her, even though she had signed a legal waiver promising not to hold the Zimmermans or Rose Books liable should she be hurt.

Brad stopped and took a minute to catch his breath. Marianne idly found herself wondering if Kyle would be as winded as Brad after so short a run.

How ridiculous was that? But then, she hadn't been able to get that man out of her thoughts since Brad had "rescued" her from him. Especially Kyle's wonderfully tight rump, which had been begging her for a covert fondling.

Too bad she had lacked the courage even to try and grope him.

Well, at least she'd gotten one really good kiss out of this experience.

Hmmm . . . Maybe she should plead a headache and venture to the other side of the island again in search of the only man who'd turned her head since she'd stepped off the plane three weeks ago.

Not that Brad wasn't gorgeous. He was. In fact, he was almost pretty. But his looks didn't make her weak the way Kyle's rugged handsomeness had.

Just as she was about to lament the lack of fireworks, a large unidentified object went whizzing over her head. The next thing she knew, something exploded to her right.

A tree crashed down.

"What the . . . ?" Brad whirled around to face a man in green camouflage.

His features obscured by the paint, the unknown man swung at Brad and knocked him back, then he turned on her, and before she could see much more than a blur, he tossed her over his shoulder and ran for the trees.

Draped over him, she caught sight of an exceptionally nice ass.

Kyle?

The hope hung in her heart as they raced away from the others.

Marianne couldn't form another coherent thought as he sped with her through the dense brush. His shoulder wasn't exactly comfortable as it slammed repeatedly into her middle.

She was about to tell him to put her down when more explosions sounded.

He turned sharply, narrowly missing another bomb.

"What's happening?" she asked in a broken voice that reminded her of Katharine Hepburn as her first real wave of fear went over her.

This wasn't part of the book.

"It's the Big Bad, love. Keep your head down or lose it."

She would have recognized that deep, husky voice anywhere. "Kyle? Is it really you?"

He stopped and slid her down his body, which made her instantly wet and needy. Oh, but he had a body and build made for sinning. But she hated the fact his face was completely obscured by the green and black paint.

"Shh," he said, placing a finger over her lips.

He cocked his head as if listening for something.

She heard the faint sound of firecrackers.

"They're coming for us," he said. Taking her hand, he pulled her deeper into the woods.

"Who?"

"Tyson Purdue."

Her scowl deepened at the unknown name. "Who's that?"

"A nasty arms dealer. He's been looking for me for a long time now."

She looked at him skeptically. "Tyson Purdue? Why do I have a feeling that's a name you made up while at the grocery store?"

Kyle ground his teeth. Damn, she was a little too intelligent. Coming up with cover stories had never been his forte. He left that up to operatives such as Retter and Hunter. They were slick and fast with a lie.

His forte was explosives and muscle.

Still, the other agents had taught him one thing. People would believe anything provided you said it with enough conviction.

He gave her a sincere stare. "Well, we call him the Chicken Man. He kind of looks like a chicken. It's why he has such an inferiority complex. Imagine being tagged with such a name. You'd be psychotic, too. What can I say? The man wants me dead."

"So why am *I* running?"

Kyle froze at her question. The only thing he could come up with was a lame excuse he'd seen once in a bad spy movie.

"You kissed me," he answered partially. What the hell, it made about as much sense as anything else. "One of his minions saw it, and now he's after you. I had to go back for you to save you before he used you to get to me."

By the look in her brown eyes, he could tell she wasn't buying it. "Yeah, right. I don't—"

He pressed the trigger for another remote explosive. Marianne took the bait. She cringed in his arms. "Are you serious?"

"Baby, I never lie about minions out to get me." At least not unless it was helpful, and not unless it would keep her in his arms.

"Is this for real?"

He triggered another explosion. "We have to get moving," he said, letting just a hint of an edge into his voice. "It's going to get ugly if we don't."

Marianne swallowed at that. Part of her still doubted that this could be real, but the look on

Brad's face had been sincere. The man wasn't that good an actor. He'd had no idea that Kyle was going to show up.

Any more than she'd known.

"Where are we going?" she asked.

"Don't worry. I have a safe place."

Not sure if she should trust him, but having no other choice, she followed him through the woods until they came to a sheer drop-off near the crashing waves.

Kyle gave her a heated stare. "Feeling adventurous?"

"I can't go down there."

"Sure you can, love. I won't let you fall."

I must be insane.

She hated heights. She hated the thought of falling into the ocean below, and yet something inside her trusted Kyle implicitly. Not to mention the fact he seemed to know what he was doing, while she had no clue whatsoever.

With him helping her, they carefully slid down the steep side of the cliff and moved across the beach until they came to a small cave.

Marianne looked at it skeptically. "You know, I have a really nice room back at—"

His peeved look interrupted her. "And it's just as likely to be riddled with bullet holes. Trust me, being shot hurts." He gave her a devilish grin. "Don't tell me my little teacher has lost her sense of adventure."

"No, but . . ." She paused as his words sank in. "How do you know I'm a teacher?"

"Aren't you?"

"Yes, but how did you know that?"

He hesitated before he answered. "The way you dress."

Marianne looked down at her khaki shorts and white button-down shirt. There wasn't anything to mark her as a teacher. She looked just like anyone else out for a stroll on the beach. "My clothes don't say anything."

"Sure they do," he said, moving closer to her.

Closer and closer until his large muscular body overwhelmed her with desire.

He unbuttoned the top button at her throat, making her entire body instantly hot with sexual anticipation. When he spoke, there was a deep, erotic timbre in his voice. "Only a teacher would have her collar buttoned all the way up to her chin. What? You afraid of driving your students wild?"

"Hardly!"

He smiled down at her as he unbuttoned the next one. "I'll bet the guys you teach spend hours in your classroom staring at your ass while you're at the chalkboard, trying to imagine what you're wearing underneath all this conservative dressing—"

Marianne cut his words off with an outraged squeak. "Stop that. You're skeeving me."

"Skeeving?" he asked with a laugh. "What kind of word is that?"

"A perfectly good one that means I don't want to even think about what you're describing." She narrowed her gaze on him. "You're trying to get me off the topic, aren't you?"

Yes, he was. Damn, she was good. If he didn't know better, Kyle would think she really was a special agent. "Why would I do that?"

"I don't know."

Kyle couldn't keep himself from touching her lips with his thumb. She had a mouth that had been made for long, hot kisses, and the memory of her taste was still fresh in his mind. Under his skin.

Simmering in his blood.

"You are beautiful," he breathed.

She actually snorted at him.

"What was that?" he asked with a light smile.

"Disagreement. They must be paying you a lot to do this."

"No one's paying me for anything where you're concerned," he said, lacing his hand through her hair. "I've done a lot of bad things in my life, Marianne, but I would never toy with someone's emotions. I'm not that cruel."

He lowered his mouth to hers.

Marianne sighed as his arms tightened around her. This man had more magic in his touch than every member of Harry Potter's school. She'd never seen anything like Jungle Jim.

He was incredible, and the woman in her was completely captivated by him and his powerful touch. His sensuous taste. His warm, male scent.

His mouth blistered a trail from her lips to her neck, where his breath scorched her. She buried her face in the soft locks of his dark brown hair and inhaled the warm, manly scent of his shampoo and skin.

Goodness, but this man set her on fire.

He pulled back to stare down at her with those captivatingly blue eyes. He rubbed gently at her face, letting her know he must have gotten some of his camouflage paint on her skin. "Have you ever made love to a stranger before, Marianne?"

"No," she said, her voice weak. In truth, she'd never before wanted to.

But she did now, and the depths to which she wanted him scared her.

He was truly irresistible.

Kyle took her hand into his and led it to the swollen bulge in his pants. She could feel the whole outline of his cock in her palm. Feel it straining toward her hand as if as eager for her touch as she was to touch him.

She should be offended by his actions.

She wasn't.

"Would you like to take a walk on the wild side with me, little teacher?"

This was insane. The very thought of it was . . .

Heavenly.

Decadent and frightening.

Dare she?

He trailed her hand up to the top button of his pants, where he lifted his shirt ever so slightly so that she could touch the hard, warm skin of his lower abdomen. He curled her fingertips into his waistband, then released her hand so that he could cup her face with his large hands.

She swallowed at the sensation of the short, crisp hairs that led from his navel downward.

"It's entirely up to you, Marianne," he whispered. "Do you have the courage to live out your fantasy?"

Did she?

How many nights had she lain awake dreaming of this? Dreaming of a some hot man saving her from something bad and then taking her madly into his arms and making love to her in some wildly erotic location?

More times than she could count.

Seize it or leave it.

Woman or weasel?

I'm a weasel. I'm a weasel. I'm a weasel.

No, her days of weaseldom were over.

Taking a deep breath, she undid his pants.

Her heart stopped beating as she saw the size of the swell of him underneath the thin white boxer briefs. He was huge!

His smile was tender, warm, and if she didn't know better, she'd swear she saw relief in his gaze.

This time when he took possession of her mouth, his kiss was demanding. Bold.

His kiss literally made her dizzy. He pulled back long enough to jerk his olive green T-shirt over his head. He took a moment to wipe the paint off her mouth and then his, but ended up only smearing it more across his face.

Marianne laughed as she took the shirt from him and carefully removed the paint from his skin. "I suspected there might be a human somewhere underneath all of this." She'd meant the words to be light and funny.

He didn't take them that way.

Instead, he made an odd noise in the back of his throat. "Not really. Once I don the garb and assume the mission, the human in me is trained to be shoved deep into the background."

With his chin in her hand, she paused while wiping a particularly stubborn bit of camouflage from his temple. The sincerity of those deep blue eyes scorched her. "You were trained?"

"What they didn't kick out of me from birth, the military finished."

His words tugged at her heart, and she felt strangely close to him, as if he had just shared something with her that he didn't normally share with others.

As gently as she could, she wiped his tawny skin clean.

He watched her with a hint of suspicion behind his eyes, as if it were more habitual than anything she'd done or might do to him, and at the same time she felt his trust. It was a heady contradiction.

And as she toweled the last of the color from his face, she let her gaze roam his hard body.

Her breath caught at the sight of his wide chest and broad shoulders that tapered down into a narrow waist and lean hips. He was built like a professional athlete.

Every single muscle in his chest was discernible.

But what caught her attention most was the sight of several scars over his ribs and the two in his chest, which looked vaguely like healing bullet wounds. Or at least what she thought healing bullet wounds might look like.

Having never seen a real bullet wound, she didn't have a basis for comparison. Still, those scars looked authentic, not like makeup or window dressing.

Before she could ask him about them, he picked her up, cradled her against his chest, and took her deeper into the cave. He laid her down on a pallet that was made up of several military blankets and an air mattress.

He turned on a small battery-operated lamp.

"What is all this?"

"Boy Scout motto. Always be prepared."

She trembled as he slowly unbuttoned her shirt. Her heart hammered in anticipation as she felt trapped between her common sense, which told her to run, and her lust, which told her to rip the pants off him and have her wicked way with all that lean, masculine strength.

"Are you always prepared for a tryst in a cave?"

"No, ma'am. But I was hoping you'd take me up on my offer."

"Because you were bored?"

He paused with his hand at the last button and gave her a hot, intense stare. "No, because I happen to think you're sexier than hell."

She had a hard time believing that, but there was no doubt he was sexier than hell. He had a body that had been torn from her dreams.

He undid the last button.

Marianne gulped for air.

Kyle slid his large, callused hand through the opening of her shirt to cup her breast through her white lace bra. She moaned at the feel of his palm against her swollen nipple. Even with the fabric of her bra between them, his hand was scorching.

It had been way too long since she'd last made love to a man.

For that matter, it had been a long time since she'd really wanted to make love to a man. Now all that repressed sexuality thrummed through her, wanting him desperately.

But with that desire came the fear that he might think her lacking in her inexperience. She wasn't the kind of woman who played the field, and in spite of what she'd done with Kyle, she'd never fallen into bed with strangers.

What was he expecting from this?

He pulled back from his kiss to smile down at her. His eyes were blazing and hot.

"Say the word, Marianne, and I'm out of here."

She answered him with a demanding kiss of her own.

Kyle closed his eyes as he inhaled the scent of her hair, combined with the sweet scent of some kind of womanly perfume. But it was the earthy smell of woman that made his heart race even faster. Made his mouth water for more.

He'd never been with a woman like her before, and for the first time in his life he was nervous.

As a teenager, he'd run with the worst sort of New York gang. At fifteen he'd lost his virginity in the backroom of a run-down slum in the Bronx to a woman in her mid-twenties who was on the make and looking to nail any handy dick she could find.

He'd fought his way out of the streets to enlist in the Navy. At age eighteen he had done his best to turn his life around and not become another statistic of urban poverty and bad parenting. Even so, he'd never dared dream a woman like this would want to be with him.

Someone soft and gentle. A teacher. Not a woman on the make. Not an operative out to blow his cover or a criminal wanting a fast lay before she blew his brains out.

Marianne was just a nice, average lady from a small town in the Midwest.

She was safe. That word alone was so alien to him that it made him ache even to think of it.

He'd never known safety. Never known unconditional acceptance.

He could vaguely remember his mother once telling him that sometimes the best dreams were simple ones. He'd never understood that.

Not until this moment.

He didn't crave the excitement that was his life. He craved the slice of normality Marianne offered. The simple taste of wholesome woman.

The simple taste of Marianne Webernec.

Marianne was breathless as Kyle moved down her body to unlace her shoes and pull them from her feet. She couldn't believe she was doing this with a complete stranger.

It was so out of character for her.

And yet she couldn't stop herself.

"Tell me something about you, Kyle." She needed to know something so that she wouldn't feel so self-conscious.

He pulled her other shoe off and massaged her sensitive arch with his thumb. Oh, but it felt sinfully wonderful as it made her stomach tight. She felt a rush of moisture between her legs.

"What do you want to know?" he asked, his deep voice intoxicating.

Everything. There was nothing about him she didn't want to know.

"What do you do for a living?"

He tossed her socks by her shoes and gave her an impish stare as he nibbled the arch of her foot.

She moaned in ecstasy.

He blew a stream of warm air over her skin before he spoke again. "Honestly?"

She nodded, unable to breathe from the pleasure that rippled through her.

"I'm a federal agent."

For a second she couldn't move as his words sank in. Then she laughed at the absurdity. "Can you break out of character for one minute and be serious?"

"I am serious," he said earnestly.

But she didn't believe it. It was too perfect to be real, and what were the chances of a federal agent being here with her right now, when that was her fantasy?

He was just one of the men playing on the island. She didn't want that. She wanted to know about *him*. The truth. "Who do you work for?" she asked skeptically. "The CIA?"

"The Certified Idiots Association?" he asked, as if offended by her question. "Hardly. We eat those wannabes for breakfast. I'm with BAD, the Bureau of American Defense."

She scoffed. "There's no such agency."

"Yes, there is."

Part of her wanted to believe him, but the rational part of her knew better. She'd never even heard of such a thing. "And what part of D.C. are you located in? The White House?"

"We're not. Our offices are in Nashville."

She laughed even harder at that. "Oh, please. What kind of agency would have their headquarters there?"

His look was devilish. "The smart one. If D.C. gets wiped out or bombed, we're still able to function. No one's ever going to take out Nashville. It's barely on the terrorist map. Besides, we don't do anything by the book. Hell, our director is so whacked, he put us on the ground floor of the bat tower just for shits and giggles."

She arched her brow at that. "Ahh, the bat tower. Let me guess? Your director is Commissioner Gordon."

She groaned as he sucked her toe into his mouth and used his tongue to gently massage it. He nipped her large toe, then pulled back. "Trust me, BAD would make mincemeat out of Commissioner Gordon, Sergeant O'Hara, and Batman combined."

"BAD, huh?"

"Mad, bad, and dangerous to know."

"Have much luck with that line?"

He laughed gently as he crawled up her body like a languid panther and pressed his lips to her belly. His breath tickled her stomach as he parted her shirt more. "So far it's working."

Yes, it was. Much better than it should be. Who would have ever thought that she could be seduced by some cheesy little line?

No, she realized. She wasn't seduced by a cheesy line, but rather by his stunningly blue eyes. His tender lips.

Oh, who was she fooling? It was that sinful body that she wanted.

All of it.

She'd never made love to a man who looked like this. One who was so handsome he should be on the cover of a book or in a movie.

One who set her blood on fire just by being with her.

She stared down at him while his hot mouth skimmed the flesh of her stomach. He lay between her spread legs with his chest pressing against the center of her body.

Oh, how she ached for him. Marianne ran her hands through his dark hair, letting the swirls of his tongue sweep her far away from what they were doing.

She arched her back as he sat up slightly and pulled her shirt off. Then he reached behind her and unfastened her bra.

"Mmm," he breathed as he bared her. "What have we here?"

"Breasts," she said simply as she fought the urge to cover herself. "Two of them."

He laughed at that. "Good, 'cause I was afraid you might have three."

"Nope, no Anne Boleyn here. Just two, like any other normal woman."

Kyle smiled at her teasing and her intelligence. He couldn't recall ever being so at ease with a lover. It didn't feel as if they were strangers.

There was an odd sense of belonging with her. It didn't make any sense.

"Tell me something, Marianne," he whispered in her ear. "Tell me what schoolteachers dream about when they're all alone at night. Tell me what fantasies keep you awake while you lie in bed, wanting to feel someone inside you."

Her face flushed.

"Don't be embarrassed," he said, teasing the corner of her mouth with his lips.

He'd always wondered what "good" girls dreamt of. The scenes in the romance novel he'd read had shocked him more than the first time he'd read a *Penthouse* letter. He still had a hard time believing Marianne read such things.

"I don't know," she said with a small shrug. "I think of someone dangerous. Deadly. A larger-than-life officer or agent who can come in like Rambo and yet still be tender to me." Her brown eyes seared him with a heartfelt longing. "Someone who sees me."

He frowned at her words. Who in their right mind couldn't see her? "I see you, Marianne," he whispered, kissing her, tasting the warmth of her mouth.

Her tongue was heaven. He loved the sensation of it stroking his while her breasts were flattened against his chest.

Marianne sighed as he left her lips and trailed scorching kisses over her. His lightly whiskered cheek scraped her while he moved down to her shorts.

She lifted her hips as he slowly, sensuously slid them down her legs and left her completely bare to him.

She'd never felt more vulnerable.

Kyle's gaze locked and held hers as he rose to his feet and kicked his boots off.

She held her breath as he reached to the waist of his unbuttoned pants and then slid them and his briefs down his long, hairy legs.

If she lived to the end of time, she wouldn't ever forget the way he looked standing there in the dim light of the lamp, his cock erect, his body perfect. He was pure male beauty. Completely unadorned and completely stunning.

With a charming smile he moved to a small backpack and pulled out a box of condoms and an army green bandanna.

"What are you doing?" she asked as he started folding up the olive green cotton fabric.

"Remember the scene with Ren in the cavern?"

Her face heated up instantly. "What about it?"

His smile turned ravenous. "I couldn't find the chocolate sauce, but . . ."

She stiffened as he put the bandanna over her eyes. "I don't know about this."

"Trust me, little teacher. I promise you, you won't regret it."

"I'd better not."

He knotted the blindfold over her eyes. Marianne swallowed as she tried to see through the fabric.

It was useless.

She had no idea where Kyle was. Not until she heard the sound of foil tearing. Then Kyle was back, his warm hands urging her toward the back of the cave.

"What are you doing?"

It felt as if he was seating her on a large rock that he had covered with one of the blankets. "I'm going to take my time savoring you, little teacher."

He rested her hips against the rock, then nudged her legs open. Marianne leaned back, unsure why she was allowing him to do this, and yet it was so wildly erotic that she couldn't bear the thought of stopping him.

Her entire body sizzled and throbbed with anticipation. With demanding hunger that longed to feel him deep inside her.

He trailed his hands from her knees, up the insides of her thighs. She shivered in expectation of him touching her where she ached for him.

He didn't, and she almost whimpered in disappointment.

Instead his hands skimmed up her ribs, massaging and tormenting her more.

"Touch me, Kyle," she whispered.

She felt his lips touch her breast. Marianne groaned as he swirled his tongue around her nipple, drawing it deep into his mouth while his hand skimmed down the outside of her thigh until he finally trailed it to the center of her.

His long, hard fingers parted her nether lips before they stroked her swollen cleft. She shivered as he massaged her clitoris.

She hissed as he finally gave her a modicum of relief.

Kyle growled at how good she tasted and at how well she responded to his caresses. He liked a fiery woman, and this one had more fire than her share.

Wanting more of her, he left her breast and kissed his way down to the part of her he wanted most.

She actually yelped the first time he licked her cleft. Laughing at her reaction, he spread her nether lips wide and ran his tongue over the hard edge of her clit, sucking and teasing her until she was on the brink of climax.

Marianne struggled to breathe. She leaned back on her arms, giving him as much of her as she could. Never in her life had she felt anything more incredible than him tasting her.

Wanting to see him, she started to remove the blindfold, only to find his hands stopping her.

"I thought you wanted to be Ren," he said.

She hesitated. Ren was the kind of woman who would be in this cave with a stranger, not Marianne Webernec. Marianne always played by the rules. She always played it safe.

Today she didn't want to be a Goody Two-shoes. "Okay."

Kyle kissed her shoulder, then turned her over so that she was leaning on her arms and stomach against the rock. Her back was completely exposed to him.

"Mmm," he breathed, running his hand over her hips as his nails gently scraped her skin and made her tingle all over. "You have the nicest ass I've ever seen."

He licked his way down her backbone until he reached the sensitive spot at the base of her spine. His hands massaged her thighs, sending ribbons of pleasure through her while his tongue delivered stroke after ecstatic stroke to her flesh.

He slid one finger down her cleft, making her shiver again. "Do you want me inside you, Marianne?"

"Yes."

He slid two fingers deep inside. She moaned at the ecstasy of his touch as he teased her unmercifully while she slowly rode his fingers.

He leaned his body against her so that she could feel his erection against her lower back as he rained kisses on her neck and shoulders.

She was breathless and weak from the pleasure of his touch. No one had ever been more attentive to her. With Kyle, she actually felt beautiful. Desirable.

And that made her melt.

He moved his hand and then shifted behind her.

Marianne moaned as he slid himself slowly, inch by lush, incredible inch, inside her until he filled her to capacity.

Kyle growled at the feeling of her body welcoming his, of the way she felt as she lowered herself from her tiptoes down until he was even deeper inside her. It took every piece of control he had to make love to her slowly, gently, when what he really wanted to do was ravish her.

Since the moment he'd met her, he'd wanted nothing more than to have her.

And she was so worth it.

He held himself perfectly still as she rode him with soft, long strokes. Grinding his teeth to hold off his orgasm, he cupped her breasts with his hands and let her take her satisfaction first.

Every woman had a rhythm to her, and Marianne's was sweeping and sweet. Slow and sensuous like a gentle breeze.

He savored the sensation of her hips grinding against him, of her sweet low moans of pleasure.

He leaned forward over her back and braced one hand beside hers on the rock so that he could use his other hand to stroke her clit in time with their movements.

Marianne groaned aloud as he touched her again. She reveled in the feeling of him behind her and in her while his hand teased her, and when she came, it was so intense that she screamed out.

"That's it, baby," Kyle whispered in her ear. "Don't hold back on me."

She didn't. Nor did he. He continued to stroke

and tease her until the very last tremor had been gleaned from her body.

Weak, she fell forward.

Kyle picked her up, carried her back to the air mattress on the floor, and removed her blindfold. His smile was dazzling as he covered her with his body and entered her again.

Marianne arched her back, groaning as his hard shaft slid back into her sensitive sheath.

Kyle's heart hammered as he thrust against her, wanting his own satisfaction. Her legs and arms were wrapped about him, cocooning him in her softness.

It was all he'd ever wanted.

Her body was paradise.

And when he found his own release, his head reeled from it. Growling, he buried his face in the fragrant sweetness of her neck and let the pleasure rip through him until he could barely breathe.

Every spasm, every wave, shattered some part of him until he couldn't do anything more than whisper her name.

Now, that had been the best sex of his life.

Weak and spent, he gathered her into his arms and held her against his chest.

Neither spoke for the longest time as they lay there, sheltered together, completely relaxed.

Kyle didn't care if he ever moved again. Nothing could top what he'd just experienced.

"Do you think Tyson will be back after us?"

It took him a second to remember who Tyson was.

"No," he said. "I secured the perimeter. I'd know if he was anywhere nearby."

"You sure?"

"Absolutely. I made certain this place was safe from any intruders."

Marianne sighed as she lay in the shelter of his arms.

Kyle ran his hand over her soft skin as he savored the feel of her breath on his naked skin. He'd always loved the sensation of feminine flesh against his, but never more than he did at this moment.

How strange that he'd been honest with her, when he'd never told any woman before what he really did for a living. BAD had been set up as a covert, ghost agency. The government, even those who had commissioned their bureau, denied all knowledge of its existence.

The BAD agents answered directly to Joe, who only answered to the president, and not even the president would acknowledge their mandate. Each and every member of BAD was an orphan who had been recruited to lie, steal, cheat, and/or die or kill for their country. Whatever it took to secure their objective, they would do without anything as cumbersome as morals or ethics getting in their way.

They were the modern-day Spartans who either returned with their shield or upon it.

There was no such thing as family for them. The agency was the family.

In this world they only had each other, and up until now that had been fine with Kyle. But his last bout with terrorists that had almost cost him his life had got him to thinking. . . .

He had been trained zealously to guard his country. But what was he really fighting for?

It wasn't until Marianne smiled up at him that he'd remembered.

He fought for those who couldn't fight for themselves.

"Kyle?" Marianne paused as she traced one of the smaller scars along his ribs. "What is this from?"

He glanced at it and the two similar ones below it. "A bullet."

Marianne frowned at his words. From the sincerity of his eyes, she could tell he was being truthful. "It looks recent."

"About a month ago."

Her jaw went slack. "And these?"

"Same."

She leaned up to study his chest. Now that she was closer, she saw even more of them, and no, they weren't makeup. The scars were real. "How many times have you been shot?"

"What are you asking? How many *total* bullet wounds or how many times has someone shot me up?"

There was a difference? She was aghast at his nonchalance. "Both."

He actually had to pause to think. "I've had a total of twenty-two bullet holes. Though we're still debating one of them. The doc said she thought it was a bullet that passed clean through, but I think the wound was caused by some shrapnel that hit me when the grenade went off. As for assholes who've taken shots at me, I'm at the unlucky thirteen mark."

Marianne's jaw opened even more. "Are you serious?"

He nodded, then turned his head and showed her a scar behind his ear.

"That was the first one," he said, placing his finger over the small round scar. "I was only seventeen and it was a drive-by from a rival gang. They took out my best friend Angelo as we came out of his house, headed for a movie. I got caught in the crossfire." He shook his head. "It's what got me out of the gang and made me want to do something with my life other than be target practice. Little did I know it would lead me into a field where drive-bys are even more likely than they were in New York."

She didn't know what to say. Part of her believed him, and part of her found it hard to swallow. It was too close to what she would expect from a Rachel Fire hero, and too alien to the sheltered world she'd known growing up.

She couldn't imagine being shot.

"You really, truly—swear to the Lord above—are a federal agent?"

He made an X over the center of his chest. "Cross my heart. And hope not to die on my next mission."

She sat back on her heels. "How long have you been an agent?"

"The last two years."

"Before that?"

"I was a Navy SEAL."

Yeah, right. "You almost had me going. But for the record, the SEAL thing blew it."

"I swear," he said, as if offended by her doubt. "I really was a SEAL. I'd still be one if I hadn't been recruited for BAD."

She looked at him suspiciously. "What does BAD do?"

"That I can't tell you. Well, I could, but then I'd have to kill you, and no offense, I'm rather attached to you." He ran his hand down her backside and over her rump. "Especially this part here."

She squeaked as he clenched a handful of her buttocks.

He pulled her on top of him. Marianne straddled his waist and watched as he closed his eyes and sighed contentedly. She felt him stiffen against her hipbone.

Opening his eyes, he stared up at her and cupped her face in his hands. "You have no idea how beautiful you are, do you?"

"I've never had anyone call me beautiful before. Heck, I had a guy in high school run screaming from the room when he lost a bet and was told he'd have to take me to the prom."

"He was an idiot."

She smiled at his words, amazed by them. "Who did you go to the prom with?"

"I didn't."

"Why?"

He shrugged. "My junior year I spent prom night in jail, waiting for my dad to sober up long enough to bail me out, and I didn't have the money to go senior year."

"Jail?" she asked. "What did you do to go to jail?"

"Nothing too bad. I was in for fighting."

"Over what?"

"Bella Marino. She broke up with her boyfriend and then threw herself at me. He got pissed, and we got into it at the mall. He pulled a knife, I pulled a knife, and they called the cops on us."

"Kyle!" she said, stunned by his confession. "You're not making up any of this, are you?"

"No."

She let her breath out slowly as she stared into his blue eyes.

He laced his fingers through her hair. "I'm not proud of my past, Marianne. I've spent most of my life trying to forget it. I just . . ."

She waited a few minutes until it became apparent he wasn't going to finish his sentence. "You what?" she prompted.

"I don't know. I feel like I can tell you things, and I don't know why. It's not something I normally do. Hell, I barely talk to anyone. And then I meet you on the beach, and I can't seem to shut my mouth or re-sist you."

She leaned forward and kissed him. "I can't resist you, either."

His cock hardened to full size at her words. He pulled back with a wicked grin.

Marianne melted at the look. He was better than anything she'd ever read in one of her books.

A real-life hero. One with a very sad past. How she wished she could make it up to him.

She moaned as he lifted her up and set her down on top of him. He was so hard and full inside her, and the tip of his shaft went straight into her G-spot from this position.

"Ooo," she moaned. "You keep doing that, and I might not ever let you leave this cave."

He guided her hips with his hands as he watched

her. "You keep doing that, and I won't even try."

Marianne covered his hands with hers and felt the strength of him in his grip. She trailed her gaze over his tawny skin, pausing at the multiple scars. He was her fantasy come to life. Only he was real. His scars were deep, and she suspected he carried a lot more inside than those she saw on his body.

How many more did he carry in his heart?

"Have you ever killed anyone?"

"That's a strange question to ask while I'm making love to you."

"I'm sorry. I guess it was rather nosy."

He trailed his hand up her body and sank it deep in her hair. "Yes, I have," he said softly. "And no, I'm not proud of it. My life has been very ugly."

She held his hand against her cheek and kissed the scars over his knuckles. "I wish I could make it better."

"Trust me, love. You are."

She smiled at that.

Kyle raised his hips, tossing her forward, onto his chest. He wrapped his arms around her and rolled over with her until she was pinned under him.

How he loved the way she felt beneath him. The feel of her breath falling gently on his shoulder. The warm, sleek wetness of her around him.

How he wished he could make love to her without a condom. To feel the whole of her wetness surrounding him.

She was magnificent, and he didn't want to leave her body. Not even when they came together in one swirling moment of blissful orgasm.

He still held on to her while she ran her hands over his bare back and shook under him. He was worn out and sated to a level he wouldn't have thought possible.

He laid his head down against her hard nipple so that he could feel the puckered areola against his cheek. It was the tenderest moment of his life.

But he knew it wouldn't last. Good things never did.

CHAPTER THREE

Marianne woke up mid-morning to find Kyle already awake and dressed. Or at least partially dressed. He wore a pair of faded jeans and those biker boots again, but the rest of him was gloriously bare and glistening in the bright sunshine.

Yum!

Resting on his knees, he had his back to her while he cooked over a small Coleman camping stove.

Wow, the man really was prepared for anything.

She felt a tiny shiver as she stared at him and remembered the night they had shared. They'd made love so many times and in so many different ways that she was sure she wouldn't be able to walk straight today. Not to mention, they would definitely need another box of condoms—which might be her only saving grace from all that glorious temptation he offered.

The smell of coffee and bacon made her empty stomach growl.

"How long have you been up?" she asked.

He looked at her over his shoulder and grinned as he came out of that deadly crouch like some lethal, languid panther who had been tamed only by her. "Morning, little teacher."

"Good morning."

He made her a paper plate of eggs and bacon and brought it to her, then went to the small cooler to fetch some butter for her toast and a small carton of orange juice.

"Wow, full service in bed. I like that," she said as she sat up on the air mattress, which had been surprisingly comfortable while she slept. Marianne made sure to keep the sheet wrapped around her.

His eyes turned dark, seductive. "I have to say that servicing you in bed gives me a great deal of pleasure."

She blushed even more.

"Not to mention you gave me quite an appetite after last night."

She smiled at the depth in his voice, knowing exactly what it heralded, and one quick glance at his groin confirmed it. Kyle Foster was a sex machine.

"So, what's on the agenda for today?" she asked before she took a bite of her bacon.

Kyle drew a deep breath as he thought it over. In the book they were supposed to be outrunning the drug dealers who were enemies to the arms dealer, or some shit like that. For all he knew, it could have been a car dealer chasing them.

He'd spilled coffee on the book earlier that morning and hadn't been able to finish the chapter. Not that it mattered. With just the two of them, there wasn't really a way to fabricate a group of people pursuing them.

He was good, but that was beyond even his abilities.

So he'd have to think up something else for them to do.

"Well, I think we're safe here on our private beach. I say we enjoy the day. What about you?"

Her smile dazzled him. "It sounds like a plan to me."

Marianne finished her breakfast and dressed while Kyle cleaned up and shut down the stove. As soon as he had it cleared, he got up and pulled a gun out from under his folded shirt. Ejecting the clip, he checked his ammunition, then returned it to the hilt. He put the gun back in the concealed holster and then fastened it around his waist before he put his shirt on to cover it.

His movements appeared reflexive, as if he wasn't even aware of what he'd done.

"You always do that?" she asked as she tied her shoes.

"Do what?"

"Check your gun."

He frowned. "My gun?"

"The one you just put behind your back."

"Oh," he said, his face lighting. "My weapon. Yeah, I guess I do. I never thought about it."

She sucked her breath in between her teeth. "You're a scary man, Kyle Foster."

"So they tell me. But how about I put Scary Kyle away for the day?"

"I think I would like that." She pulled his shirt up. "Want to leave *that* behind?"

He cringed at her suggestion. "I don't think I can. That's like asking me to leave my arm behind."

"Yeah, but I don't want either one of us to get shot in the event I get a little frisky with you later."

One corner of his mouth twisted up at that as he pulled her into his arms. "Frisky, huh?"

She nodded.

He dipped his head down and kissed her while reaching behind his back to unfasten the gun. "All right, teacher. For you, but only for today."

He moved away to unload the ammo, and then placed the gun and clip in a small box near the stove.

Marianne sighed in relief. She might like to read about cops and robbers, but real guns made her very nervous.

Kyle grabbed a hand shovel and bucket, took her by the hand, and led her down to the beach.

"You like clams?" he asked.

"Yes, why?"

"Want some for dinner?"

"Sure."

She frowned as he walked around the beach, studying the sand. After a second he bent over, presenting her with an exceptionally nice view of his butt.

He started digging.

It was awfully hard not to walk over to that butt and cup it. Or better yet, to cup the nice-sized bulge that she had become more than just a little acquainted with the night before.

"What are you doing?" she asked, moving closer to him. She had to fist her hand to keep from stroking him while he worked.

He glanced up from his task. "Digging up dinner. Want to help?"

She was astonished when he produced a clam from the beach. "I've heard of doing this, but I've never seen anyone do it before."

He examined the clam, then put it in the bucket. "Want to try it?"

"Sure. What do I do?"

He took her hand and pulled her along the sand. "We're looking for airholes," he explained. He paused by a small dimpled circle in the sand and indicated it with the toe of his foot. "That one's called a keyhole. Clams make it so they can breathe. All you have to do is put the shovel a few inches, away and then you can dig it up."

Marianne was a bit timid at first. "How is it a New York City boy knows about digging up clams?"

"Travis Lamb, one of the guys I was in the Navy with, showed me how to do it when we were on leave in Charleston years ago. His mother took the whole house full of guests out at dawn, and we dug up enough clams for her to make a shitload of chowder for an Independence Day party that night."

"You really were in the Navy, weren't you?"

"Hell, I can even fax you the discharge papers if you want. They have the official seal on them and everything." Kyle smiled warmly, then helped her dig.

Marianne closed her eyes for an instant as she felt his warmth surround her. She'd never done anything like this or enjoyed anything more than just feeling him behind her as the sun shone down on them.

This was peaceful. Comfortable.

She laughed in triumph as she uncovered a clam of her own. Kyle reached for the bucket. His hips brushed against hers, letting her know he was hard again.

She felt heat sting her cheeks.

"Why are you always blushing?" Kyle asked.

"I . . . uh . . ." She cleared her throat, not sure what to answer. The truth was, her sexuality had always embarrassed her, and Kyle was so at ease with it.

Then again, she'd never been more sexually aware of anyone else. Every time she looked at Kyle, she wanted to take a bite out of him. Pull him into her arms, throw him down on his back, rip his clothes off, climb on top of him, and then ride him madly until they were both sweaty and spent.

Of course, she'd done a lot of that last night, and it still wasn't enough to satiate her.

She wanted more of him.

He stared at her intently as he took her hand into his. He laid a gentle kiss into her palm, all the while staring into her eyes.

"What's the matter, Marianne?" he whispered. "Are you scared of how much you make me want you?"

"A little."

He brushed a light, tender kiss across her lips. She moaned at the taste of him as he moved her hand so that her palm was pressed against his swollen erection. "Have you ever made love on the beach?"

She cringed at the thought. "Someone might see us."

His look turned mischievous. "Afraid? I thought you were Ren Winterbourne. Woman of adventure."

She bit her lip to keep from laughing. "Ren doesn't have to live with herself or the embarrassment of being caught in flagrante delicto by a stranger."

He pulled his shirt over his head and tsked at her. "So much for fantasy, huh?"

Marianne stared at his tanned, muscular chest. He really was scrumptious. Irresistible.

And this time when he kissed her it was fierce, demanding. Every part of her thrilled at the taste of his tongue dancing with hers. At the way his hand felt cupping her face.

He laid her back on the beach.

The sane part of herself told her to push him away, but the repressed part of her refused. She'd lived sheltered and safe the whole of her life.

Kyle hadn't. A man who was riddled with bullet scars knew nothing of fear. Nothing of trepidation.

He only knew how to live in the moment.

How she envied him that.

He pulled back and reached for the buttons of her shirt. "Well?"

Marianne swallowed. "If *anyone* catches us, you're a dead man."

He laughed at that. "I'll even loan you my weapon to shoot me."

"Promise?"

"Absolutely."

Taking a deep breath, she slowly unbuttoned her shirt.

Kyle watched breathlessly as she opened her top for him. It was the most erotic thing he'd ever seen. Strange. He'd had much better looking women striptease for him. Watched them peel their clothes off like a pro.

None of that had ever turned him on the way Marianne's timid movements did.

Her quiet hesitancy was a breath of fresh air. She wouldn't do this for someone else. He wasn't just another lay to her.

He liked the feeling of being special.

In his life, that was something that had always been sorely missing. The type of women he'd dated had always known the score. Always known their way around a man's body.

Not Marianne. She was just an unassuming woman from Middle America, living a life that was nothing special.

Nothing special to anyone but him.

He found her remarkable.

She moved her hands away from her shirt and ran them down his back. Kyle dipped his head down so that he could taste her bared flesh.

"Hmmm," he breathed as he flicked his tongue around her navel. "I think I'm addicted to your taste."

Marianne closed her eyes while his hot breath

scorched her. This was the most unbelievable moment of a life she had spent playing it safe. A life made up of daydream fantasies of something like this happening to her.

To her surprise, she found herself laughing.

Kyle lifted himself up to stare at her with a stern frown. "You know, it's not a good thing to laugh at a guy when he's trying to seduce you."

She brushed his hair back from his face and smiled up at him. "I'm sorry. I was just thinking of how you swept me off my feet yesterday. Literally."

His frown faded as his face relaxed into a heated, intense stare. "Any time you need a hero, baby, you just call me."

She moaned as he dipped his head down and kissed her fiercely. Mmm, how she loved the taste of his mouth. The way his muscles rippled around her.

Marianne wrapped her body around his and reveled in the sensation of his bare chest against the part of hers that was bared by the opening of her shirt. She felt him from her lips all the way to her toes.

Her heart thundering, she ran her hands down his back, feeling the dips and welts of old scars there. Her heart wrenched at the thought of how much pain he must have lived through.

"I don't know," she whispered against his lips. "I

think you need a keeper a lot more than I need a hero."

Kyle froze at her words. "Would you care to volunteer for the job?"

"Would you let me?"

Her question hung in the air between them.

"I've never had anyone interested in it."

"Never?"

He shook his head as the truth of that sank in. "No, it's why I joined the Navy. All those sappy, stupid commercials about teamwork got to me, and I thought it might be nice to be part of some kind of family."

She toyed with his hair as she watched him quietly. "Did you find it?"

"I did with the SEALs. I knew with them I had a kindred bond."

"Then why did you leave?"

"Joe came in and selected three of us from my unit. Tony and Doug had been like brothers to me, and I didn't want to let them down. When they signed up for BAD, I followed suit."

"Do you regret it?"

"Not until they dumped me on this damned island and told me to rest here for a few weeks."

She gave him a peeved stare.

He offered her a wicked grin. "Now I'm thinking I should thank them for it."

"You'd better be thinking that."

He rubbed himself against her, letting his body caress hers. "Believe me, Marianne, I am."

Marianne sighed as his kiss swept her into heaven. She didn't even protest when he removed her shirt and laid her back against the scratchy sand. Strange, this didn't look uncomfortable in movies and such, but in reality . . .

She groaned as Kyle unzipped her shorts with his teeth, then pulled them down her legs. And when he did the same with her panties, she almost came just from the sheer eroticism of the act. He was like a wild predator set loose on her.

One who wanted only to devour her.

What was it about him that made her burn like this? That made her forget the fact that they could be discovered at any moment?

"You do like to live dangerously, don't you?" she asked as he crawled sinuously up her body, nibbling every inch of the way.

"There's no other way to live." His hot breath teased her taut nipple before he opened his mouth and claimed it.

Marianne sighed in satisfaction as she cradled his head to her. His hair teased her skin while his tongue encircled her areola, teasing it to a hard, bitterly sweet nub that made her stomach contract every time he licked it.

The waves ran up the beach, lapping gently against her bare feet, while the hot sun heated her almost as much as Kyle's touch did.

Kyle pulled away only long enough to remove his jeans.

Marianne couldn't fathom why a man like this was interested in her. "Are you sure you're not one of the actors they hired for this?"

"Positive. Why do you ask?"

"I don't know. You just seem too good to be real."

He snorted at that, then turned over with her so that she was on top of him. He reached for his discarded jeans and pulled out a condom, which he opened with his teeth, then reached around her so that he could put it on.

"I think you're the only person in my life to ever say such a thing to me. Most people I know curse the day they met me."

"I don't believe that."

She gasped as he lifted her up and set her down on his hard shaft. Marianne moaned at the feel of him inside her. The tip of his cock tickled her deep, making her entire body throb from the feel of him there.

Bracing her hands on his shoulders, she rode him slow and easy, savoring every lush stroke of his body with hers.

"I can't believe I just met you," she said. It felt as if she'd known him much longer.

Kyle watched her as she milked his body with hers. Her hair fell around her lightly freckled shoulders, which had just a hint of red to them from their exposure to the sun. She was so beautiful there. Like some ancient goddess who had been washed up on the shore to seduce him.

He took her hand into his and suckled the pads of her fingers. He let the salty taste of her skin whet his appetite for her even more.

She was unlike any woman he'd ever met. She was cut from the same cloth as the pure, innocent homecoming queens he had dreamed about in his youth. The women he'd passed countless times on public streets and elevators. Decent women who knew nothing about espionage or lies. Deceit.

She was the kind of woman who would turn in the wallet that contained a thousand dollars without stealing a single bill.

His head reeled as she quickened her strokes. He reached up for her and pulled her lips to his so that he could feel closer to her.

Let some of her decency creep inside him.

He wanted to crawl inside her body. To find a safe, warm spot where such a thing as goodness lived.

Maybe if he stayed with her just a little longer, some of her decency would rub off on him.

She came calling out his name.

Kyle didn't move as he watched the ecstasy on her face. When the last tremor had shuddered through her, she collapsed against him.

He rolled over with her again so that he could take control.

Marianne held him close, brushing the sand from his back as he slid himself in and out of her, thrusting against her in a demanding rhythm.

He was incredible. Powerful. Every stroke went through her, exciting her, and when his orgasm came, he cried out, then lay down on top of her.

She held him there, letting his breath stir her hair as his heart pounded against her breasts.

She closed her eyes and sighed contentedly. "Wow," she said quietly. "I think I felt the earth move."

He chuckled, but didn't make any move to leave her. "More likely it's just the waves moving the sand out from under us."

She blew him a raspberry. "You're such a spoilsport."

He kissed her lightly on the lips, then pulled her into the surf so that they could bathe in the crystal clear water where little tropical fish swam around their feet.

It was a perfect, surreal day.

"I feel strangely like Jane in some *Tarzan* movie."

Kyle beat his arms against his chest in imitation of an ape and made a Tarzan cry.

Before she could draw the breath to laugh at him, he bent at the waist and rushed toward her, lifting her up and tossing her over his shoulder.

Marianne shrieked and laughed at his antics. Until she saw the sight of the pink wounds in his back. She had felt them while they made love, but this was the first time she had really seen them up close in the light of day.

Her heart thudding, she touched one long, ragged scar that ran just under his shoulder blade. "What is this from?"

"I think that one's from the razor-wire fence I slid under in Beirut about a year ago. Thank God I had my leather jacket on, or it would have done some serious damage."

"From here, it looks like it did."

"Nah," he said, setting her back on her feet. "It's a flesh wound."

She rolled her eyes. "You're like that psycho knight in *Monty Python and the Holy Grail,* aren't you? The one who has his arm lopped off at the shoulder who looks at it and goes, 'Ah, it's just a scratch.'"

"Hey, in the neighborhood where I grew up, any sign of weakness was an invitation to a serious asswhipping."

"And where I grew up, we went to the hospital and got ice cream afterward."

Kyle frowned at her words and the idyllic world she described. "I don't think such a place as that really exists."

"Didn't you ever have anyone kiss your boo-boos?"

He thought about it a minute. "No. My mom was killed in a car wreck when I was five. There wasn't anyone around to kiss much of anything after that."

She shook her head at him, then pressed her lips to the scar on his chest, the one just an inch to the side of his heart that was fresh and pink.

Closing his eyes, Kyle enjoyed the feel of her lips on his flesh. The strange warmth that rushed through him from her actions.

So this was tenderness . . .

He liked it a lot more than he should.

"Marianne!"

They both jumped at the sound of someone calling from somewhere in the trees.

Kyle moved away from her long enough to scoop up their clothes and hand her hers.

"Wait here," he said, pulling his jeans on.

Barefoot and shirtless, he reached for his weapon, only to remember he didn't have it with him.

Damn. His military training snapped, making him creep toward the sound of the intruder. . . .

Marianne dressed quickly as she wondered what Kyle was going to do.

As soon as she was dressed, she headed off after him. No sooner had she reached the trees than she heard something snap.

A man yelped, then Kyle came running toward her, laughing.

He sobered instantly.

"What was that?"

"Nothing," he said, clearing his throat. "It was just one of Tyson's men."

"Let me down!" The unknown man's voice rang out through the trees.

She looked at him suspiciously. "What did you do?"

"I put him someplace where he can't follow us or tell Tyson where we are."

Unsure if she should believe him, she frowned. "Are you sure about this Tyson?"

"The Chicken Man is deadly, love. I promise. Come on, we need to go quickly before he sends more guys after us."

Still skeptical, she followed after him as he gathered their clams and shovel and headed off down the beach, far away from where he'd left "Tyson's" man.

They walked down the surf for quite some time before Kyle judged it safe again to dig clams. Once they had the bucket full, Kyle led her carefully up the rocky slope that led back to the wooded area of the island.

"Boo!" she said at one point, making him jump.

"Don't do that," he said in a hushed, peeved tone.

"I couldn't help myself. You look so serious."

"This is serious. One of those bastards could get his hands on you and take you away from me. That's the last thing I want." The sincere anger in his voice set her back.

"Really?" she asked.

"Really."

Marianne bit her lip as warmth gushed through her. She laced her fingers with his and let him sneak her back to their isolated cave, where they made steamed clams and made love until the very wee hours of the morning.

They made love until she was weak and breathless, but so well sated that she just wanted to sleep in the shelter of Kyle's arms for eternity.

For the next few days they hid in their cave, running during the daylight from Tyson's men and spending their nights getting to know each other and every detail of their lives.

There was nothing she hadn't shared with Kyle, and as she fell asleep snuggled against him on the fifth day, she knew all of this would end soon. She only had a few more days on the island, and then her fantasy was over.

Would Kyle still want her then, or would he put her on a plane and make ready for the next contest winner?

The anger and fear that question evoked startled her.

But what stunned her most was how much it hurt to think of letting Kyle go.

Chapter Four

Kyle and Marianne sat on a blanket on the beach long after dark with a small fire crackling before them. He was leaning back against a large piece of driftwood with Marianne sitting between his raised legs, cradled against his bare chest while she wore his T-shirt.

He adored the sight of her in his clothes, which she had been wearing every day since he'd "kidnapped" her. There was no way he was going to let her return to her hotel room, where one of the others might be able to keep her from him.

Not that they could. He just didn't want to have to hurt someone unnecessarily. But he would hurt anyone who tried to pry her away from him even a minute earlier than he had to let her go.

She was braless underneath his shirt, and the thin material reminded him constantly of the fact that she was ready for him at any time. Her nipples were puckered nicely against the thin white cotton fabric, begging him to reach out and touch her while she had her head resting back against his shoulder. Her hips were nested firmly against his groin, and every time she moved, his cock jerked with awareness of her warm softness so close to him.

With the awareness of just how much he enjoyed her company and her body.

It was quiet now, with only the sound of the surf and fire to intrude on their peace.

But Kyle was concerned. The men from her side of the island were getting more resourceful and insistent that Marianne return to her "fantasy."

He'd be damned if he was going to let her go. Not until she asked him to, and so far she seemed utterly content to stay with him.

But those pesky vermin kept running after them, and today they'd gotten a little smarter.

One of the buggers had almost caught up to them on the cliffs. But a few well-tossed grenades had sent the man running back the way he'd come.

Tomorrow Kyle would have to move them to a new location farther down the beach.

Marianne continued to play along with the idea of their pursuers being Tyson's henchmen out to get them, but by the light in her brown eyes whenever he spoke of it, he could tell she didn't believe him.

It was just as well. Tyson had been a stupid idea, but it had brought him the best moments of his life, and if she didn't call his bluff, he wasn't going to confess the truth to her.

He just wanted to enjoy what little time they had left.

Marianne snatched her stick up as her marshmallow caught fire. She quickly blew it out. Her long hair tickled his skin as she moved, stirring the air between them so that he could smell the fragrance of his shampoo in her hair.

He loved the smell of his scent on her. It touched him on a level that was profound and frightening.

Entranced, Kyle watched as she pulled the gooey mess from the tip of the stick and carefully took a bite.

The sight of her tongue flicking back and forth over her lips undid him.

His body burning, he pulled her close to taste the sugar on her lips. She moaned the instant he swept his tongue against hers.

"Are you burning your marshmallow, Kyle?"

He rubbed noses with her and inhaled her womanly scent before pulling away to see his stick and marshmallow buried deep in the fire. "It would seem so."

She tsked at him. "And that was the last one, too. Shame on you."

Shaking his head at her, he tossed his stick into the fire. They were running low on supplies. He'd snuck over to his hotel to get a few more essentials such as soap and shampoo while she'd slept last night, but the truth was they would have to go back to the real world all too soon.

Their time was so limited.

"If I have to die for my country, Joe, then I'd like to know what the hell I was living for."

Those angry words haunted him now as he remembered saying them to Joe right after he and Retter had blown their way out of the Middle East.

Marianne was the answer, but he couldn't stay with her. His duties were elsewhere. Men like him didn't have liabilities, and Marianne Webernec was a huge liability. He didn't need to have the stress of worrying about the widow he would leave behind if he died.

Such things guaranteed death with cold-blooded certainty. In the field the best soldiers were the ones who had nothing to focus on or worry about except the job.

The job was everything.

But at least now he understood what it meant to be alive. To feel deeply for a woman and to know, while he was getting the crap shot out of him, why his job was so important.

It kept people like Marianne safe. She was no longer some faceless stranger. An abstract ideal.

He had something real to hold on to.

Closing his eyes, he leaned his cheek against hers and just held her in the quiet solitude, wishing that time could stand still and that he could make this moment last for eternity.

He never wanted to leave her.

He never wanted to leave this island.

Marianne sighed as she absorbed the sensation of Kyle's whiskers lightly scraping her skin. His strong arms were wrapped around her chest as if he were afraid to let her go.

She loved that feeling, but more than that, she suspected that she might actually love *him*.

These last few days they had shared so much of themselves with each other. She had told him of her fears of dying alone without ever having one spectacular moment to say Marianne Webernec had lived. That she was important to someone other than her rogue tomcat.

Kyle had listened, and he, too, had shared his sad past with her. And with every nugget he had entrusted her with, she had fallen for him more.

No one had ever been closer to her. Never meant more to her. Kyle was wonderful.

She didn't know how much of what he'd told her was truth and how much was made up, but she didn't think he was lying about the important things, such as his best friend and mother dying. The pain in his eyes when he spoke of them was too real to be faked.

No, he had opened himself up to her, too.

Her heart thrilled at the thought. Warmed by him and his concern, she turned around to face him. The firelight played in his hair and across his face, making shadows along the sharp, handsome planes.

"You are so delectable," she said.

He arched a brow at that.

Smiling wickedly, she reached for the button of his jeans.

"What are you doing?" he asked.

She unzipped his fly. "Why, I'm having my wicked way with you, sir."

His swollen cock, nestled by his short, dark hairs, jutted out, arching back toward his stomach. Luckily his underwear was still drying from where they had washed their clothes earlier, so now he was all naked and exposed to her.

Mmm, how she loved the sight of him like that. Hard and ready for her. She ran her hand down the length of him and delighted in the way his cock followed the motion of her caress. The way it lifted and arched in reaction to her touch.

She brushed her hand along the sensitive tip, letting his wetness coat her fingers.

Kyle watched her with hooded eyes as his breathing changed to sharp, intense breaths.

Marianne licked her lips and lowered her head so that she could draw the tip of him into her mouth. She closed her eyes as she tasted the salty sweetness of him. How she loved the taste that was Kyle.

He hissed in reaction.

She growled deep in her throat as she took more of him into her mouth, while running her tongue around the large vein, and allowed the vibration of her voice box to add to his pleasure.

He cupped her face in his hands and ran his hands through her hair while she cupped the soft sac of him in her hand to massage him in time with her long licks.

Kyle's head swam as he leaned back to allow her more access to his body. There was nothing better than the sensation of her sweet little mouth teasing him. Her timidity was gone now after the days they had been together. She was bold with him.

And he liked that most of all.

She no longer hesitated to touch him. She'd learned he couldn't deny her anything. Whatever she wanted was fine by him, and in truth, he liked being her chew-toy.

She sucked him gently, then licked her way from the base to his tip. His pleasure was so intense, he swore he could see stars.

And when she reversed direction, it was all he could do to not cry out in ecstasy. Oh, the feel of her mouth on him, especially when she kept going and drew one of his balls into her mouth to suck and nibble.

He dug his heel into the blanket as he carefully balled his hand into a fist in her hair without hurting her.

She didn't take an ounce of mercy on him. Instead, she continued her bittersweet assault. Breathless, he ran his hand down her jaw while she returned to his cock and took him all the way into her mouth again.

The sight of her there was enough to finish him off. Unable to stand it, he let his orgasm tear through him. His entire body shuddered and convulsed.

Weak and spent, he collapsed back against the driftwood. Marianne kissed her way up his body slowly, as if savoring every inch of his skin as much as he savored hers.

He groaned when she paused at his nipple to draw it deep into her mouth and flick her tongue back and forth over it. "I love the way you taste," she said, her breath scorching him.

"I love being tasted."

Her smile made his heart pound even more.

Then she dug into the pocket of his jeans and pulled out a quarter.

"What are you doing?" he asked suspiciously.

"Turn over."

He laughed nervously. "I'm not sure about this."

"C'mon," she said, wrinkling her nose at him. "It's something I've been wanting to do."

When he hesitated, she shook her head. "Don't be a baby, Kyle. Trust me."

Reluctantly he moved so that he could lie down on his stomach. "Okay," he said slowly. "But I want to be able to use that quarter later. You know what I mean?"

Laughing, Marianne pulled his pants down to his buttocks. "You are such a worrywart. Relax."

Suddenly very nervous, he lifted himself up on his forearms so that he could stare at her over his shoulder.

She stared at his butt, then took the quarter and bounced it off his left cheek.

"I knew it!" she said triumphantly. "Your butt is so tight, the quarter actually bounces."

"What?"

She smiled even wider at him. "You have the tightest ass in the world, you know that?"

"Yeah, okay," he said again. This had to be the strangest moment of his life, and when you considered the fact he spent a great deal of time with drug dealers and terrorists, that was saying something. "You do this a lot?"

"Nope," she said, putting the quarter into her pocket. "I just wanted to test my theory."

"And now that you have?"

Her look turned wicked. "I have plans for that tight butt cheek."

She placed her hands on his cheeks and gave a hard, pleasurable squeeze before she leaned forward and took a nip in the same spot where she'd bounced the quarter.

Kyle laid himself down, content to let her have her way with his body.

Marianne never ceased to surprise him. He found the challenge of her the best part about all of this.

And as the night sped by, he realized something.

For the first time in his life, he was in love with someone.

Someone who had come to mean everything to him.

Someone he was going to have to leave behind forever.

———

Kyle woke up inside the cave the next morning so sated that he was sure he must have died and gone to heaven. This last week with Marianne had been unlike anything he'd ever known.

The more he got to know her, the more he liked her.

No, it was more than like. She made him feel things he'd never felt for anyone.

And he adored the scent of her on his skin. The feel of her hands on his body. He loved waking up with her lying next to him.

Dreamy and warm, he rolled over to pull her close for some serious snuggling, only to find himself alone on the air mattress.

Frowning, Kyle opened his eyes to see the strangest sight of his life.

Someone had placed a toy rubber chicken on Marianne's pillow.

"Marianne?" he called, laughing at what he assumed was a prank. She had an odd sense of humor at times.

No one answered.

And now that he thought about it, where would she have gotten a toy chicken?

Extremely concerned, he sat up instantly. His gaze fell to the handwriting on it, and his blood ran cold.

If you want to see Marianne alive again, call Tyson Purdue, 212-555-6209.

What the hell?

His heart pounding, Kyle shot out of bed and dug his cell phone out of the small backpack he'd brought along days ago. For the first time in a week, he turned it on and dialed the number.

"Kyle?" The voice was electronically distorted.

"Who is this?" he demanded.

"It's Tyson Purdue, and you have been a bad boy.

Literally. I'm sick of you interfering with my business, and it's time I taught you a lesson."

"What are you talking about?"

A sharp click sounded. It was followed by Marianne's terrified voice. "Kyle? What's going on? Who are these people who have me?"

He saw red at the fear he heard from her. He'd kill whoever had scared her like this. "It's okay, baby. Don't worry. I won't let them hurt you. Can you stay calm for me?"

Marianne didn't answer. Another sharp click sounded, and then the electronic voice responded. "Don't worry, Foster. She's okay so long as you do what we say."

"What do you want?"

"I want *you*, Kyle Foster. I want you dead for what you've done."

"Who the hell are you?"

"You know who I am. Don't be stupid. And at the risk of being clichéd, if you want Marianne to remain healthy and living, meet me at dusk on the south beach. Oh, and you'd better be unarmed."

The phone went dead.

❦

Marianne was so scared she couldn't breathe. Couldn't move. All she knew was that one minute she'd been sleeping happily wrapped around Kyle, and the next minute someone had pressed a pungent-smelling rag against her face.

Then everything went black again.

She'd awakened a short time ago with a ferocious headache to find herself blindfolded, with her hands tied behind her back and her feet tied to the wooden chair she sat on.

From what she could tell, there were three men with her. The one who had awakened her to talk on the phone seemed to be an American. His voice was extremely deep and seemed to have a very light hint of an unknown foreign accent to it.

The man on her right spoke with a heavy Spanish accent while another man's voice was definitely German.

"Why did you tell him to wait until sunset?" the man with the Spanish accent asked. "I'm ready to get this done and go home."

"Reno, you were born impatient, *mi'jo*. The beauty of dealing with your opponent is playing with his head. Let's make him sweat a little. By nightfall he'll be so rattled, he won't even be able to think straight."

Marianne heard something click that sounded like a gun being cocked or maybe loaded.

Reno laughed. "You are an evil bastard."

"Yes, I am, and if you were wise, you'd be taking

notes. Learn from the master, boys, and learn well."

Marianne was so afraid that her teeth chattered. She was freezing cold, shaking even though her hands were tied behind her back.

She wanted to be brave for Kyle, but she wasn't a secret agent. The character in her novel would be able to get out of this. A small-town high school teacher couldn't.

What was she going to do now? This wasn't supposed to happen to her. She was . . .

Marianne paused as the men started talking about blowing up the cabin she was in.

Wait, this was familiar to her. She knew this part. Being tied to the chair, the phone call.

The cabin explosion.

Chapter 9!

Her mind raced as relief coursed through her. *That's right. Halfway through the book Ren ends up captured by the villain and Brad has to come to the rescue, only Ren ends up being the one who rescues him.*

It was the book!

These men must be more actors, and they had finally recaptured her from Kyle.

Well, it was about time. They'd been woefully inadequate up until now.

She relaxed at the discovery. This wasn't real. It was only part of her fantasy.

Oh, thank God no one was going to kill her or

Kyle. She let out a long breath as she tried to wiggle out of the ropes.

"Okay, guys," she said, her voice surprisingly steady. "You can untie me now."

"Untie you?" the American repeated, his tone filled with disbelief. "Why should I?"

"Because I asked you to?" She waited expectantly for them to untie her.

They didn't. Nor did they say anything, and she had a sneaking suspicion they were staring at her.

"Look," she tried again, "I realize that you guys finally managed to get me away from Kyle. Bully for you, you did good for once. But now we're back to the book, and since I'm the heroine and I'm supposed to escape, I need some help. This chair is really uncomfortable, and my hands hurt."

She waited for them to obey her, and again they didn't make a move to undo her.

Time stretched out interminably.

"C'mon," she said, hopping in the chair. "I can't undo these knots. See, I know Ren Winterbourne, Secret Agent, is supposed to be able to get out of the chair, but Marianne Webernec from Peoria can't, and until I get loose, we can't move on to the next scene, so would you guys help?"

"What is she talking about?" the Spanish man asked.

"Who is Ren Winterbourne?" the German asked.

The American laughed.

Another ripple of fear went through her.

They're just playing with you. You heard them, they like to play with people's heads.

Play with Kyle's head.

Marianne paused as she realized this wasn't about her. They might really be after Kyle after all. Otherwise, why use the name Tyson Purdue?

Dear Lord, what if Tyson Purdue was a real man?

Stay calm, Marianne.

"C'mon," Marianne said again, hoping she was wrong and they were just being mean for all the times Kyle had scared them off. "I know this isn't real. Just let me go, and I won't tell Mr. Zimmerman how bad you scared me."

"Do you guys know a Zimmerman?" the German man asked.

Marianne felt someone move closer to her.

"Not real?" The American stood so close that his voice was nothing more than a growl in her right ear. "Lady, do you know what BAD is?"

"Bureau of American Defense. It's the agency Kyle made up."

She heard the American move away from her then. It sounded as if he might have huddled with the others.

The men began speaking to each other in German. Little did they know, German was one of the languages she taught at her school, and she understood them perfectly.

"If she doesn't believe him, then we can let her go, right?" the German man asked.

"How much did Foster tell her?" the Spanish man asked. "You were the one who had him bugged."

The American answered, "A lot more than he should have. I don't know . . ."

There were a few seconds of silence, and again she heard something that definitely sounded like a gun being cocked this time.

"I'm thinking she's a liability, and you know what I think of liabilities."

"Put your weapon down. You can't just kill her," the German man said. "I'm tired of cleaning up body parts after you get through."

Oh, God, it's real!

These weren't actors from the island.

Someone pulled the hair back from her neck, and then something sharp and cold was pressed against her throat.

"Are you scared, teacher?" the American whispered in her ear. "You said you wanted to be an agent. Were you really prepared for it?"

I don't want to die! The words tore through her mind. No, she didn't want this any more than she wanted Kyle to die.

Against her will, she started sobbing uncontrollably.

"Hey, hey, hey!" the American said as he moved whatever was against her throat away from her. "What is this?"

She couldn't speak past her wrenching cries.

"Ay caramba! What have you done? Look at her."

The blindfold came off instantly, and she realized she was inside a very small cabin that had next to no furniture. Her chair and a table appeared to be it.

Well, that and a whole lot of ammunition and guns. There were boxes all around her bearing the words *Fragile, Danger, Explosives, Ammunition, Grenades,* etc.

Marianne saw the three men through her blurry eyes. The one in front of her was gorgeous for a psycho. He had shoulder-length black hair that fell around a face that belonged to some Calvin Klein model. His dark skin was perfectly tanned, his eyes so pale a blue they didn't look real.

He reached out and wiped the tears from her face. "Don't cry," he said, letting her know he was the American. "C'mon, I can't stand to see a woman cry."

Reno cut the ropes on her feet.

Angry and scared, she reacted without thinking. She kicked the American in the leg.

"Ow!" he snapped, moving away from her.

Reno untied her hands, flipped closed his knife, then slapped a hand against the American's shoulder.

"Pendejo!" he snarled. "I told you not to tie her up like this."

The American hissed and took a fearsome step toward Reno, who stepped back instantly. "Don't come at me, *maricón,* unless you come bearing a weapon."

"I've got your weapon, right here," Reno said, flipping open the large black butterfly knife he'd used to free her with.

The tall, blond German stepped between them. His hair was cut short, and he wore a pair of black aviator-style sunglasses. His white T-shirt was tight over a body that was huge and well built like a major bodybuilder. A colorful tattoo spiraled down his right arm.

"Enough!" the German said, keeping them at arm's length with his body between them.

Marianne decided to take advantage of their fight to run for the door.

She'd barely reached it before the American caught her. He swung her up in his arms.

She kicked with everything she had and screamed while trying to claw his eyes out.

The other two men laughed.

The American sat her down hard in the chair and held her there with an ease of strength that was truly terrifying.

He turned his icy gaze back to hers. "Look, no one's going to hurt you, okay?"

"You're going to kill Kyle."

A lopsided grin broke across the man's face, showing her a set of perfectly white teeth. "Not today, I'm not. I just want to teach him a lesson."

She launched herself at him.

He actually laughed as he held her easily away from him. "Well, the little teacher has spunk." He set her back in the chair. Again. "Listen to me, Marianne. You had a fantasy to be a damsel in distress, right?"

She swallowed her tears as she looked back and forth between the men. "You don't look like actors."

"Yeah, well," the American said. "That's because we're not."

"Then what are you?"

"We're friends of Kyle's."

The German snorted at that. "Since when?"

Marianne glared at the American. "I knew you were lying."

"Look, I swear, I'm not lying about this." He looked at the German. "Dieter, really, don't help me here, okay?"

"Fine, Retter. Don't call me the next time you need some *Scheiflekopf* to help you."

That diabolical half smile played across the American's face. "Your words, not mine."

Marianne froze as the man's name registered in her mind.

Retter ...

The name went through her like glass. She knew

who this man was. Kyle had told her much about his pseudo-partner who didn't listen to anyone except himself. Kyle's exact words had been, "Retter is a dick-head, but he gets the job done with scary reliability. The man strikes like lightning."

Retter turned back toward her. "I'm just playing a joke on Kyle for making me have to come out here to retrieve him. Since you wanted to be a damsel in distress, I was going to give you what you wanted while I jerked his chain. I'm sorry I scared you so badly. I'm used to dealing with agents who would sooner have their hearts cut out than cry."

She narrowed her eyes on the man before her. Still skeptical, Marianne wasn't sure what to believe. "How do I know you're who you say you are?"

"You'll just have to take my word for it."

"If I don't?"

Reno laughed. "I really like this woman, Retter. She thinks you're an asshole, too."

He gave Reno a cold, brutal look before those piercingly blue eyes moved back to her. "You'd be wise never to accept my word on anything, but if I kill Kyle, I'd have to explain it to Joe, and then he'd get bent and then I'd have to kill him, too, and that would make his woman go wild on me. And it's all just more trouble than even I want to deal with at the moment. So, see, he's safe."

There was a light in his eyes that said he would enjoy the challenge of the fight in spite of what he said, but there was also something charming and oddly warm about this man.

Marianne nodded quietly at him. "He'd better be safe," she warned him. "I don't know who Joe or his woman is, but if you do anything to Kyle, I swear Joe's woman going wild on you will seem like a walk in paradise compared to what I'll do to you."

         —

Kyle stalked back and forth in anger as he tried to figure out who could have taken Marianne while he slept.

He discounted the morons on the other side of the island. He'd been hanging them from trees and escaping them with barely more than a fierce growl. They could never have perpetrated anything like this.

It would have to be someone stealthy. Someone who knew how lightly he slept and how to move about without waking him . . .

He cursed as one name resonated in his head.

Retter.

There was no one else it could be.

Kyle's sight clouded at the thought. It had to be. Retter was the only man Kyle had ever known who could maneuver around him while he slept and not wake him. The man was part ghost.

But how did Retter know about Tyson Purdue?

He'd made the name up and . . .

He paused as he glanced back at the chicken and the crisp handwriting.

There must be a bug on him somewhere. There had to be. Joe was ever paranoid about losing agents and bugged almost every piece of equipment they had. The only reason Kyle hadn't thought of it sooner was the fact that every time he called Joe demanding a ride out of this place, Joe had laughed at him and told him to get lost.

It had never occurred to him that Joe would have the stuff on the island tagged, but since he'd raided the BAD supply closet for supplies, he should have known.

"Damn it."

Pissed and wanting blood, he called the number again.

No one answered.

So he dialed Joe's office, where Joe's assistant director, Tee, picked it up on the third ring.

"Tee, this is Kyle. Is Joe in?"

Tee Ho was the extremely attractive assistant director of the agency. She was a Vietnamese immigrant, and her intelligence was off the scale. So was her memory and her need to exact revenge on anyone dumb enough to mock her name. It was a mistake Kyle had made only once, and he was lucky he didn't have a permanent limp from the experience.

She was a top-notch agent and Joe's right hand, and she never let anyone forget those two facts.

"Well, well, Mr. Foster," she said in her crisp, flawless English—Tee could speak somewhere in the neighborhood of fifteen languages fluently—"how nice of you to finally check in. Blown up any busboys lately?"

"I beg your pardon?"

"Please, don't beg, it's not becoming of you, Mr. Let-Me-Kidnap-a-Woman-and-Drag-Her-Back-to-My-Cave. Joe is so hot about you right now, you're lucky you're still living. He's on the phone with Wulfgar Zimmerman from Rose Books trying to assure him you haven't hurt Marianne and that she will be returned to him shortly."

"I'm not the one who hurt her. Retter kidnapped her from me this morning."

Silence answered him for a few heartbeats until Tee started laughing.

"It's not funny, Tee."

"Sure it is. You're just mad he got away with it. At least he didn't punch you in the nose before he grabbed her. The actor playing Brad Ramsey, in case you're wondering, is fine, but bruised. He also quit his job and was threatening to sue us until I introduced him to Tessa and convinced him that a lawsuit would be extremely hazardous to his health."

Tessa was Tee's prized Glock 33. Which was only slightly more deadly than Tee's other lethal weapon, Petey the killer Pomeranian.

"I swear, I'm going to kill Retter for this."

"Uh, no, you won't, hon. He's vital to national security and falls under extreme protection."

Kyle growled into the phone. "Then tell me how to get a hold of Retter and call him down."

"Ooo," she breathed. "I don't think that's possible. See, he was off in Rio having a grand old time on the beach when Joe had to call him in to come get you away from Wulfgar's tourist. You were bad, Kyle, not BAD. So sorry. If you want to talk to Retter, then call him. There's nothing I can do."

She actually hung up the phone.

"Fine," he said loudly, hoping that whatever mic was hidden, it picked up his voice. "You'd better hide, Retter, because tonight I am going to kick your rotten ass all over the beach."

Three hours later Kyle came across the beach, loaded for bear, or in this case, loaded for Retter.

He'd fought beside the bastard enough to know what he needed to beat him. And beat him he was going to do.

For the last three hours Kyle had done total recog

on the island. There was only one place where Marianne could be.

One place Retter would deem "secret."

He already had the small cabin in his sights. It sat alone at the base of a small mountain. It was used for supplies that Joe didn't want near the hotel in the event of a fire or something else that might make it explode.

Kyle didn't break stride or hesitate as he headed for it. He was less than three yards from the door of it when he heard a sharp click.

Cursing, he dived away from it an instant before the shack blew apart.

Debris rained all around him.

Kyle couldn't breathe as terror overwhelmed him. Marianne!

"It's not sundown, Kyle."

Kyle saw a two-way radio in the sand a few feet from him. He got up and grabbed it. "Where the hell are you, Retter?" He looked around, scanning everything.

"Look up."

He did and found Retter, Reno, and Dieter standing on the cliff. Marianne was nowhere in sight. "What kind of game are you playing?"

"Hide-and-seek. If you can find Marianne, I'll let you keep her."

"And if I don't?"

"Your loss. Literally." He saw Retter motion for

Reno and Dieter to leave. Once they were out of hearing range, Retter spoke again. "Do you feel her loss, Kyle? Tell me the truth."

Yes, he did. He'd been feeling the emptiness of it since he'd awakened and found himself alone again.

Every minute he'd been away from her, he hurt. The desolation inside him was unlike anything he'd ever known.

He didn't want to live without Marianne.

But Lucifer would freeze solid before he ever admitted that to Retter. "Go to hell."

"I most likely will, but in the meantime the clock is ticking for you. If you don't find her by nightfall, it's over, and you, my friend, are on a plane out of here."

It was all Kyle had wanted. But that was before he'd met Marianne and had learned to have fun without explosives. Fun without someone taking potshots at him.

What would he do without her?

He didn't want to find out. Tossing the radio down, he backtracked through the woods and tried his best to focus on where Retter would have hidden her now.

—

Marianne sat in the lobby of Kyle's hotel, wrapped in Kyle's jacket. The scent of his body clung to it, making her want to bury her face in the sleeve and just inhale it until she was drunk from the scent.

Sam sat behind the concierge counter, staring at her. His old basset hound lay beside him on its back with all four of its paws up in the air.

"Are you sure that dog's not dead?"

Sam glanced at him. "Nah, ole Roscoe always sleeps like that."

She nodded, then frowned. Sam was a strange bird. "How long before Kyle gets here?"

"I dunno. Depends on what Retter does to him for taking you."

"Do you think they'll be really harsh on him?"

"Well, back when I worked for the CIA, we'd have killed him for being such a pain, and Retter might yet. He's got a lot of the old school in him."

Marianne felt the color drain from her face.

"But his boss, Joe, is a bit more understanding about such things, so it's hard to say. I figure the worst thing that could happen to Kyle is nothing."

"What do you mean?"

"Well, he must have thought a lot of you to keep them actors and all on their toes. He had to have known that sooner or later Mr. Zimmerman would call in Joe to come get him. So to my way of thinking, he must have thought you were worth the trouble that's now coming his way."

Before Marianne could speak, Aislinn Zimmerman came running into the lobby. She was followed by an extremely tall, devastatingly handsome man. There was an air of refined elegance to the man, who wore an expensive tailor-made suit.

"Oh, Marianne!" Aislinn exclaimed. "Thank goodness they found you. We have been worried sick."

The man with her rubbed his brow as if Aislinn's dramatics were giving him a headache.

He held his hand out to Marianne. "Hi, Ms. Webernec. I'm Wulfgar Zimmerman, and I just wanted to tell you personally how sorry I am for your ordeal."

So this was the mysterious owner of Rose Books. He was devastating and rumored to be one of the richest men in the world. Marianne shook his hand. "There really is nothing to apologize for. I've had the time of my life."

Aislinn snorted. "Yes, but that was before that lunatic Kyle Foster ruined it."

"You're the one who put her here, Ais," Wulfgar said calmly.

Aislinn turned on her brother with a snarl. "Well, the next time the island is occupied by *them,* I wish you would put something down on paper."

He arched an elegant brow. "Forgive me, but I thought the word *occupied* on the schedule was self-explanatory."

"I thought you meant it was occupied by *our* people, not *theirs*. You're supposed to put *training* down when they're training here."

"Excuse me," Sam said, interrupting them. "But I take exception to that. Me and Roscoe are always here, and we definitely fall under the *them* category."

"You're you, Sam," Aislinn explained. "You don't count."

Sam looked extremely offended by that.

Wulfgar shook his head. "You'd better stop while you're behind, Ais. You're just getting in deeper at the moment."

Aislinn ignored the men and took Marianne's arm. "Don't worry, hon. I'll take care of this mess. We'll extend your stay another week and get back to your fantasy."

"It's okay, really," Marianne said. "I've had a great time with Kyle." She stared up at Wulfgar, hoping to make him understand. "Look, I don't want Kyle to get into trouble. Had he not shown up, I was ready to call you and ask for the fantasy to be canceled."

"Really?" Wulfgar asked.

She nodded.

He looked at his sister, who appeared horrified. "Well, how was I to know Brad was having an affair with Spencer?"

"I don't want to go into that again, Ais, but this is the last time I leave a fantasy package up to you."

"Fine," Aislinn snapped. "I don't want to do another one anyway. You get entirely too cranky when the guest goes AWOL. So I leave it up to you from now on. I'm through." Aislinn stalked out of the hotel and left Marianne alone with Wulfgar.

Wulfgar gave her a patient stare. "Tell me something, Marianne. What could possibly make this story turn out to be a happily-ever-after for you after everything that's happened?"

Marianne opened her mouth to say having Kyle as her own, but the minute the thought occurred to her, she realized something.

Mr. Zimmerman might be a billionaire magnate. But he couldn't give her the one thing she needed.

Only Kyle could do that.

And right now she had no idea if he even wanted to.

CHAPTER FIVE

Kyle searched all the likely places Retter might have stashed Marianne.

He was out of options.

Disgusted and angry, he leaned back against a palm tree at the edge of the beach and raked his hands through his hair. If he closed his eyes, he could feel Marianne with him. Feel the touch of her hand on his skin. The warmth of her body under him.

He just wanted to see her one more time.

"C'mon, Kyle," he said to himself. "Think through this. You've never given up on anything in your life. You can do it."

Nothing had ever been more important to him.

He had to find her.

The best hiding place is always the most obvious. No one will ever think you're dumb enough to put something there. Kyle froze as Joe's words from training went through his mind.

Most obvious . . .

Surely Retter wouldn't have done that. He was

never obvious. The bastard loved being complicated and vague.

But the more he thought about it, the more sure he was that Retter had chosen someplace easy. After all, Retter wouldn't think he'd think to look there.

Running as fast as he could, Kyle headed back to his hotel. Time seemed to slow down as he ran. He couldn't remember anything ever taking longer.

Please let me be right. . . .

If he was wrong, then he was totally screwed.

As soon as he reached his hotel, he went crashing through the door, only to find Sam sitting at his desk, watching TV.

There was no one else in the place.

No one.

Damn it to hell!

It had been a stupid thought.

His heart heavy, Kyle actually wanted to cry in frustration. What would he do now?

"Welcome back, Mr. Excitement," Sam said, looking up from the TV. "Heard you've had a high time with them weirdos from the other side of the island. I told you not to go over there, didn't I? Told you they'd do strange things to you." He paused as he adjusted his glasses and frowned. "You okay, boy? You don't look right."

Kyle couldn't speak. All he could do was struggle to breathe past the pain in his chest. One that had nothing to do with his mad sprint and everything to do with what he'd lost.

"Where's Marianne, Sam? Have you seen her?"

Please tell me she's here. . . .

Sam scratched his cheek. "Well, she was here a while ago, but that Mr. Zimmerman from the publisher came and took her away."

Kyle's heart leaped with hope. "Where did he take her?"

He shrugged. "Marianne said she wanted to finish out her fantasy. I'm not sure what that means."

She must be on the other side of the island again, which meant he could find her.

Sam opened up the small red Igloo cooler at his feet and pulled out a cold beer. "Here," he said, twisting the cap off. "You look like you could use a drink."

"No, thanks. I've got to find her."

Sam nodded as if he understood. "You know, I had a woman I loved once. Long time ago." He sighed dreamily. "Her name was Ethel Burrows. Oh, she was beautiful. Smart. Quick as a whip. She made me feel like I could fly."

Kyle frowned at his words, wondering why Sam was sharing this with him when Sam usually shared very few personal things. "What happened to her?"

A sad, faraway look covered Sam's face. "Me, mostly. I didn't ever tell her how I felt about her. I was about your age and working for the CIA all the time. I was afraid to take a wife. Afraid I'd get killed, or she might be in danger. Either way, I knew I wouldn't be home much to be with her. I didn't think it would be fair to her to be married and have to go off on missions while she stayed behind with my kids." He pierced Kyle with a dark, meaningful look. "I never stopped to think about what would happen if I *didn't* die."

"What do you mean?"

"Well, at the time I had fourteen more years of active service before they sent me to the desk or retired me. Fourteen years seemed like forever when I was twenty-eight. It didn't dawn on me that I'd be spending more years than that alone, wondering what would have happened to me if I'd just asked her to marry me." Sam reached over to scratch Roscoe's ears. "But that's okay. I've got Roscoe here to keep me company in my old age."

Kyle stared at the man and his dog, and in that instant he saw a very sobering future for himself. One he didn't want to even contemplate.

"Thanks, Sam."

Sam nodded at him and started drinking the beer he'd offered him. "Don't make my mistakes, Kyle. Go find your woman and tell her what she means to you."

Kyle tore out of the hotel and headed for the other side of the island.

He had a destiny waiting for him, and come hell or high water, he was going to find it.

⟡

At least that was what he thought. By five o'clock Kyle knew it was hopeless.

Marianne was nowhere on the island. Nowhere.

He'd searched every place he could think. Every corner, every cranny.

It was as if she'd vanished off the face of the earth. Of course, none of the busboys or actors from the other side would help him. Hell, they barely spoke to him after the trouble he'd given them while they had tried to find her and he'd scared them off.

It seemed they thought turnabout was fair play.

One of the little bastards had even laughed at him when he'd asked if the man had seen her.

That was okay. He'd stopped laughing the minute Kyle shot out his tires.

At four-thirty he'd finally found Aislinn Zimmerman in Marianne's hotel, debriefing the staff for their next guest, who would be arriving within the next few weeks. The redhead had promptly read him the riot act for screwing up the one and only fantasy her brother had entrusted her to run entirely on her own.

"You want Marianne?" she'd snapped at him.

"Then find my brother. Last I checked, she was flying off on his private plane back to civilization."

Kyle had gone immediately to their airstrip, only to find out Wulfgar Zimmerman was long gone.

Which meant so was Marianne.

Damn it!

Defeated and tired, Kyle walked the long distance back to his side of the island. He didn't stop to say good-bye to Sam, though he should have. He just couldn't face the old man right now.

So he bypassed the hotel and went straight to the private airstrip they used, which wasn't all that far from where he'd been hidden with Marianne. His throat tightened at the thought.

Retter was standing by the small luxury jet, waiting for him.

"You're right on time."

"Stay away from me, Retter. In the mood I'm in, I just might kill you."

"No luck, huh?"

"Shut up."

Retter stepped aside so that Kyle could reach the stairs to the plane.

Kyle snarled at him as he paused by his side. "I really hate you for this. Couldn't you have given me twenty-four hours before you came crashing in?"

"Would that have been enough?"

No, it wouldn't have. It wouldn't have made any of

this a bit easier to swallow. Shoving Retter aside, Kyle ascended the stairs and bent his head down to enter the plane.

Retter was only a few steps behind him.

He saw Reno in the cockpit, wearing the pilot's headgear, waiting for them.

"So what did you do with her?" he asked as he took a seat up front, not far away from Reno.

Retter shrugged as he sat down in the row across from him. "Talked to her for a while. I found her fascinating."

Kyle saw red at his words. "Don't talk about her like that. She's too good for you."

"She's too good for *you*," Retter shot back.

Kyle didn't say anything. It was true.

It still didn't lessen the pain he felt.

Reno started making their flight plan.

In that moment Kyle knew what he needed to do.

He stood up again. "Reno," he said as he neared the cockpit. "I want you to fly us to Peoria."

Reno's jaw went slack. "Excuse me?"

"You heard me."

"I can't do that, *mi hermano*. Joe wants you home."

"Fuck Joe and what he wants."

"Whoa," Retter said, moving to stand behind him. "I think you need to take a more civil tone, bud. Have you any idea how much your little 'date' has cost us already? There are countries with a smaller

GNP than the tab you've spent on Marianne. Now you want us to fly your ass to Peoria?"

"Fine," Kyle said angrily. "I'll just book the flight when we land in Nashville and head out then."

Retter shook his head. "Are you insane? Joe will fire you for this."

"Then let him."

Retter's face hardened. "Think about this for a minute, Kyle. You'll lose everything. Is she worth it?"

He didn't even have to hesitate. "She's worth everything in the world to me."

To his surprise, Retter stepped back and smiled.

Three seconds later the rear emergency door was ripped off the airplane and a smoking canister was thrown into the aisle.

Before Kyle could reach for his weapon, a small commando dressed all in black tripped through the doorway, carrying an M-16.

She paused at the opening and stared agape at the plane. "Wow, this is really nice."

Kyle smiled the instant he recognized that less-than-fierce voice. Not to mention he'd know that body anywhere, even when it was decked out in ill-fitting fatigues and her face was covered in black paint.

It was Marianne.

And she was joined by another commando he recognized as Dieter, also dressed in full commando gear. "Terrorists," Dieter whispered to her loudly, "hostage, remember?"

"Oh, yeah," she said, gripping her weapon and looking fierce, or at least as fierce as a high-school teacher could look. "Don't anyone—" She started coughing from the smoke as she moved through it.

Dieter pounded her lightly on the back and nudged her out of it. "It's okay. Breathe deeply."

Marianne coughed a few more times and nodded. "Don't—" She coughed more.

"She says don't move," Dieter finished for her.

She started toward Kyle, only to be stopped the instant her gun got wedged between the two seats on opposite ends of the row. She *whoofed* as it caught against her middle.

"That thing's not loaded, is it?" Kyle asked Retter.

"Hell, no. I told you I spent the day with her. Last thing I want is to be shot dead by friendly fire."

Dieter helped her get unhooked.

Retter held his hands up.

"You!" Marianne said, waving Retter aside with her gun. "Stay out of my way or I'll blow your head off."

"Yes, ma'am." Retter moved toward Reno.

Marianne took another step forward with her gun a little higher this time. "I'm Ren Winterbourne, Secret Agent, and ... um ... um ... um ..." She paused, thinking. "Wait a second . . . I'm Ren Winterbourne, Secret Agent, and . . ."

"And I'm here for the hostage!" Reno shouted out.

Kyle turned to see Reno in the cockpit with a copy of the book for Marianne's fantasy.

Marianne took a step toward him, but Dieter caught her and showed her how to walk down the aisle without catching the gun on the seats.

"Move, you scum," Reno prompted again.

Kyle stared at Marianne as she came even with him. He couldn't take his eyes off her.

"Hey," Reno said, raising his voice. "Move, you scum. This is the part where you make the terrorists get down on the ground and tie them up."

"Bullshit," Retter said. "This is the part where she shoots the pilot."

"*Nein,*" Dieter joined in, moving past them toward the other two. He pulled a copy of the book out of his back pocket and opened it up to a bookmarked page. "She makes you get down, Retter, and eat the floor. It says so right here. You must get down."

"Yeah and this is the part where you get sent back to Pakistan, Adolph. I'm not kissing dirt for nobody."

"I am not Adolph, I am Dieter."

Kyle was only vaguely aware of the others arguing about the book. His attention was solely on the woman before him.

"Were you really going to fly to Peoria?" she asked him.

"Well, yeah. I thought that's where you were. Aislinn told me you were on Wulfgar's plane."

She smiled. "I am, kind of. We both are."

Kyle glanced around the luxurious jet. He hadn't noticed just how nice it was earlier. It should have dawned on him the minute he entered it.

But then Marianne always had a way of distracting him.

"You know," she said quietly, "I always wanted to be the heroine in the book."

"Funny, I only want the woman who is reading the book."

She smiled up at him, and his groin jerked.

"So how does the story end?" he asked her.

"You kiss her, sheez!" the guys said in unison.

"Didn't he read the book?" Dieter asked. "It says right here—"

"Shut up, Dieter," Retter snapped. "I think we should leave them alone."

Laughing, Marianne stepped into his arms and held him tight. "It ends like all good romances do. We live happily ever after."

"CAPTIVATED" BY YOU

CHAPTER ONE

In her life as a covert agent, Rhea Stevenson had done a lot of things she hated: cozy up to cold-blooded killers, make goo-goo eyes at drug lords, pretend to be a Russian mail-order bride, walk unarmed in a low-cut, almost nonexistent dress into a nuclear arms deal.

But nothing in all her years as an agent had ever prepared her to do . . .

This!

"You want me to do *what*?" she asked Tee, the managing director of the Bureau of American Defense, or BAD, as it was known to most of the people who worked there.

A shadow antiterrorism agency that most of the country didn't even know existed, BAD had a lot of "interesting" people in it, and Tee was definitely one of the more colorful characters. At five feet even, Tee shouldn't have been intimidating at all, and yet the small, beautiful Vietnamese-American woman held a look to her that let anyone know she was far deadlier than any cobra.

And she was.

Tee gave her a flat, emotionless stare. "You're going to be a dominatrix."

Rhea couldn't do anything more than gape as she heard male laughter from the desk in the office cube across from hers.

Her gaze narrowed as a bad feeling came over her. "And whose bright idea was this?"

Ace rolled his chair back so that he could look from the entrance of his cube into hers. He smiled at her like the Cheshire cat.

"Oh, no, no, no," Rhea said firmly as she handed the file folder back to Tee. "Not on your life. Let Agent Hotshot over there go in with studded leather and whips. Then the deviants can hang together."

Ace, who really was sexier than any man had a right to be, gave her a hot once-over. "I can't, love. I don't have the ass for it. But you, on the other hand . . ." His dark blue gaze dipped down to her hips, and his smile turned lecherous, as if he was imagining cupping her derriere.

Rhea wasn't sure what she hated most, the boldness of that look or the way her body reacted to it. And yet her body always betrayed her with this man. She'd never understood how a woman could be both repulsed and turned on at the same time.

Surely something was seriously wrong with her.

"Is this not sexual harassment?" she asked Tee, even though a part of her was humming in excitement. "You know, I do have friends in the EEOC."

Tee looked rather amused by her question. "Well, in this case, Ace is right. We need a female agent to pose, and Ace thought you'd be the best one for it."

Rhea directed a gimlet stare at him. "I'll just bet he did."

Ace got up and sauntered toward them to stand in the cube's doorway. At six-two, he towered over Tee. The look on his handsome face was that of a kid at Christmas. An image that was helped by his tousled, dark blond hair and teasing, blue eyes.

He cast a devilish grin at Rhea. "Ah, just think, Rhea. You . . . me . . . chains and whips . . . Recipe for a hot night, huh?"

Recipe for a disaster, in her opinion. "Recipe for a nightmare, you mean. I wouldn't do this for all the money on the planet. Sorry, Tee, get yourself another agent for this."

Tee sighed irritably. "We need you, Rhea. You're the only one in the home office who fits the profile. Put aside your personal distaste and work with Ace just this once."

"I am not going to take my clothes off around him, even if I do get the benny of beating him."

Arching a brow, he folded his arms over his chest.

"But would you do it to stop a known terrorist?"

Rhea paused at his words. That was her one hot button, and everyone in the agency knew it. They just didn't know why. The reason was private and personal, but she had spent her entire adulthood on a crusade to stop such needless violence. That one word could get her to do anything.

Even take her clothes off around Ace Krux, male god, personal demon.

"That's another reason we thought you would be perfect," Tee said solemnly. "We all know how you feel."

No, they truly didn't. Rhea took the file back. "Do I have to work with Ace?"

Tee shrugged. "It's his baby. He's been working on the case for a year now and knows all the ins and outs."

"Don't worry, Rhea," he said. " You'll feel differently after you see me naked."

She snorted at that. "Yeah, someone remind me that I better bring along gallons of Pepto-Bismol, an industrial bottle of Tums, and some bicarbonate."

Ace rolled his eyes. "Yeah, right. Like you wouldn't sell your soul for a shot at me."

Rhea pulled her weapon out from the holster at her back, then ejected and checked her clip. "You got that much right." She slammed the clip back in and switched the safety off. "You want a ten-second head start, or can I just shoot you now?"

Tee shook her head at Ace. "Why must you always torment her? One day, she really is going to shoot you, and I just might authorize it." Tee turned back to her with a warning stare. "Put it away, Rhea."

Grumbling, she reactivated the safety and complied.

"Ah, she wouldn't shoot me anyway, Tee. She's just covering her infatuation for me by being a hard-ass."

Rhea stood up to confront him. "You know, Ace, you're not nearly as irresistible as you think you are."

"Sure, and just how many times have you dreamed about having me naked and in your bed?"

Rhea counted to ten in her head and forced herself not to rise to his baiting. But the worst part of it all was that he was right. She did find him physically attractive, but the minute he opened his mouth, she wanted to gag him.

"Oh, yeah," she said sarcastically. "You set my entire world on fire. Oh, baby; oh, baby. I must have your hot bod. Why don't we just strip naked and do it right here in the cube?"

Hunter Wesley Thornton-Payne stuck his handsome, albeit pompous, blond head up over the wall of the cube beside Rhea's. "Jeez, people. Could you cut the crap? You know some of us are actually trying to work over here."

"Since when do you work on anything other than

your stock portfolio, Payne?" Carlos Selgado asked in his accented voice as he popped up over Rhea's other wall to glare at Hunter. "Some of us are enjoying the fireworks."

"My name is *Thornton*-Payne," Hunter corrected.

Ignoring him as he always did, Carlos looked over at Tee. "If Rhea is really going to get naked, can I bump off Ace and take over his case?"

Tee gave them all a withering glare. "Agents, down, or there will be a vicious virus that attacks the payroll system and locks you all out of the loop. It's called the Pissed-off Tee Virus, and it could make it so that none of you get paid for at least six weeks . . . maybe more."

Carlos and Hunter immediately vanished.

Tee turned back to Rhea and Ace. "You two, play nice."

Rhea scoffed. "Play nice? I'd rather pet a scorpion, bare-handed."

That devilish grin returned to Ace's face as he raked her with an appreciative stare. "I'll show you my stinger if you'll show me yours."

She screwed her face up in disgust. The man was truly a reprobate.

"Hey, Carlos," he called, "you used to do a lot of work with scorpions. How do they mate, anyway? You know they got those stingers and claws and—"

"Enough with the mating rituals of scorpions,"

Rhea said from between clenched teeth. "Why don't we discuss the praying mantis instead? You know, the female rips the head off the male. She's a wise woman."

Ace wagged his eyebrows at her. "Yeah, but what a way to go, huh? If you've got to die, it's always best to go out with a good bang."

Tee cast a withering stare at them. "Yo, Marlin Perkins and crew, let's get back on topic here."

Ace leaned nonchalantly against Rhea's desk and folded his arms over his chest. "Okay, we'll get back on the subject now and save the banging for later."

Rhea just continued to glare at him. This was one of those times when she really hated this man.

But then Thaddeus "Ace" Krux was a man of many talents. He could scale a building in a manner to make Spider-Man proud. He could drive better and faster than Jeff Gordon and Mario Andretti combined. He could construct a lethal bomb from an empty Coke bottle, a piece of tissue, and simple household cleaners.

Most of all, he could render any woman on the planet speechless at first glance.

It was a hell of a combination that was deadly to any woman's defenses. He had the sleek, seductive movements of a beast in the wild, the smile of Don Juan, and the intelligence of Einstein, all packaged into the body of a Bowflex ad model.

He was the epitome of everything she found desirable in the male species. . . .

And everything she despised.

His calm, cool rationality bordered on dispassionate. His arrogance knew no bounds, and his ego . . .

Someone really needed to take him down a few notches.

Since he seemed to live for no other purpose than to torment her, he was completely distracting to her peace of mind.

"So has she racked him yet?" Joe asked as he joined them.

Barely in his thirties, Joe was young to hold the position of senior director for such an important agency, and yet Rhea couldn't think of anyone more suited to controlling the motley, often illegal bunch that made up the BAD task force.

For all his youth and handsomeness, Joe was even more lethal than Tee. He never compromised, never took prisoners. Something that was at odds with his pretty-boy features.

He had on a black leather shoulder holster with the ivory handle of a .38 Special peeking up (Joe had once said he liked being a cliché on the surface), but it was the stiletto he kept strapped to his calf that he was most famous for using (that was for the surprises he liked to give after someone mistook him for a cliché).

His dark brown shoulder-length hair was worn in

a ponytail, and for once he had the sleeves of his blue dress shirt rolled up to show off the telltale colors of the dragon tattoo on his left forearm—a remnant, Rhea had once been told by Tee, of the days when Joe was a member of a vicious New York street gang.

"Does this mean I have your permission to rack him?" Rhea asked Joe.

Joe gave Ace an amused smirk.

Ace snorted. "I don't think so. Remember, I do know where you live and sleep."

"Yeah, but not even you could get past my security system."

Joe was probably right. His specialty was wiring and demolition work. He could booby-trap just about anything. It was a special talent that Rhea couldn't imagine a New York City boy acquiring legally.

"So who are we after, anyway?" she asked, opening her folder.

"Lucius Bender," Ace said. "Ever heard of him?"

Rhea nodded. Of course she had. It was a case she'd been begging Joe for, and why he'd assigned it to Ace, she couldn't imagine. She was twice the agent he was. At least, she was when it came to research and reconnaissance. When it came to physical case execution, Ace had her beat only because the man had a flagrant disregard for human life, especially his own.

"He arms a lot of the West Bank terrorists," she said.

"Yeah," Ace agreed. " I've been aching to nail this bastard since I worked for the Secret Service and one of his flunkies made an attempt on the president's life, but he's slippery as hell, and we haven't been able to pin anything on him. The IFT just told us that a few days ago the German authorities picked up his favorite dominatrix, who they've had under surveillance for contraband. Now the brothel she worked in is looking for a replacement."

"And I'm the replacement?" Rhea asked.

Ace nodded.

Joe reached into her folder and pulled out the most recent photo of the unattractive bald, middle-aged man for her inspection. "The GA have a bug in Ute's cell, where she's been talking with other cellmates about Bender's odd habits. Seems he likes to talk a lot during his beatings, and one of the things he brags about is how many terrorist acts he's either funded or committed. He has a thing for women who look like Bettie Page, so we want to send you in as Latex Bettie, his newest toy. You go into a wired room, get him to confess, and then we come in with the GA and arrest him."

It sounded simple enough. Too simple in fact, and nothing was ever that simple.

"All I have to do is beat him?" Rhea asked suspiciously.

Joe nodded.

"He's a real fucked-up bastard," Ace said as he showed her another photograph of Bender at a party with a dark-haired Bettie Page–looking girl who couldn't be any more than fifteen . . . and that was stretching it.

"Okay. If this will get him off the street, then hand me the thong and stiletto heels."

"You're killing me, Rhea," Carlos said from the other side of the wall.

Rhea huffed audibly at the comment. "Go to work, Carlos."

"Joe?" he called over the wall. "I want a transfer to Ace's case."

"Why, Carlos?" Joe asked. "You aching to wear high heels and a woman's thong?"

"Hell, no."

Rhea cleared her throat to get Joe's attention. "So how do we prep this?" she asked.

Ace smiled. "Me and you are meeting with a coach to learn about bondage and dominance. You're going to be the mistress, and I get to be your slave." He looked to be enjoying this way too much.

"You really are a perv, aren't you? Admit it."

Ace laughed.

Joe rubbed his head, as if they were starting to give him a migraine. "Since the two of you are going to be extremely intimate over the next few days, why don't you leave early and have dinner together tonight so you can discuss the case and get to know each other before you actually get naked."

Now she was the one developing a migraine at the prospect of what this assignment entailed. "Thanks, Joe," she said sarcastically.

"Any time, Rhea. Hell, I'll even let the two of you put it on the company card."

She gave him a droll look. "You're just so damned generous."

Ace indicated the way to the door with a tilt of his head. "Are we taking him up on it, Rhea?"

Rhea took a deep breath as she fought an urge to run in the other direction, but this wasn't about her and Ace and his obnoxiousness. It was about stopping a cold-blooded killer who didn't care whom he hurt.

For that, she was willing to do anything. Even put up with the most arrogant male in existence.

She looked at Tee. "I do get to beat Ace, right?"

"He'll be your slave for training. I say make him cry for mercy."

Ace looked completely undaunted by the prospect. "Beat me, hurt me, call me Ralph."

"Yeah, call you Ralph. I'll be lucky if I don't ralph from the sight of you naked, all right."

"Ooo," Ace said in an appreciative tone. "Swift on the uptake, Stevenson. I'm impressed."

Before she could respond, Ace returned to his

cube and grabbed his jacket. Rhea went ahead and shut down her computer while Joe headed back to his office.

Tee opened up the folder again and sorted through the papers until she found one in particular, which she handed to Rhea. "This is the dossier for Bender. Memorize it while you learn to beat the crap out of him."

A distinct, evil glimmer in her eye said Tee would enjoy being in Rhea's position. "If you want this so badly, why aren't you doing it?"

"Because he doesn't have a thing for short Vietnamese women. Wish that he did, though."

"Me too. The thought of going in in nothing but a teddy doesn't appeal to me."

"Don't worry. We'll cover you."

And they would, too. BAD always took care of its own. "I know."

Tee stepped back as Ace rejoined them.

"You two have a nice night and get friendly." Tee handed a small business card to Rhea. "First thing in the morning, I'm having the instructor meet you at your house, where I'm sure you'll feel a little more comfortable. In the meantime, I want you two to get into character early. This is the address for an adult store here in Nashville. Head over and stock up on toys."

Ace gave that wicked grin of his as he gave Rhea a

once-over that made her stomach tight. " I'm definitely *up* for it."

Rhea was completely unamused by his humor. "You better be *down* for it."

She took the card from Tee, then looked up at Ace. "You are really enjoying this, aren't you?"

"Absolutely. So what's first?" Ace asked playfully as he took a step toward her. "Dinner or sex?"

"Excuse me?"

He took the card from her hand, letting his fingers brush hers in a warm caress, and smiled like a wolf in sheep's clothing. "C'mon, Rhea. Have you ever been to an adult store before?"

Hardly. Kinky sex had never appealed to her at all, and she'd heard enough tales from her odder friends to know she had no interest in haunting adult stores for the aids they provided. "Have you?"

He looked completely unrepentant. "I'll plead the Fifth to that."

"I knew you were a pervert."

"Hey, it's not my fault the customers took me along whenever my dad made them watch me."

Rhea shook her head as Ace stepped back, then led the way from their offices toward the elevator bank.

Ace's father, Alister Cross, was a renowned director who had won several Academy Awards. Ace's grandfather, Osker Krux, owned one of the largest movie studios in the world, and Ace's younger brother was an Academy Award–winning special FX guru. Ace himself had once been a stunt double before he'd gone on to work for the Secret Service.

"You know, I've never understood why you're a BAD agent, anyway. Why didn't you follow your family's business?"

He shrugged. "Movies are boring. Actors are fake, and I figured if I wanted to live my life on the edge, I might as well be doing it for real. Why take a chance on dying from a blank gone bad when I can dodge real bullets intended to kill me and save the world?"

In a weird way that made sense to her, and she actually managed a grudging respect for him.

"What about you?" he asked as they waited on the elevator. "What made a respectable CIA agent follow Joe to a shadow agency that has no known ally?"

"I respect the hell out of Joe and Tee and their agenda, and I didn't like all the rules of the CIA." That's what BAD was best at. No rules to bind their hands. Each agent was licensed as a civilian contractor. They were funded under the Treasury Department and hidden away as a federal insurance agency, which in an ironic way they really were. Only, "insurance" took on a whole new meaning for them.

In reality, they were an antiterrorism special task force that no one other than the president knew about. The individual agents answered to Joe, and he answered to the head man alone.

No one else knew they existed, and they all liked it that way.

The elevator doors opened.

Ace stood back to let her enter first. She didn't speak again until they were enclosed inside, and he'd pressed the button for the lobby.

"Besides," she said, continuing their conversation, "I like the different kinds of agents we have. You guys are a lot more fun than the other agencies."

He laughed at that. "Yeah, we're not your average crew."

Rhea smiled as she watched Ace from the corner of her eye. Even though he worked her last nerve into an apoplexy, she had to admit he was incredibly sexy standing there with his hands in his pockets while he looked up at the floor numbers overhead. Something about him was absolutely irresistible.

Too bad he knew it.

His presence was mammoth in the elevator, or then again, anywhere. He was one of those rare men who possessed an aura that was intense and all-encompassing.

As much as she had tried to stay angry at him for his pomposity, a tiny part of her had always been attracted to him. A really *tiny* part.

When he was silent and serious, he was actually breathtaking, which had always made her wonder just how many hearts he'd left broken.

"So tell me, Ace. When was the last time you went out with a woman on a date?"

He looked at her. "A real date, or an I'm-pretending-to-be-someone-else-and-am-prying-you-for-information date?"

"A real date."

He let out a low whistle. "Probably a year. What about you?"

She sighed wistfully at the painful truth. "Three years, at least."

"Yeah," he said with a sigh. "Our job doesn't exactly lend itself to dating, does it?"

"No. I'm never sure what to say when they ask me what I do for a living. Most guys are heavily intimidated by the thought of dating a federal agent."

He snorted at that. "I tell women I'm a federal agent, and they laugh and think I'm handing them a line. So I usually make up bullshit about being a salesman or something."

The door opened. Rhea walked across the lobby as she continued to smile while thinking of Ace in a bar with some giggling woman who had no idea just what the man was capable of. He was incredible in the field. He could speak a dozen languages fluently and held no fear of anything.

While in the Secret Service, he'd been shot three times and had brought countless criminals to trial. She was actually amazed that Joe had been able to pry Ace loose from their clutches. He'd been a celebrated hero to his group.

"You want to ride with me?" he asked.

She shook her head vigorously no. "You can ride with me. I've seen the way you drive."

"What?" he asked, his face a mask of innocence. "I have a perfect driving record."

"Only because you charmed your way out of the last three tickets you got," she reminded him.

"Those were minor speeding offenses."

"Sure they were. And I'm a three-armed alien."

Her words seemed to only amuse him. "Fine, Cha-Cha. You drive."

She frowned. "Cha-Cha? As in Shirley 'Cha-Cha' Muldowney?"

"You know racing?" he asked, as if surprised.

Rhea nodded. It wasn't something she ever really mentioned to anyone, but then the topic seldom came up. "Are you kidding? She's the first and only female Top Fuel Champion in NHRA history. When I was a kid, I wanted to be just like her when I grew up. My father was an old friend of her crew chief, Connie Kalitta, and I actually have her autograph. Oh, I love that woman!"

"Then why is it you now drive like an old lady?"

She scoffed at that. "Old lady, nothing. I can J-turn a bulletproof Lincoln limo with the best of them."

Ace chuckled at her reference to agent training, where they all learned how to handle a variety of vehicles under stressful circumstances. One in particular that all BAD agents had to pass was the ability to jump into anything available and drive it out of any possible danger, including heavy artillery fire, and grenade and bomb attacks.

He leaned over and whispered in her ear, "You still drive far too cautiously for my tastes."

Rhea shivered at the unexpected sensation of his breath on her skin and did her best not to think of other, much more intimate things that would cause him to be so near her.

And she had the distinct impression that he wasn't really talking about the way she handled a car.

Unwilling to go there, she led him to the parking deck where her red Mustang was parked.

Ace didn't say anything as they got in and headed out.

"Do we really have to go to the sex shop?" she asked, even though she knew the answer.

"That depends. You got any whips and chains at home? And if you do, I will definitely have to change my opinion about what Agent Rhea Stevenson does on her days off."

Rhea groaned. "The only chain I have is the small gold one around my neck, and as for whips . . . do half-empty containers of Cool Whip count?"

"It does for what I have in mind."

She let out a tired breath. "Does everything I say to you have to do with sex?"

"Since you're supposed to dominate me, baby, yeah."

Ace watched her stony face while she wove her way through traffic in a much more sedate way than he would have.

Rhea was a hot woman with a cool exterior that he'd wanted to melt for quite some time. But then, business and pleasure didn't mix well. He knew that better than anyone, and yet he couldn't help wondering what the petite brunette would taste like.

What those lean, supple limbs would feel like wrapped around his.

She was beautiful. Not so much in her looks, but in the way she could make him feel better by doing nothing more than smiling at him. She was extremely quiet and seldom said much even when her phone rang.

While in the CIA, she was supposed to have been one of their best field agents.

But in the last three years since BAD had come together, she hadn't taken many field assignments. Most of her work was done online, making Ace wonder what she'd be like undercover.

In more ways than one.

He'd always had a theory that silent, quiet women

were much more uninhibited in bed. But since he hadn't known that many who were quiet, he'd never been able to test his theory.

She glanced over at him. "What are you thinking?"

Ace fell back into his standard male reply. "Nothing."

"Nothing? Then why do you look like the cat eyeballing the canary?"

He gave a wicked grin at that. "Okay, so I was thinking of you dressed in black leather, wielding a whip over my naked ass."

She didn't look at him as she made a left turn. "I think I like 'nothing' better."

"Excuse me?" he asked, stunned and excited at her words. "You really *want* to whip my naked ass?"

"No!" she snapped sharply. "I said I like 'nothing' better, not I'd like nothing better. Oh, jeez, Ace, grow up!"

He continued to smile at her, which was something he didn't do around many people. There was just something about her that attracted him against all common sense or reason.

Not even he fully understood his incessant need to tease her. Other than the fact that he thoroughly enjoyed her snappy comebacks and the way those brown eyes would flash at him whenever he made her angry. It was almost as sexy as foreplay.

Almost.

"I figured you would, which is why I said 'nothing' to begin with."

She slid a censoring look to him. "I can't believe I'm going to do this."

"You? I'm the practice slave. I think if anyone should be embarrassed, it should be me."

Rhea glanced at him as she pulled into the parking lot of the large blue building covered in triple X's, which had no windows whatsoever. "Look, Ace, it's your home away from home."

———

Rhea stood in the doorway of the adult novelty store as total horror engulfed her. She'd never seen anything like this in her entire life. Cages were set up in the corners with mannequins dressed and chained in the most sexually graphic manner imaginable. Did people really use this stuff?

She paused next to a display of penis-shaped suckers and scowled at them.

"What's wrong?" Ace asked as he brushed past her into the store.

It was all she could do not to gape. "Where do I begin?"

He shrugged nonchalantly as if missing her point. "Well, we could begin with one of the swings over there."

Rhea couldn't help gaping now as he pointed to something that looked as if it had come from the planet Porno. The large, black contraption held a spread-eagled female mannequin completely subdued and gagged.

Yeah . . .

Unwilling to let him know she was bothered by it, she quickly recovered her facial expression and paused at the display of leather blindfolds and masks that were covered in spikes.

"Can I help you?"

Rhea actually jumped at the sound of the shaky female voice behind her. She turned to see an elderly woman with white hair and black-rimmed glasses staring at her. Jeez, it was someone's grandma! She even had the black SAS shoes and a white dress with little dark blue flowers that matched her dark blue sweater. She looked kind and frail.

Why on earth would she be here working as a porn store clerk?

"No. Just . . . looking."

The older woman laughed and lightly patted her arm. "This must be your first time, sweetie. Just relax and have fun. Don't let me worry you, I've tried most everything in here, so if you have any questions, please let me know."

"Um . . . yes."

Grandma smiled as she watched Ace. "Well, you're

a lucky woman to have that for a playmate. Why, he's simply delish."

Delish? Grandma knew *delish?*

Okay, I'm in an episode of Twilight Zone *with Grandma as the zookeeper. Just go with it, Rhea.*

Grandma continued to study him. "You know, he reminds me of my dearly departed Herbert. Oh, hon, he was the best. He just lived for sex. Would throw himself into it anywhere, anytime. In fact, we once got arrested for indecency on a subway while we were in New York."

This was way too much information.

"Have you two been arrested yet?"

"No," Rhea answered quickly and honestly. At least, she hadn't been. With Ace . . . well, she wouldn't make a bet on it.

"Then you two ain't doing it right." Grandma winked at her.

Grandma was without a doubt the most frightening thing in this store.

"Oh, you'll like those," Grandma said to Ace, who had paused two aisles over. "The strawberry are the best, though my Herbert liked the lemon-flavored."

Rhea looked to find Ace examining packages of edible panties. She inwardly cringed as he inspected them. "Don't even think it, Ace."

He held up one of the packages. "They have grape."

Then he looked to Grandma. "You ever try these?"

"The grape isn't the best. They have a bit of a bitter taste to them."

Ace put them back. "You said to try the strawberry?"

Rhea's gaze narrowed as he picked up a package. Fine. Two people could play that. "You also have whips, right?" she asked the woman.

She nodded.

"Do you have nice spiked ones?"

"Absolutely, sweetie."

"No!" Ace said, putting down the panties and moving back toward Rhea. "No spiked nothing."

She arched a brow. "I can't believe I've finally found something to make the big, bad Ace craven. What on earth could make you fear spikes?"

"A Goth girlfriend in high school who left lasting scars on my flesh. I don't ever want to cozy up to another porcupine as long as I live."

Rhea was amazed he'd admitted that. "You went out with a Goth chick? How unlike you."

"Not really. I always had a thing for women in leather." He looked meaningfully at a mannequin dressed in an extremely revealing leather corset that left its breasts bare except for two tiny leather pasties.

The expression on his face said he was picturing her in that getup.

Rhea decided to fight fire with fire. Determined,

she walked over to the rack of leather Speedos, which would have to be laughable on any male no matter how sexy or fabulous he was. She picked up one that was of a thong design and looked back at Ace, who grimaced.

"Trust me, baby, that would be like trying to cover two bowling balls with a slingshot."

"Oh, that's disgusting!"

He flashed her one of those taunting smiles. "But it makes you curious, doesn't it?"

She hated to admit it, but he'd won this round. "No, it just makes me pity whatever woman ends up permanently shackled to you. Do womankind a favor, Ace, get neutered."

"Oh, no, honey," Grandma said. "No one should neuter something as fine as him. Take my word for it. I've seen lots of handsome men in my day, but yours . . . He's definitely worth keeping around."

"See, she likes me."

Rhea bit her tongue to keep from saying Ace should train Grandma for Bender. But rule one was never to disclose an agent's mission to an unknown, no matter how harmless he or she appeared. Words could kill even faster and more effectively than a handgun.

Rhea took a deep breath and looked around. "So what appeals to you, Ace?"

He picked up a jar of chocolate body paint that

even came with its own paintbrush and came to stand next to her. In that moment, there was something extremely compelling about him and the soft way he was looking at her. "Rhea al dente."

An unexpected shiver went over her, and she knew it was caused by the hot, seductive curve of his mouth. Ace Krux was a man to be reckoned with.

"If you like that, we have a sample," Grandma said as she brushed past Ace.

She went to the shelf and opened a tester jar, then took a white, plastic spoon and ladled out a bit of chocolate into a small plastic cup.

When Rhea reached for it, she pulled the cup back. "Give me your finger."

Before Rhea could really comply, the old woman took Rhea's finger, dipped it in the chocolate, and held it up for Ace to sample. He didn't hesitate to open his mouth and capture her.

Rhea's stomach fluttered as his warm, sensuous tongue encircled the pad of her fingertip while he held her hand in his to keep it in his mouth. He nipped her flesh ever so gently with his teeth while he stared at her with a hot, needful look. His masculine scent of aftershave and shampoo filled her head, making her heart pound.

Never in her life had she been so unexpectedly turned on by any man. This was intrusive and rude and . . . and she was dying to know what his lips would taste like.

Get a grip!

Rhea pulled her finger out. "I hope you've had a rabies shot lately."

He laughed at that, then dipped his finger into the cup. "Your turn."

"That is so not sanitary."

"Chicken?"

Rhea couldn't believe he was relying on the childhood tactic. Even worse, she couldn't believe it was working. She wasn't about to let Mr. Perfect Agent get away with it.

It was time Mr. Krux learned a lesson.

Taking his hand into hers, she opened his palm and blew her breath across it. She gave him her best "do me, hotshot" stare before she licked the palm of his hand and took the entire length of his finger into her mouth.

Ace ground his teeth to keep from cursing in blissful agony the instant she started tonguing his finger. That woman had a tongue that poets should write about.

At the very least it deserved a major letter to *Penthouse Forum*.

Every hormone in his body fired as his cock hardened to the point of pain. And with every tiny, erotic stroke of her tongue, he hardened even more.

She growled low in her throat before she took a gentle bite of his skin, then pulled back. "Hershey's is better."

Ace was completely dumbstruck. Since all of his blood had drained to the center of his body, there wasn't much left to understand her words. He only knew she'd stepped away from him, and that was the last thing he wanted.

In fact, the only thing he wanted right then was to take her into his arms and taste that sweet, sassy mouth. To pin her to the wall behind her and sate the painful ache in his groin that wanted nothing more than to be naked and sweaty with her.

Rhea was a lot more turned on by what she'd done than she wanted to admit. The truth was, Ace had tasted wonderful. And the look on his face as she tasted him was branded into her consciousness. Her breasts were still swollen and heavy with desire.

How could she be attracted to him? Yeah, he looked great, but he was a pest.

Trying to distract herself, she strolled down an aisle with the most incredibly odd vibrators she'd ever seen. Some of them looked like penises, and some of them just looked weird. One in particular had two penises pointing away from each other.

Tilting her head to study it, Rhea paused and frowned.

Ace gave a low, amused laugh as he came up behind her. He was so close, she could actually feel the
heat from his body. Feel the intensity of his presence.
He might as well be touching her, for all the damage
he was doing to her willpower.

"You really haven't ever been in one of these
stores before, have you?" he asked her.

She shook her head. "I had no idea that these"—
she gestured toward the myriad of battery-operated
boyfriends—"came in so many shapes, colors, or tex-
tures. Good grief. Do people really use these?"

As his body brushed against her, she could feel his
taut erection. He'd been right. He was a large man,
and the thought of that electrified her as he reached
for one of the illicit packages. "Yeah, they do—at
least, I know they use them in porn flicks."

She gave him an arch, censoring look.

He actually looked offended. "What? My cousin
Vito produces porn films for a small, independent
studio. Much to the horror of my grandparents, he
talks about it at every Christmas party."

Relieved more than she wanted to admit, she
shook her head. "You have the strangest family."

"And you've spent as much time in Beverly Hills
as you've spent in adult stores if you believe that.
Trust me, where I grew up, my family were the most
normal ones on the block."

"And now I know why I've never made it a habit

to frequent either place." Rhea folded her arms over her chest. "So what exactly will I need for this . . . excursion?"

Ace returned the "item" in his hand to the shelf. "I vote we ease our way into this. For one thing, no gags, since gagging Bender would defeat the purpose of getting him to talk."

"That makes sense."

Ace headed over two aisles to where they had a display of restraints. "Something simple. Handcuffs."

Rhea studied the variety of manacles they had. An unbidden image of Ace spread out naked on her bed flashed through her mind, and in spite of what she would ever admit, she had to say it was an incredible thought.

Oh, jeez, don't make him right! He would be flattered to no end to know that you really are picturing him naked.

"Some of this stuff looks like it ought to be illegal," she said, trying to distract herself again.

Ace shrugged. "Personally, I'm not into the rough stuff, but there are all kinds out there."

"I'm just glad I'm not one of them and that I'm licensed to carry a concealed weapon should I ever have the misfortune of meeting one in a dark alley."

"Yeah." Ace grabbed two pairs of velvet-lined cuffs. He held them like a man who truly had no interest in using them.

"You really aren't into it, are you?" she asked in

surprise. As gung-ho and adventurous as he was in everything else, she would have thought he was a regular porn-meister.

"No. I like my sex the good old-fashioned way. Down and dirty."

She rolled her eyes at him. "You know, there for a minute, I was starting to like you."

"Only a minute?"

"You're right. It was more like ten seconds."

"Okay, for that, I vote for this." He picked up a cat-o'-nine-tails that was made of thick leather straps.

"Fine." She left him and went to the bustier rack, where she quickly found a frilly red number made out of satin and feathers. "What do you think of this?"

He grinned. "I like it."

"Good. What size are you?"

"Pardon?"

Grandma laughed. "I have his size in back."

"No!" Ace snapped. "I only have one rule in life: no drag."

"Why not?" Rhea teased. "You allergic to satin?"

"No, but this"—he picked up the thong part of it—"would give me a wedgie from hell. No, thank you."

She tsked at him, then put it back.

Ace stopped as they passed a tall, thin silver canister that held several long feathers. His look turned speculative, then wicked. "Tickle your ass with a feather?"

"Excuse me?"

He cleared his throat. "I said, particularly nice weather?"

Rhea screwed her face up. "Oh, please, don't tell me you're a fan of *Up the Academy?*"

Ace was stunned that Rhea knew his vague reference to the offbeat early-eighties film. "So how many times have *you* watched it?"

"More than I cared to. It was my older brother's favorite movie in high school, and I curse the day they ever turned it into a videotape."

Ace laughed, amazed at just how much he enjoyed their verbal sparring and her unique views of the world. "Hey, I defend your brother's taste in movies."

"You would." But the dancing light in her eyes said that she wasn't as offended as she pretended.

Better still, she picked up one of the feathers and added it to the cuffs.

"You gonna let me?" he asked hopefully.

"Oh, no, you're the slave, remember? You have to do what I say."

"Yeah, but don't slaves get rewards?"

"No." She sashayed past him.

Maybe slaves didn't get rewarded, but before they finished this detail, Ace fully intended to. He'd been too hot for this women far too long to not at least get a small taste of that wisecracking mouth.

As for the rest of her . . .

Ace wasn't the kind of man to let something he wanted get away from him, and he wasn't about to let Rhea tie him down without both of them getting a taste of something decadent.

CHAPTER TWO

Rhea kept glancing up from under her eyelashes while she ate. Ace seemed incredibly focused on her.

Too focused. She was beginning to feel like a piece of prey under the hungry stare of a powerful lion. Little did he know that this bunny, much like the one in *Monty Python and the Holy Grail,* had sharp, vicious teeth.

She sipped her wine. "If you're trying to make me nervous, Ace, you can hang it up. I don't scare easily."

He arched a brow at her comment as he continued to watch her. "I'm not trying to make you nervous, Rhea, I'm only trying to figure you out. You're normally so cool at work that I find it amazing how much you're not when you're out of the Bat Tower." The Bat Tower was the pet name of the BellSouth building in downtown Nashville where the BAD offices were hidden under the guise of a BellSouth department door in a secured area of the building that no one but their people could access.

Rhea set her glass aside and answered snidely, " It's all the chemicals in the air there. They solidify my blood cells until I'm nothing but a statue."

His warm laughter washed over her. Ace was a lot easier to talk to than she would have thought. Her first impression of him when they'd met three years ago had been less than flattering.

Okay, she'd hated him.

He'd shown up to work in a pair of ragged jeans with a T-shirt and a flippant attitude that had set off her ire immediately. She took her job seriously, while Ace took few things seriously—or at least it had seemed like that in the beginning.

It wasn't until she'd seen him in action that she'd developed some respect for his abilities and learned that he really did take his job with the same grave responsibility as the rest of them.

Since he came from a Hollywood family, he was a consummate actor. But that too left her wondering what the real Ace Krux was like. How much of even this charming man eating with her was real, and how much of it was an act?

He paused while cutting his steak and looked at her. "Why do I have the sudden feeling that I'm some lab experiment gone wrong, and you're the scientist trying to figure out why?"

"You're perceptive. Not about being an experiment. I was just wondering how a guy like you ends up working for the government."

He wiped his mouth before taking a drink of his beer. "In a nutshell, Joe."

That wasn't what she was expecting to hear. "Joe?"

"Yeah. We went to college together out in California. I didn't know what I wanted to do with my life, other than anything that didn't have Hollywood in it. I didn't even know what to major in. When I started my second year, Joe was my roommate, and even though he was only nineteen, he knew exactly what he wanted. While the rest of us went out drinking and partying all the time, he stayed in the room studying."

"That sounds like Joe to me."

"Yeah. One night, I actually got him totally bombed out of his mind and found out a lot about him. He wasn't there for an education, he was there because he wanted to make a difference. He wanted his life to matter to people, and he could care less if he made any money so long as he could help the people who needed it. He was the most driven human being I'd ever met, and it was the first time in my life that I ever really respected anyone."

Rhea agreed. Joe was a hard man not to respect. "I still can't understand why a guy like you wanted to save the world. You just don't strike me as an altruist."

He snorted at that. "You want to know the real truth of why I'm here?"

She nodded.

"While we were roommates, I found out that Joe had never been to D.C. before and that one of the things he wanted most was to see the Smithsonian before he died. It was the same year that they were doing the *Star Trek* exhibit, which I thought would be cool to see since one of the costumes they had on display was one my mother had worn when she played some alien princess out to seduce Kirk."

In spite of herself, Rhea was intrigued that she had probably seen that episode a dozen times in her life without ever guessing that one of the women after Kirk would have a son who would one day end up working with her. "Your mother was in a *Star Trek* episode?"

"Oh, yeah. She made tons of appearances in shows and movies before she married my dad and started having us."

Rhea hated to admit it, but she was fascinated by Ace's past. He'd had quite a childhood out in Hollywood. "Given that, I can see why you wanted to go, but it was really nice of you to take Joe along."

"Yeah, well, like I said, I admired him, and it wouldn't have been half as much fun alone. So the two of us were there in the Smith along with several hundred other people, including families with small children and babies in strollers, when this voice came over the intercom telling us that there was a bomb threat and that the entire building had to be evacuated immediately."

Rhea saw red at that. It was just that kind of needless panic and fear that she hated.

"I don't think I've ever been more scared in my life," Ace confessed.

"*You* were scared, and you admit it?"

He shrugged. "Hard to believe, but, yeah, as we filed down the halls and then single-file down some metal back stairs, I really did expect a bomb to go off and kill us all. I kept looking around at all the faces of the people who had innocently gone there that day for no other reason than to see a little bit of our history, and I thought, what kind of dick would blow up the Smith? I mean, I knew such things happened, but it was the first time it was personal.

"And as we stood out in the Mall, waiting for the bomb squad to search the building, I got really angry as I looked around at all the different buildings that make up the Smith and thought about the irreplaceable items each one held. All the pieces of history that could have been lost to future generations . . . the *Spirit of St. Louis,* the Hope diamond, the original "Star-Spangled Banner," hell, even my mother's costume and the Lone Ranger's mask. But worse than that were all the children who were around me who would have been history themselves. It wasn't right, and for the first time, I really understood what motivated Joe to right the wrongs of the world. So I decided I wanted to do something with my life too. After graduation, we packed our things, moved to D.C., and started applying for jobs. Within six months, he ended up in the CIA while I joined the SS."

She was impressed at the timetable and their impetus, especially for Ace. "That must have been scary for you guys to head out across the country on your own."

He shrugged. "Not really. When you have the kind of money and connections my family does, there's not a lot of risk in much of anything. My dad bought me a Georgetown brownstone for graduation, so it was just a matter of finding our places in the world."

"Wow," she said sarcastically, remembering how many times in her childhood they had barely made ends meet. "It must be nice to chomp the silver spoon and know that no matter what you do, you have a safety net."

He seemed to ignore her sarcasm. "Sometimes, but if you're not careful, that safety net can quickly turn into a noose to hang you."

His perception stunned her. Ace had real depth . . . that really was the last thing she'd expected from him, and it made him all the more alluring to her. "How do you mean?"

"I've seen a lot of my friends and family end up on drugs and totally screwed up emotionally because they have no concept of how hard life is for those who lack. To them a crisis is that the detail place didn't deliver the Ferrari in time for the party and now they have to take the Bentley instead. God forbid."

She watched the way the candlelight played in his dark blond hair while he ate some of his steak. The light danced on the sharp angles of his cheeks and jaw, making her wonder what it would feel like to trace that strong jawline with her finger. She shivered with the thought of it. It had really been far too long since she'd been with a man. Even longer since she'd last felt this insane need to reach out and touch one.

Why she would feel that with Ace, she couldn't imagine. Though to be honest, he was starting to grow on her now that he was talking to her and not sniping at her.

"How is it you escaped that fate?" she asked, more interested in the answer than she should have been.

"Again, I have to say Joe. He was the first poor person I'd ever really gotten to know. Here I was stressing out over whether I should go to Cancún or Rio for spring break while he was sneaking fruit into his backpack so that he'd have something to eat over the weekend rather than starve. I shudder to think what I might have become had I not lucked out when they were handing out roommate assignments."

Rhea thought about that in silence while Ace continued to eat. He really was beginning to intrigue her with his stories.

And that terrified her.

Even so, she wanted to know more about him. "So how did you end up with the name Thaddeus?" she asked, changing the subject. "That just doesn't seem to fit you at all."

He groaned as if the name pained him greatly. "Before my dad was a director, he was a stunt double. My mother thought it would be funny to name all of us after whatever character he was playing when we were conceived."

"Really? How fun." But for her life, she couldn't think of a single movie from the time of their birth with a character by that name. "So who was Thaddeus?"

He took another drink of beer. "It's an old TV western from 1971. *Alias Smith and Jones.* Ben Murphy played Jed 'Kid' Curry, aka Thaddeus Jones, hence my name. I suppose it could be worse. Had Dad been dark-haired, I'd have been named Hannibal after the Pete Deul character."

She cringed for him. "Lucky you, indeed. So where did you get the nickname Ace?"

"John Wayne."

She rolled her eyes. "I was being serious."

"I *am* serious. He was a longtime friend of my

grandfather's. One night, about a year before he died, he was at my grandfather's house playing cowboy with me. I wanted a cool outlaw name, so the Duke dubbed me Ace Hijinx, Kid Outlaw."

A rush of warmth went through her. How sweet.

But Ace's face turned deeply sad. "I was only eight when he died, and when my mother came in to tell me he was gone, I told her I would never use another name again. The Duke had named me Ace, and Ace I would be."

Her heart ached for him and the pain she saw on his face. "You loved him."

"Yeah. He was like another grandfather to me." Ace returned to his meal.

Rhea sat quietly as she thought over all of the stories and things he'd told her tonight. "You must have had a fascinating life, knowing all those celebrities."

He took it with an uncharacteristic dose of humility. "Yes and no. At the end of the day, fame is fleeting, and it really is true, we all get dressed the same way every day. The only difference between someone who works at McDonald's and a Hollywood diva is the size of the paycheck and ego. I've seen fame destroy far more lives than it's built."

Yes, there was a lot more to Ace than she would have given credit for.

He met her gaze, and the intensity of those blue

eyes made her shivery. "I have a lot more respect for someone like Joe, who had every mark against him and yet he fought his way out of poverty, turned his life around, and made something out of himself, than I do for all the rich kids who take their trust funds and party in the Caymans. Trust me, I'd much rather hang out with the Joes of the world."

He took another bite of his steak. "So what about you? Where did you grow up?"

Rhea sighed wistfully as she remembered her small hometown. "Starkville, Mississippi. The biggest celebrity I ever met growing up was the man in Tupelo who sold Elvis his first guitar."

Ace smiled at that, as if Mr. Hollywood really was impressed.

"I hope you gave that man a big thank-you."

She didn't respond.

"So what about your parents?" he asked. "You never really talk about them."

Rhea's heart wrenched as she thought about her mother and father. "No, I don't." Uncomfortable with the turn in conversation, she cleared her throat. "So tell me about Bender."

"Let's go back to the parent thing. I've spilled my guts to you, the least you could do is tell me something about your parents." Ace watched as her brown eyes actually teared up. "Rhea?"

"There's nothing to tell."

He didn't need his instincts to tell him she was hiding something. It was painfully obvious.

Before he could ask her anything else, she excused herself and headed for the restroom. Ace got up to follow her.

"What are you doing?" she asked as he pulled her to a stop in the lobby. " You're not planning on following me into the ladies' room, are you?"

"No. I just want to know why the thought of your parents upsets you so much. Most people don't get teary-eyed when they think of them."

Rhea covered her lips with her hand as she struggled with the pain that still ached raw and deep inside her soul. She always got emotional when she thought of her parents. How could she not?

It was something she struggled with every day, and not even the passage of time could take away the sting of it. That was the bad thing about senseless violence. It left a haunting mark on the lives it scarred.

She didn't want to talk about it, and yet she found herself confiding in him for some reason she couldn't even begin to understand. "Do you remember Pan Am Flight 103?"

"The Lockerbie, Scotland, bombing?"

"Yeah," she said, forcing herself not to get emotional. But it was hard. "My parents were on that flight, coming home for Christmas from a business trip. My grandmother, brother, sister, and I were putting up the

Christmas tree, listening to the news and talking about what we'd do when they got home, when we heard about it."

She choked as she saw that day again clearly in her mind. "My grandmother had been about to put the glass angel on top of the tree when they announced it. It was a special edition Lenox ornament that she had guarded all my life. She dropped it to the floor, where it shattered like our hearts. My sister started screaming, and I just stood there in complete shock as I stared at the broken glass on the floor, unable to move or breathe. My grandmother was so upset by the news that she ended up having a stroke later that night."

Ace could see the agony plainly on Rhea's face, and it made his own chest tight.

The look she gave him tore through him. "Do you know what the human soul sounds like when it screams in utter agony? It echoes through your body until you're sure it will shatter your eardrums. Only no one else can hear it. Only you do. One minute, I was just a kid, dreaming about picking out a prom dress with my mother, having my dad teach me to drive that summer, and in the next everything about my life was irrevocably changed.

"I no longer had parents to be there when I graduated, to nag me to get married before I turned thirty. No Mom for the mother-daughter tea at my sorority or Dad to help me lug boxes into my dorm room. And all because of a senseless act of violence. It is harsh and it hurts, and no child should ever feel like I did in that moment. No one should ever lose a loved one like that. No one."

He didn't know how she held herself so composed. Nothing but absolute anguish was in her eyes.

"Two hundred and fifty-nine families were shattered that day, and I want to make sure that no one will *ever* feel the pain that went through me when I realized my mom and dad weren't coming home ever again. So that, Mr. Krux, is why when you say the word *terrorist,* I get pissed."

"And you have every right to. I'm sorry, Rhea. I really am."

She nodded. "I know. Now if you'll excuse me, I really need to go to the bathroom for a minute."

Ace stood back and watched as she headed toward the door. She walked slowly and methodically, but he had a good idea she was going in there so that she could fall apart.

Damn. He shouldn't have pushed. But how could he have guessed that? His stupid story at the Smith was paltry compared to hers. And people like her were why his job meant so much to him. It was what kept him going on no sleep, and why he never wanted to get serious with a woman.

His job was stressful enough; the last thing he

needed was a woman who wanted time from him that he couldn't give her.

Sighing, he went back to the table to wait for Rhea to return.

When she came back a few minutes later, he could tell she'd been crying. Her features were pinched, her eyes only a little red, but it was enough to let him know what she'd done in the bathroom.

"You are without a doubt the strongest woman I have ever met," he said, toasting her with his beer. "I really admire you, Rhea."

Rhea frowned at him as she reached for her wine and clinked it lightly against his beer bottle. "Now I'm really suspicious of you, Ace. What do you have up that sleeve of yours?"

"Nothing but bare flesh, which you will see all for yourself tomorrow morning." He winked at her, which caused her to get that familiar angry spark in her brown eyes.

Now that was much better than her sadness. If he kept her angry, she wouldn't be able to focus on anything else.

"You know, I've always read about incorrigible men, but you really are, aren't you?"

He laughed at that. "Beat me with all your whips and quips, baby."

She gave him a half-teasing, half-sinister smile. "I plan to."

"That's all right. It'll be worth it so long as you kiss all my boo-boos afterward."

"Oh, you are a quick one, Mr. Krux."

"But the real question is, am I charming you out of your pants?" He wagged his eyebrows at her.

"You're working on it, aren't you?"

"I'm trying to."

She gave him a heated once-over. "You might stand more of a chance if I didn't know how many other women you've already charmed out of *their* pants and then danced right out of their lives."

He held his hands up in mock surrender. "Those are all lies. I was framed."

"Yeah, right."

And yet she was beguiled by him and that infectious debonair attitude of his. He really was starting to charm her out of her pants, and that scared her more than the thought of dominatrix training.

She really did want him. How could she not? He had been strangely understanding about her parents, and now she realized he was trying to distract her to get her mind off it.

Ace really did have a heart and a soul underneath that trying facade.

"So let's do some business," she said as she returned to her grilled chicken. "Tell me all about Bender."

"He's a total freak. Just your kind of guy."

She laughed. "Sounds more like your type. Maybe I should have gotten you that bustier after all."

"Stop with the bustier jokes." He shuddered. "Every time you talk about it, I get this image in my head that has scarred me for life."

"What image?"

"My aunt was one of the women who did the makeup for *Tootsie*. To get ready for it, she practiced on my dad. I came home from school to find him decked out in the complete getup: sequins, wig, earrings, makeup, you name it. Forget horror, that was the scariest thing I've ever seen. My dad made one ugly woman."

Rhea laughed again. "Are you serious?"

"Oh, yeah. You couldn't pay me enough to ever get me near female clothes . . . unless I'm taking them off a female body."

"Ace!" she growled. "Focus on something other than your hormones."

"I would try to focus on your hormones, but you get pissed every time I do."

"We are here to work."

"Yeah, but for once my work entails me getting you naked."

"I am not getting naked for you."

"Nearly naked then."

"Ace . . ."

"Okay, okay, I'll stop and brief you for real."

And for once he held to his word. They finished up dinner while he went over every nuance of the case and every sick fetish he had uncovered about Bender.

The more Rhea learned, the more she became aware of just how important it was to get this man out of commission.

After Ace had paid their check, they walked out to the parking lot and got back into her car, where he was just a little too close to her. It was hard to ignore a man whose presence dominated the small area. The warm scent of his skin filled her head, and it was all she could do to focus on traffic and not those teasing lips that she suddenly wanted to taste.

"So how do I find my way to your bed, anyway?" Ace asked as she backed out of the space.

Rhea gave him a hooded stare. "You don't have enough charm, wit, or money to ever get into my bed."

His face was a mask of wickedness. "Wait a sec. I'm supposed to be at your place tomorrow so you can tie me to your bed, remember? I can't do that if I don't know where you live."

Oh, yeah. "Well, you are a superspy. You could sic Carlos on me and find out."

He laughed. "Yeah, but Tee has the payroll. She'd be faster."

"True, but lucky for you, I'll make it even easier than that. I live in Franklin, down on Church Street."

"The historic area?"

She nodded. "It's a small 1930s cottage, painted creamy yellow with a burgundy door and black iron fence. You can't miss it."

"Creamy yellow? That's different from regular yellow how?"

"It's lighter, paler."

She could see from the corner of her eye that he had that man face that said, "Women and their weird colors."

They were quiet as she drove him back to the lot where he had his car parked. She pulled up beside his Viper. "See you tomorrow."

The intensity of those eyes on her body made her hot. Feverish. "Yes, you will. *All* of me." He glanced to the bag she'd tossed in the back seat. "Don't forget to lay out our toys."

"I shudder at the thought." But the real problem was that after tonight she didn't truly shudder in revulsion. She shivered in anticipation.

A foreign part of her was actually looking forward to it.

"You shudder, huh?" Ace leaned over, and before she realized what he was doing, he kissed her fiercely.

Her entire body sizzled at the taste of those firm lips against hers. She opened her mouth to taste him fully and let the scent of warm, spicy cologne and Ace fill her head.

This man really knew how to give a kiss. Forget his gun, his mouth should have been registered as a lethal weapon. His tongue swept against hers in a promising, hungry fashion that left her completely breathless before he pulled back to give her a hot, lustful look. Her entire body was on fire, and it was all she could do not to pull him back to her and taste him again.

"That was daring of you," she said, her voice remarkably calm given the havoc of her body. "Especially since you know I'm packing heat."

He laughed. "True, but I thought I should at least kiss you before you see me naked." He opened the car door. "Night, Rhea."

"Night, Ace."

He got out and slammed the door shut, then got into his Viper.

Rhea watched as he buckled himself in. He paused to give her a devilish grin before he squealed out of the parking space and headed for the entrance.

Her body still on fire from the passion of that kiss, she followed him out of the lot at a much more subdued pace, even though a part of her was racing even more than he was.

"It's just a kiss."

But it had been a great one.

And tomorrow she really would see him naked . . .

Ace pulled his black Viper into Rhea's driveway. He still couldn't believe he was going to do this. He should actually thank Bender for being such a sick bastard, since Bender was the one finally giving him a way to get close to Rhea.

God help him, but he'd been in love with her since the first time he'd seen her. And she had shined him on without a second glance.

Unused to having to beg or fight for a woman's attention, Ace had walked away, wishing he knew of something to make her attracted to him. She'd always been so reserved toward him, if not downright nasty. No matter what he tried, it always seemed to be the wrong thing with her.

Until last night.

His lips still sizzled from her kiss. His body burned from the thought of having her tie him up . . .

You're a sick man yourself, Ace.

No, he was a desperate one. There had always been something about Rhea that set his entire body on fire. It was why he'd bribed Hunter to change cubes with him in the office. Hunter had pretended that being under the air vent was messing with his allergies. So Ace had "volunteered" to take his desk.

It had been the best and worst $3,000 he'd ever

spent. The best because it forced Rhea to acknowledge him when he was in the office. The worst because being so close to her was complete torture.

Ace pulled off his sunglasses and set them in the
passenger seat.

It was the moment of truth.

Getting out, he slammed the door shut and sauntered up the driveway when what he really wanted
to do was sprint. But the last thing he wanted was for
Rhea to know just how badly he wanted her.

No, coolness would win this. Or if not, it would at
least save his dignity.

Rhea saw Ace leave his car and saunter with that
masculine, predatory lope toward her front door. He
looked totally edible as he came closer to her lair.

Yes, he was sexy. Yes, he was hot, but she wasn't
about to play into that overinflated ego of his. She
had to be cool and dispassionate about wanting to
take a bite out of that man. She should never have
spent time with him last night. Somehow, he'd actually become human to her and not a total scumbag. A
tiny part of her was even starting not only to like
him, but respect him as well.

He knocked on her door.

Rhea clenched and unclenched her fists, then

shook them in an effort to calm down. She had to get a grip on herself. Quick.

Taking a deep breath, she opened the door to find Ace standing there with one hip cocked and a seductive smile on his face.

"Morning, sunshine," he said.

"Morning." Rhea stepped back to let him enter.

He gave her that wicked, charming smile. "Now this is where in Hollywood they would cue 'Bad to the Bone' to play as I entered your house."

Rhea rolled her eyes. "Oh, please! Ace, you're so bad."

"To the bone, baby," he sang.

"Stop that!"

He didn't—instead, he broke into a perfect rendition of George Thorogood. The man really did have a great voice.

Rhea closed her door. "All right, I get it."

He didn't stop; worse, he literally pinned her to the door and held her trapped between the wood and his long, lush body. He lowered his tone so that he could sing in her ear without causing her pain. His voice was low and sultry, and it reverberated though her.

The pain came not from his body pressing against hers or her voice ringing in her ears, it came from the deep-seated ache at the core of her body that throbbed with a piercing need for him.

"I want to be yours, pretty baby, yours and yours alone."

That sounded too good to be true, and she knew that things that seemed to be too good, always were.

"Should I get my saxophone?" she asked, trying to get her thoughts on something other than him being naked in her arms.

That succeeded in breaking his song. "You got one?"

"Yeah, I do."

"Cool. Can you play?"

He still hadn't moved back, and she couldn't move away without brushing even more of her body up against his.

If she did that, she'd be lost, as badly as she wanted him. There was no way she could feel all that hard, lean muscle and not kiss him again.

Or do something she might later regret.

She cleared her throat before she answered his question. "Not well, but I can hammer out a few notes now and again that don't make the neighborhood dogs bark."

He laughed as he lifted one hand to play with a stray black curl of her hair. She had to force herself not to lean her head forward the few inches it would take to bury her nose in the hollow of his throat and just inhale his spiced, manly scent.

Or better yet, lick the tawny skin that covered the hot tendon in his neck. . . .

"In that case, I need to introduce you to my little brother, Aramis. He used to torture his guitar to the point I sold it for a dollar to our gardener."

"You did not!"

"Yeah, I did. Still have my father's handprint on my butt to prove it. Want to see?"

Rhea snorted at him, even though the offer was extremely tempting. "Why does everything have to get back to me seeing you naked?"

He smiled at her. "Ulterior motives."

The worst part was that Rhea really did want to see what he kept hidden under those clothes. She'd spent many hours last night after their kiss wondering how much of his ego was boasting and how much was true.

He dipped his head down to nuzzle her cheek.

For a full second, she couldn't move as she savored the feel of him there. But somewhere in the back of her mind, warning bells went off.

"Would you like some coffee or juice?" she asked, pushing him away before she headed toward her kitchen. Yowza, but he had a hard body. Just the brief contact of her hand on his chest was enough to let her know he was built of solid muscle.

Disappointment flashed across his face, only to be quickly replaced by a grim determination. "Juice would be great." He followed after her and took a seat at her breakfast counter while she went to her fridge.

She could feel his gaze on her body. Turning her head, she saw confirmation. He was staring at her butt as if he were caressing her in his mind. Her entire body burned.

Rhea almost dropped the juice. Tightening her grip, she pretended to ignore him and went to get a glass. "So your brother is named Aramis, huh? Your dad must have been in *The Three Musketeers*."

"Yes, and Aramis is grateful every day of his life that Dad didn't double for Christopher Lee."

"Why?"

"He played Rochefort."

She laughed as she poured the juice. "Yeah, I can see where that might be bad. But had your father doubled for Michael York, Aramis would be D'Artagnan. That could have been cool." She handed him his juice.

"Maybe," Ace said before he took a sip. "But no one would ever be able to spell it."

The doorbell rang.

Grateful for the interruption, Rhea put the juice back in the fridge. "That must be our instructor."

She headed back to the door, unsure of what to expect. The woman's name was Beullah Mueller, and for some reason she pictured an extremely rigid German woman who looked like the gym teacher from the movie *Porky's,* complete with hair rolled into sausages around her head.

The reality was worse.

"Hi," the woman said, not in a German-accented voice but in a normal American one.

"Beullah?" Rhea asked, unsure if this was the right woman.

Surely not.

Around the age of forty-five, the woman in front of her was of average height, slender, and was dressed in pink designer sweats. She had a large navy blue gym bag slung over her shoulder. Something about her reminded Rhea of Meredith Baxter-Birney from *Family Ties.*

She looked wholesome and sweet.

Beullah smiled warmly. "I know. I look like someone's middle-aged mother and not a dominatrix instructor. But in my day . . . I have to tell you, I have whipped many a man's ass and enjoyed it thoroughly."

There was something extremely incongruous about that coming out of the mouth of a woman who looked as if she ought to be in a peanut butter commercial.

"Okay," Rhea said, stepping back to let the woman in. "I don't suppose I want to ask how it is Tee knew to call you, do I?"

"We go to the same spa and health club. I have to

tell you that Tee is something else. She bends like a pretzel."

"Oh, jeez, now there's an image I want burned out of my memory. I'll never be able to look Tee in the eye again," Ace said as he joined them.

Beullah smiled. "You must be Ace. Tee told me to give you an extra hard time."

"I'm sure she did, just as I'm sure you will."

Rhea had to admit she didn't like the way Beullah was looking at Ace, like a starving woman staring at a steak.

Beullah waltzed into the living room and placed her bag on the coffee table. "Tee said she liked the two of you a lot and that you were ready to get more adventurous in your relationship, so here I am."

"Pardon?" Rhea asked.

Beullah waved her hand. "Oh, don't be bashful. I've worked with lots of couples who have gotten bored with the missionary position and are looking for new ways to spice up their sex. I had this couple once who started out normal as pie, and the next thing I knew, they had more body piercings than Marilyn Manson and Christina Aguilera combined. He really liked feeling the cat-o'-nine-tails whip across his pe—"

"TMI," Ace said quickly, cutting her off. "Way too much information for me."

Rhea agreed completely, but couldn't resist teasing

him. "I don't know, Ace. That sounds like fun. Sure you don't want to give it a try?"

"Nothing painful comes near the area," he said, indicating his entire groin. "Nothing."

"Now, now," Beullah said as she unzipped her bag. "You two have to learn to trust each other. That's rule number one about being a couple. If you're to have a healthy relationship, you have to learn to express your needs and fears to each other without dread or inhibition."

So that was the story Tee was using for this. Rhea and Ace were supposed to be a couple wanting to add spice to their sex life. Nice lie. Tee could have filled them in on it first.

"Well," Rhea said wistfully, "you know how it goes. Even the hottest piece of cheese eventually goes bad. I never thought I'd get bored with Ace, but look at him . . . My cheddar turned into Gouda on me."

"Hey, I resent that." Ace's tone was offended. "I'm not the prude here. You're the one who walks around in shirts buttoned all the way up to your nose and pants or long skirts. You know it wouldn't hurt you to wear a miniskirt and low-cut blouse once in a while."

Rhea arched her brow at that. Ace had been paying attention to her clothes. Who knew?

"Now, now," Beullah said in a voice that held the

full authority of a woman used to being in charge." There's no need to blame each other. Two days with me, and you two will know all there is to know about how to make each other beg for your attention."

She opened her bag wider and searched through plastic bags. "You," she said to Ace. "Take off your clothes."

He went completely stiff. "Bullshit."

Beullah pulled out a whip. "Take off your clothes, slave. Now."

"No."

She snapped the whip at Ace, who caught it without flinching when it wrapped itself around his forearm. "Whips don't do it for me, baby. I'm not a lion, and you're not going to tame me like one." He jerked the whip out of her hands.

Beullah looked at him with a newfound respect. She glanced over to Rhea. "You certainly have your hands full, huh?"

"You've no idea."

Beullah retrieved her whip.

"C'mon, Ace," Rhea said. "Time to play."

He growled low in his throat before he started unbuttoning his shirt.

Beullah smiled approvingly. "That's it, Rhea. You have to take charge of your slave and show him who's boss." Beullah unzipped her sweatshirt top.

Rhea's eyes bulged as she realized that beneath that average outfit, Beullah wore a leather corset with studded metal cups that covered her breasts.

Beullah acted as if there were nothing unusual about her state of dress. "First thing you have to do, Rhea, is get used to your role as mistress. You need to be completely comfortable in this."

Beullah pulled her pants off. She wore a pair of black fishnets that were held up by blood-red ribbons. The back of the corset was a thong that left more of Beullah exposed than Rhea had ever wanted to see.

Rhea could feel herself gaping. "I could *never* feel comfortable in *that*."

"Sure you could," Beullah and Ace said at once.

"No, really," Rhea insisted. "How about a T-shirt and . . ." Her voice trailed off as Beullah pulled out three small plastic baggies.

"This should fit. Tee gave me your size and told me to pick out something extra rough."

Beullah opened one bag and handed Rhea two pieces of something she would have sworn was an arm sling . . . for a very small child.

"Don't be bashful," Beullah said. " I'm sure Ace has seen you naked enough not to care, and you haven't got anything I don't." She looked at her speculatively. "At least I hope you don't, and even if you do, I'm sure I've seen it on someone else."

Yeah . . . Little did Beullah know Ace had never seen her undressed in either of their lives. But then Bender would have the same problem. She was going to have to wear this for not only a complete stranger, but a demented one at that.

Okay, Rhea, you can do this.

No, I can't.

Yes, you can. Do it.

Determined to go through with this, she started for her bedroom. At times she really, truly hated her job, and now she knew why she'd given up fieldwork to begin with.

It sucked.

"And don't forget this." Beullah handed her another red-tinted plastic bag and a smaller bag.

Rhea was too scared to even look at what it contained. Ignoring Ace, who watched her with a hot, intense stare, she crept to her room down the hallway, where she would hopefully find her courage lurking someplace.

By the time she was dressed in the tiny, shiny PVC halter top and thong bottom, Rhea had almost convinced herself that this wasn't so bad. After all, women wore less than this on beaches in Rio.

Not that much less, but somewhat less.

Of course it would help if the bottom wasn't crawling into places the good Lord never meant neoprene to touch. Rhea opened the bags to find a pair of fishnet stockings and six-inch-spike-heeled PVC boots. Oh, yeah, these looked lethal.

And poor Ace thought his padded handcuffs would be used.

—

"How long have you two been dating?" Beullah asked while Ace waited without his shirt on for Rhea to return.

He kept his arms folded over his chest, wondering what Rhea would look like when she came back.

"Three years," he said to Beullah's question. The first rule of lying was to stick close to the truth. Since he'd known Rhea that long, it seemed a safe guess.

"Do you love her?"

Rule number two, answer question with question and let the other person draw their own conclusions. "What's not to love?"

Beullah went to her bag and pulled out a pair of tiny leather briefs. "You know, this is what *you're* supposed to wear."

He curled his lip at the thought of that little thing strapped onto him. "I'd rather keep my pants on, thank you."

She clucked her tongue at him. "Aren't you more sexually adventurous than that?"

If it were only a sexual relationship, the answer

would be, Hell no. Unfortunately, more than a relationship was at stake here. If Rhea didn't at least act as if she knew what she was doing, she'd end up killed, and since he was the one who had gotten her into this . . .

Expelling a disgusted breath, he grabbed the briefs from Beullah and realized *brief* was definitely the keyword. He might as well be covering a watermelon with a Band-Aid.

Okay, maybe that was an exaggeration, but that's what it felt like.

Ace headed for the open door in the hallway that led to Rhea's bathroom. Ignoring the feminine pink-and-white-flowered decor, he closed the door, then pulled his shoes, socks, and pants off.

Just as he reached for his briefs, the door opened.

Rhea froze at the unexpected sight of Ace completely naked in her bathroom. Her heart hammering, all she could do was gape.

Hello. He was glorious!

It wasn't as if she hadn't known he'd have a great body. She did. But this . . .

This was heaven. He was so toned, she could see every tendon and muscle. His skin was deep tawny and inviting. Warm and delectable.

He made her mouth water.

And as she stared at him, she realized he was growing hard even before her eyes.

He cursed an instant before he grabbed a pink towel off her counter and covered himself. "Did you need something, Rhea?"

"Damned if I remember what it was now," she confessed. "I have to say, seeing you naked has totally reduced me to utter stupefaction."

He scoffed at that. "Yeah, well, I have to say, I'm enjoying the view myself."

It was time to teach this man a lesson. Rhea narrowed her eyes on him two seconds before she stepped forward and grabbed the towel he was holding. Before she could stop herself, she jerked it free.

"Hey!" Ace snapped as she danced away with it.

Laughing, she ran out of the bathroom with Ace in hot pursuit. They both skidded to a halt as they entered the living room and saw Beullah looking intimidating in her role as mistress.

Rhea didn't protest Ace's taking the towel back and wrapping it quickly around his hips.

"I'll get you later for that," he whispered before he vanished back into the bathroom.

"Good, good, good," Beullah said. "You should play with your slave. Torment him until he knows who the boss is."

Yeah, but in this relationship, Rhea wasn't sure she was any more his boss than he was hers. It seemed to be a mutual game of one-upmanship.

Beullah handed her a cat-o'-nine-tails that was

made out of velvet and feathers. It looked more like a cat toy than something designed for sexual stimulation.

Ace returned with the towel wrapped around his hips.

Beullah frowned at him. "Did the briefs not fit?"

"Not in my opinion."

Before either of them could move, Beullah whipped the towel free of his hips to expose the leather briefs.

Rhea burst out laughing.

"Hey!" Ace snapped. "Galaxina, I didn't laugh at you."

"I'm so sorry. That just doesn't look right." And it didn't. Something was profoundly wrong with a man as tough as Ace Krux wearing what amounted to a leather Speedo.

"Who is Galaxina?" Beullah asked.

Rhea struggled to subdue her laughter. "A very cheesy sci-fi movie with Dorothy Stratten."

Beullah humphed, then dropped the towel. "Now we need to set a few ground rules. One, there should always be a safe word that the slave uses to let the master or mistress know when he or she has had enough. I think today we will use Pinocchio."

Amusement flashed across Ace's face. "Pinocchio? The boy made of . . . *wood*?"

Rhea rolled her eyes at him.

Beullah gave him a censoring glare. "You have something against Pinocchio, slave?"

"Well, no." He gave Rhea a playful look. "I just think it's an interesting choice."

"Okay, then," Beullah continued. "Just say Pinocchio to let Rhea know when she's hit you too hard. Remember, this is for fun and for arousal. The point of this isn't to actually hurt each other."

"Thank you, Lord," Ace said in a relieved tone. "Can I start this whole thing by saying Pinocchio now so that I can get dressed again?"

Rhea rolled her eyes at him.

Beullah looked around the living room. "Now, Mistress Rhea, where should we tie up your slave?"

Rhea grinned wickedly with a thought. "The front yard, for the neighbors to see?"

"Like hell."

Beullah laughed. "You two certainly have the relationship, don't you? All right, children. We'll start simple. The bedroom."

Ace didn't miss a beat. "Pinocchio."

Rhea put her hands on her hips. "Ace, c'mon, play nice."

Unready to face the Hun with the whip, Ace crossed his arms over his chest and followed Beullah and Rhea to the bedroom in back. He paused in the doorway as he took in the white and pink perfection of Rhea's domain. It was innately feminine.

Better still it was innately Rhea, right down to the soft, sweet scent of her perfume that hovered in the air.

His body stirred instantly, and it was all he could do not to close his eyes and just inhale the seductive scent.

"We bought these last night." Rhea handed Beullah the bag full of their toys.

Beullah scoffed at them. "Those are for amateurs."

Ace scoffed back, "Consider me an amateur."

As he reached for the velvet-lined handcuffs, Beullah pulled them away. "You are a very bad slave." She handed the whip to Rhea. "Punish him."

Rhea burst out laughing. "I don't think I can do this. I really don't. I'm just not dominatrix material."

"You have to get into the mindset. Close your eyes."

Rhea looked at Ace. "Cover me if she makes a weird move?"

"You got it."

Rhea closed her eyes as Beullah came up behind her. "Now picture yourself as the ultimate goddess. You have to embrace your inner womanhood and know that you rule the world."

Rhea could see herself as empress of the universe.

"Imagine men lining up to do your every bidding. You have the power to make them want you. To need you. To do anything to get your approval."

A woman could cozy up to that idea.

"Now open your eyes."

She did, and Beullah handed her the whip.

"Now make him serve you!"

Rhea stiffened her spine. "Get on your knees, Ace."

"Pinocchio."

"There is no Pinocchio for you!" Rhea cracked the whip, which would have been more effective had it been made of something other than velvet and feathers.

Ace felt completely ridiculous as he did what she ordered. But then, she had to get used to this. Her life would depend on her being able to convince Bender that she was a dominatrix.

What was a little damaged ego if it saved her life?

"Now grab his hair and pull his head back."

Rhea complied.

Ace stared up at her dark, sinister glare.

It lasted about three seconds before she burst out laughing. She rubbed his head where her hand had been gripping his hair. "I didn't hurt you, did I?"

"No," he said honestly.

"Dominate him, Rhea!"

The problem was, Rhea didn't want to dominate him. In truth, she wanted to kiss him as she stared at him looking up at her. She knew this had to be humiliating for him, and yet he was going along with it.

For her.

"It's okay, Rhea," he said charitably. "Think of all the times I've pissed you off and you wanted to choke the life out of me."

Strange, as he knelt there, she couldn't think of a single instance. More as if they were all an amalgam, but no one incident stood out as being all that heinous.

"This isn't about violence," Beullah said as she watched them. "It's about trust. You don't want to hurt him, Rhea, you want to pleasure him. You have to learn what his pressure points are and learn to pull back just before you really do hurt him." Beullah took the whip and showed her how to wield it.

Rhea practiced for a few minutes until she got the wrist action down that would enable her to slap the velvet and feathers against him until they made a popping sound.

"Now make him crawl into the bed."

Yeah, right.

"Jump up, Baby Judy, jump up," Rhea said, using the reference from her favorite Hawaiian Pups song. "Get on the bed."

But as Ace climbed up her comforter, all she could focus on was the glorious sight of his lean, hard body. She watched the muscles working in his back and legs as he positioned himself on her bed.

Yeah, now that was something a woman had dreams about.

"Let your fantasies go wild," Beullah whispered in her ear.

The only problem was, Rhea doubted seriously that the chubby arms dealer would ever look that good in leather Speedos.

Ace, on the other hand . . .

That butt begged for a nip. All too well she could imagine peeling that leather abomination off that delectable flesh with her teeth. Exploring every inch of the man that it concealed with her fingers . . .

Her mouth.

Beullah handed her a pair of leather manacles. "Now tie him up."

Rhea approached the bed. "Turn over, slave."

Ace wasn't sure what to think as he obeyed. A foreign part of him found Rhea's commanding tone a bit sexy. The comfortable part of him rebelled at her orders.

Luckily he had enough sense to keep playing.

Rhea grabbed his hand and secured it to her bedpost. Her hair fell against his palm as she buckled him in. She had to have the softest hair he'd ever felt, and instead of that damned whip, he wished she'd climb over him and tease him with a beating from her hair.

She walked to the other side of the bed and buckled his other hand.

Ace tried for a quick grope, only to have Rhea give him a menacing frown before she had him all buckled in and unable to get up.

That was something that made him extremely nervous. "I have a question."

"Slaves don't have questions," Beullah snapped.

"Well, this one does. In case some catastrophic event occurs and you two drop dead, is there any way for me to get out of this on my own?"

Rhea laughed. "No, babe, so you better pray nothing happens to us."

"I can see the tabloid headlines now," he muttered.

Beullah clucked her tongue. "Maybe we should gag him."

Before Rhea could say no, Beullah pulled out this strange contraption with a bright orange ball in the center.

Rhea shook her head at it. "Oh, that just looks cruel."

Beullah swung it back and forth by a leather cord as she studied Ace. "You sure you don't want to try it?"

Ace snorted. "No way that's going into my mouth until I see something legal saying it's been thoroughly sterilized and detoxed."

Rhea agreed with that, not to mention she couldn't get Bender to talk if he was wearing a gag. "I think we'll pass on that."

Her face disappointed, Beullah put it back in her

bag. Then over the next two hours, she went about explaining the psychology and toys of dominance to Rhea, whose head felt as if it were going to explode from information overload.

Just before lunch, Beullah decided to call it a day.

"I'll just head on back home," she said to Rhea. "And let the two of you practice in private for a while. It'll take you a little time to get really comfortable. Just remember, baby steps. Tomorrow I'll bring some of the more interesting toys."

"Oh, goody," Ace said sarcastically from the bed. "I can't wait."

Rhea grimaced at him. "Ace, be nice, or I will use the gag."

They left him tied to the bed while they went to the living room, where Beullah quick pulled on her sweat suit again. She packed up her "toys," then handed Rhea a business card. "Call me if you have any questions or need anything."

"Thanks."

She left Beullah out, then returned to Ace, who looked less than pleased that she had abandoned him.

"Yo, Rhea. Nice of you to go make chitchat at the door with Eva Braun, but you know I'm kind of tired of being locked to this bed while you've given me the hard-on from hell and nothing else, so either let me up or make Mr. Happy happy."

Rhea licked her lips as she let her gaze wander all

over every single inch of that divinely male form. She would never get another shot like this one in her life. All morning she had been staring at his body, examining every inch of it, and now she didn't want to beat him. She wanted to touch him.

And it was time to take exactly what she wanted.

"That's not a very nice way to talk to your mistress, slave," she said, cracking her whip against her boots. "What's the magic word for release?"

"Pinocchio."

"That's right, Pinocchio," she said with a coy smile, "and now it's time to see if you're a real boy."

CHAPTER THREE

A ce definitely liked the sound of that. But it seemed way too good to be true.

"Don't be a tease, Rhea. It's just cruel."

She sauntered toward him with a walk that stirred every male hormone in his body. She was truly the one hunger he'd had these last couple of years that he'd never been able to sate.

She dragged the whip across her halter, which cupped her breasts to perfection. The ends of it fell into the deep valley, where it caressed her bared flesh and made him wonder what the PVC obscured. His cock jerked with need.

"Who said I was teasing?" she asked.

He watched as she approached his feet. Ace held his breath in sweet expectation of her actions.

C'mon, baby, touch me where it counts . . .

Now that they were alone, he let his mind go wild with what he would love to have her to do him.

She licked her lips suggestively as she raked a hot, hungry look over his body. "Hmm . . ." She crawled

onto the bed, between his legs. "Where should I begin?"

"A little due north of your current position," he
said, his voice thick and hoarse from her torture.

She arched a brow at him. "A little north, huh?"
She inched her hand toward his swollen groin.

It was all Ace could do not to squirm at the
thought of her cupping him. He'd never felt so
alive, so on edge. So damn needful of a woman's
touch.

Her hand came closer. Closer. He held his breath
as she hovered directly over his cock.

Just as he was sure she would caress him, she
veered her hand off and started tickling him.

Ace cursed in frustration as his body spasmed to
get away from her questing hands. He wanted her
blood for disappointing him like this.

"Pinocchio!" he shouted, knowing she wouldn't
listen to him.

She took no mercy on him whatsoever.

Ace tried to grab her or throw her off, but being
spread-eagled on her bed didn't lend itself to doing
anything more than bouncing her gently. He was
completely at her mercy.

"You're going to pay for this when I get loose."

She paused in her torture. "Am I?"

Her touch turned gentle then as she brushed her
hand over his painfully erect nipple. To his amaze-

ment, she gently massaged the sensitive tip with her fingernail.

Ace growled as chills spread all over him. He tried to kiss her, but she veered her face away while she continued to stroke his chest.

Rhea knew she had no business touching Ace like this, and yet she couldn't stop herself. She'd wanted him at her mercy ever since he'd kissed her.

Now she had him right where she wanted him.

And he didn't seem to be objecting. It was still surprising to her just how much she had enjoyed their exercises with Beullah. She'd discovered a whole new facet of her personality that she hadn't known existed.

"You know, you've been remarkably good through all this." He'd only complained a few times whenever she'd hit him too hard, but overall, he'd been a really good slave as she learned to wield her whip.

Ace felt his heart hammering as she continued to massage his nipple. He was so hard for her that it was painful. "You in those clothes helped," he said, his voice thick and deep.

"Did it?"

He sucked his breath in sharply as she ran her hand across his chest, to his other nipple.

"Rhea, this really is cruel. You've got me way too excited to just cold-shower it."

"No," she said, her breath falling across his bare skin. "Cruel is having to watch you lying here looking all sexy and choice while knowing I could do anything to you I wanted to and you are powerless to stop me. There really is something very sexy about this."

"And what do you want to do with me?"

She moved her hand lower, toward his swollen cock.

Rhea knew she should let him up. She should stop this madness immediately.

If only it were that easy. But the truth was, she'd been way too attracted to him for too long to just let him leave now. Especially after the morning the two of them had shared.

"Would you let me do what I want to you?" she asked him.

"I'm in no position to stop you."

She smiled at him.

Ace held his breath as she moved toward the small leather briefs. He grabbed the leather straps as every nerve ending in his body fired and danced.

Then she did the most shocking thing of all. She bent her head down and tongued the small zipper that bisected the briefs. The sight of her between his legs made his cock jerk. He was so aroused he was almost afraid of embarrassing himself.

Tensing his body in expectation, he watched as she slowly pulled the zipper down with her teeth. It was the most arousing thing he'd ever experienced.

The most erotic thing he'd ever seen. And it was

all he could do not to pull his arms out of their sockets in an effort to free himself long enough to grab her and take her the way he wanted to.

Rhea held her breath as Ace's cock sprang free. She pulled back and used her hand to unzip the briefs all the way around to the back until Ace was completely bare to her.

He was gorgeous there.

She watched him carefully. "Beullah said you needed to learn to trust me."

"I don't trust anyone."

"No?" Rhea didn't know where she got her confidence; maybe it was because they had both been so close to naked all morning that she had gotten a lot more comfortable with him.

Or maybe it was that all she had to do was hear Ace's voice and she was immediately wet for him. Aching.

Whatever caused it, she reached around her and undid her halter top.

Ace hissed at the sight of her bared breasts. Her nipples were hard, just begging for a caress and taste.

Then to his dismay, she leaned over him and wrapped the halter around his eyes.

"What are you doing?"

"Blindfolding you. Now you really are at my mercy."

Ace shook his head, wanting to see her. It didn't do a damn bit of good.

Rhea sat back to survey her naked, blind captive. "It must be nerve-racking for you."

"You have no idea."

She laughed. It was really heady to be able to study him without his intense stare distracting her.

His tawny skin was stretched tight over a well-muscled body. He was a large man, all over. Lying beside him, she touched the tip of his cock with her finger. He was already leaking.

Ace growled as she rubbed the tip of her finger back and forth over him.

"Touch me, Rhea."

She traced the outline of veins all the way down to the base. She'd always been fascinated by the mat of hair on a man's body. Licking her lips, she ran her fingers through the coarse hair until she cupped him. He arched his back.

"Like that, do you?"

"You have to ask?"

She smiled even wider.

Ace ground his teeth as she explored him with a slow, methodical hand that left him breathless and weak. He still couldn't believe she was doing this. Rhea wasn't the kind of woman to just jump into a man's bed.

She was the kind of woman that a man took home and kept.

"If I'm asleep, don't wake me." He hadn't realized he'd spoken aloud until he heard her response.

"Pardon?"

Her hand stopped its sweet torture.

What the hell? He'd come this far. He might as well be honest with her "You have no idea how many times I have closed my eyes and tried to imagine what your hands would feel like on my body, Rhea. Your lips on mine."

Rhea gently slid her hand up his cock. "Really?"

"Yes." The word was ragged, and it excited her even more than his confession.

She pulled her hand back, then laid her body over his, reveling in the sensation of all that steely masculine flesh under her. He felt good.

Too good.

Her heart hammering, she slowly explored the chiseled outline of his jaw with her tongue. She'd always wanted to taste his jawline. He was one of those men who tended to go a couple of days between shaves. Though she didn't like the look of a beard, she loved the sight of his unkempt whiskers.

He lifted his hips so that the tip of his swollen shaft was pressing against the center of her body. She hissed at the sensation. It was making her even wetter. Hotter.

But she wasn't ready to take him in yet.

Sitting up, she leaned over him and kissed that delectable, taunting mouth of his.

Ace couldn't breathe as her tongue swept against his. Her kiss was fierce, demanding, and it whet his appetite for more.

He could just imagine what she must look like sitting on his stomach as he lay completely naked, tied spread-eagled to the posts of her bed.

"Will you take the blindfold off?"

"If I do that, I might come to my senses and chicken out."

"Forget that, then."

She laughed low and seductively. "Tell me what you've dreamed of me doing to you, Ace."

"I'm not sure where to start." He couldn't even begin to catalog all of his fantasies about her.

He felt her sliding off him.

Before he could speak, he felt something soft tickling his hip bone. "What is that?"

"The feather," she said a minute before she swept it over his cock.

Ace groaned in ecstasy.

"Have you ever thought of this?"

"Yes," he confessed. "I've seen you drizzle honey on those biscuits you get whenever Tee brings you lunch from the Cracker Barrel. And I've dreamed of coating your entire body in it and licking it off."

Rhea squirmed at the image in her mind that conjured. "What else?"

"I've dreamed of tasting your . . ." Ace caught himself before he said *tits*. Women didn't like that word. "Breasts. Of you sliding them up and down my chest until you go down on me."

"Hmmm."

She stopped tormenting him with the feather. He was afraid he'd offended her until he felt something soft against his cheek. It was her breast. Pulling against the restraints, he opened his lips and turned so that he could taste her swollen nipple as she held herself for him.

Rhea couldn't believe she was doing this, and yet she didn't want to stop. The truth was, she'd spent far too many days dreaming of him too. It was why she'd always been so surly around him. She didn't want to be just another conquest to him. She wanted to be different. Important.

You're just another one-night stand, she told herself.

No, this didn't feel like that. Maybe she was lying to herself, but somehow this felt right.

She surrendered herself to his licks until she couldn't stand it anymore. She had to taste him too.

He actually whimpered as she moved away from him.

Rhea took a deep breath. She'd gone too far to stop now, and she knew it. There was no way she could go back to just being a woman in the office where he was concerned.

She wanted more than that from him. Much more.

Her hand shaking in apprehension, she pulled her makeshift blindfold off him.

Those searing blue eyes captured and held hers. His eyes blazed with passion and need.

He was splendid.

And he was hers. At least for this afternoon.

Ace licked his lips as he watched her. He'd never been more aroused in his life, and he had yet to even touch her.

Her gaze locked to his, he frowned as she left the bed until she pulled her G-string off. Oh, yeah, now that was definitely what he wanted.

She leaned over him and skimmed the bottoms over his chest, teasing him with it until she reached his cock.

Her eyes still on his, she climbed up on the bed, then took him into her mouth.

Ace ground his teeth as pleasure assailed him. Not just from the sensation of her mouth on him, but from the sight of her tasting him.

How many times had he dreamed this? How many times had he glimpsed a peek of her upper thigh in her cube, then got so hard for her that he'd almost wanted to go to the bathroom and jack off just for peace of mind?

Now she was making love to him. And it was better than anything he'd ever imagined.

"Untie me, Rhea. I want to touch you."

She took him all the way into her mouth and caressed his sac before she pulled back and finally gave in to his wishes.

Ace moaned ever so slightly at finally being free. His muscles protested a bit from all the inactivity.

But he didn't listen to them while he had Rhea in this bed. Grabbing her, he pulled her to his lips for a kiss.

Rhea sank into his arms. There was no other word for it. She felt so incredibly safe and warm here. Cocooned by his power.

She wrapped her body around his, wanting to absorb as much of his strength as she could. He felt wonderful!

She rubbed herself against all his hardness, wanting to feel every inch of his body against hers.

"Wait," Ace said, his voice ragged. "Do you have a condom?"

Did she?

Rhea panicked as she realized what they had almost done. She wasn't on the pill, and to be honest she'd been so hot for him that she was glad he had come to his senses.

Truly she was grateful.

"I'm not sure." And she wasn't. It'd been a long time since she'd been with a man. "Do you?"

"No," he groaned. "I don't make it a habit of traveling with them."

That made her feel even better. At least he wasn't one of those "on the make" guys who kept one in his wallet "just in case."

"Hang on, let me go see if I can find one."

Ace let her up.

Rhea raced to the bathroom and started looking through her drawers.

"Come on," she said under her breath as she searched. She had to have one somewhere in here.

Please!

She felt his presence an instant before she heard his sharp intake of breath.

"You have the nicest ass I've ever seen."

Rhea backed up out of her cabinet to look up at him. "Thanks."

He knelt down beside her. "Can I help?"

"Yes. Hopefully there's one in here someplace."

"Good. You're no more prepared for this than I am." He gave her a scalding kiss before he pulled back and started searching frantically.

Rhea was about to give up before she finally found one. "Eureka!" she shouted in triumph.

The relief on his face was comical. "Oh, thank God."

Rhea leapt at him. She hit him so hard, she knocked him off balance and they both tumbled into the hallway.

Ace laughed at her enthusiasm. "How long has it been since you had sex?"

"Let me put it to you this way: it was under the former administration."

"Ouch."

"You?"

"Not since Sheila gave me the heave-ho."

Sheila had been his last girlfriend, who had left him unexpectedly a little over a year ago. "Why did she leave you anyway?"

"Honestly?"

"Yes."

"I called her Rhea while we were having sex."

His words rang in her ears, and she wasn't quite sure she'd heard them correctly. "What?"

He reached up and cupped her face in his hands. "You really don't know how much I've been wanting you, do you?"

No, and all this sounded too good to be real. "Why didn't you ever ask me out?"

"I was afraid you'd say no. At least this way, I had the comfort of believing you didn't find me a complete asshole. If I asked you out and you said no, then I'd know you didn't like me."

That didn't sound like the Ace she knew so well. "But you're not afraid of anything."

The look in his eyes seared her. She saw his heart. His soul. Most of all, she saw his sincerity. "That's so not true, Rhea."

Her heart soared at his words, but she was still hesitant. She'd been lied to too many times in the past. "Are you feeding me a complete line of bull?"

"Considering the fact that I let you tie me virtually naked to your bed in front of a complete stranger just so I could be with you, what do you think?"

"I think I wish you'd asked me out a long time ago."

Ace hissed as she bent down and kissed him. This was a dream come true. Deepening his kiss, he reached for the condom and took it from her.

She immediately took it back. "I'll do it."

His heart racing, he watched as she tore the package open and pulled it out. The plastic was cold against him as she fit it over his cock and slowly unrolled it down the length of him. It was all he could do not to come just from the sensation of her hands on him.

But he didn't want this over with any time soon. He wanted this to last.

His entire body on fire, he trailed his hand up the inside of her silken thigh until he reached the damp curls between her legs. She met his eyes as he slid his fingers down her cleft, carefully separating her folds and touching her for the very first time.

She was beautiful, and her slick, soft flesh felt incredible to him. He couldn't wait to take her.

Biting her lip, she gently rubbed herself against his fingers as he sank one deep inside her body. It was the most incredible moment of his life. Probably because he'd dreamed of touching her more than he'd ever dreamed of any other woman.

It seemed as if he had waited his entire life for this one moment.

He ran his fingers over her, letting her wetness coat his fingers as he imagined what was to come. Of sinking himself deep inside her.

She moved forward. Ace leaned back as she crawled up his body.

Rhea couldn't wait to have him inside her. She straddled his waist, then slid herself back until she felt his hard, probing tip pressing against the part of her that was aching and throbbing most for his touch.

Ace lifted his hips and slid himself in all the way to his hilt.

She cried out in pleasure at the fullness of him inside her. "Ace," she choked, rocking herself against him. It felt so good to have him there.

He gripped her hips as he met her strokes and drove himself even deeper inside her.

Ace watched her in awe as she took control of their pleasure. His little uptight agent was as wild as any woman he'd ever slept with.

No, she was better.

She braced her hands against his chest as she ground herself against him in time to his rapid heartbeat. Tilting his head up, he took her breast into his mouth while he continued to hold her waist.

He licked and teased the taut peak, letting the roughness of it please his tongue.

Rhea couldn't think straight as she felt Ace with every molecule of her body. He was so much more than she had ever thought. He touched her like a man who actually cared for her, and it had been a long, long time since she'd felt that.

They made love furiously until her body couldn't take any more. Crying out, she fell forward onto his chest and let her release claim her. All she could hear was his heart pounding while the scent of him filled her senses.

Ace growled at the sensation of her body grasping him. He quickened his strokes as she continued to climax until he found his own moment of pure bliss.

His breathing ragged, he held her close to his chest where their hearts pounded together while his body spent itself inside her. In all honesty, he didn't want this moment to end.

It was perfect.

The feeling of her head against his chest. Her body molded to his. Her breath tickling his nipple.

If he lived an eternity, he would never know anything better than the feeling of Rhea in his arms.

Rhea closed her eyes as her heart finally slowed to a normal rate. The warmth of his body seeped into hers. In all her days of bantering with Ace, she'd never have guessed he would be like this. So tender and loving after sex.

He didn't seem to be in any hurry to get up, and the floor couldn't be all that comfortable for him.

"So what's on the menu for tomorrow?" he asked.

She laughed at that. "I'm not sure. What are you thinking?"

"I need more condoms."

"Ugh!" She pushed herself up to look down at him. "Do you ever have anything else on your mind?'"

"Food. But that only lasts about as long as it takes me to get a steak."

She shook her head at him. "Stop playing on the bad stereotype."

"I am a bad stereotype so long as you're lying naked on me. How on earth am I supposed to think about anything else?"

As she started to pull away, he stopped her with a fierce, hungry kiss that set every hormone in her body on fire again. This man had a mouth that was pure magic.

He pulled back, but left his hand buried in her hair. "Thank you, Rhea," he said sincerely, his gaze burning into hers.

"You're very welcome."

Reluctantly, she moved off him and headed back

into the bathroom for the shower. "Want to join me?"

He gave her a hot once-over. "Pinocchio. There's no way I can go in there and not have another round. Since there's no more condoms . . ."

He was right. "Okay, I'll just be a minute."

Turning around, she shut the door and grabbed a towel out of her cabinet.

Rhea was still amazed that she wasn't more self-conscious around him. This wasn't like her, and yet she felt so comfortable with him that it was almost terrifying.

She showered quickly, then opened the curtain to find Ace leaning against her bathroom vanity. He was hard again.

"Did you know you can see a perfect outline of your body when you're in there?"

"No."

He moved forward and nuzzled her neck before he gently licked the sensitive flesh right below her ear. "I can't believe what you do to me," he breathed in her ear, sending chills over her body.

He kissed her cheek, gave a light grope to her breast, then released her and entered her shower as she left it.

Rhea was so aroused that it was all she could do not to rip open the curtain and pin him to her shower wall.

He was more tempting than any man had a right to be.

But neither one of them needed her to get pregnant.

Forcing herself to dress, Rhea went to her bedroom. By the time she was dressed and had remade the bed, Ace joined her.

"Thinking of new ways to torture me?" he asked as she unfastened the restraints.

She opened her mouth to respond, but the sight of him wet, wearing nothing but a white towel, made all rational thoughts flee.

"You have to stop looking at me like that, Rhea."

"Like what?"

"Like I'm a piece of chocolate you're dying to taste. It gives me a hard-on every time."

She could easily see the proof of that statement. "Sorry, but it would help if you didn't parade yourself around naked in my presence."

He indicated his clothes, which were on her dresser, as he crossed the room to stand before her. "It's not exactly my fault."

"Oh, in that case, I better leave you alone while you put your clothes on."

"I'd rather you not."

She nibbled his chin before she pulled away. "If we don't stop, we're going to do something that could get us into serious trouble."

"I know," he whispered. "Okay, time for clothes."

Before she could leave the room, his cell phone rang. Ace picked it up and answered it.

"Hey, Joe." Ace cast an amused look at her, then winked. "No, obviously I'm not tied up, since I answered the phone. . . . Thanks. So what do you need?"

Anxious as to why Joe might be calling, she moved forward, hoping to overhear something.

"Yeah, we'll be right there." He hung up.

"What's going on?"

"Joe just got word that Bender's sent out a call to his clients. Apparently he's found an abandoned arsenal of old Soviet weapons, including some nuclear. We need to get to the office for a briefing."

That succeeded in stifling her renegade passion. "I'll be waiting by the door."

Ace nodded and reached for his pants while she left him alone. Today had been a major mistake. He knew it.

As agents, they were supposed to stay detached, especially from each other. But after this morning, he wasn't feeling detached from Rhea.

Then again, he'd never been detached from her.

In fact, he was feeling extremely possessive. The thought of a bastard like Bender seeing her in that dominatrix outfit was almost enough to send him over the edge.

He didn't want anyone to see her like that. Anyone but him.

And how could he send her in there with a mad-man now?

Oh, this wasn't good. He'd never felt like this for another woman.

"Get a grip." He buttoned his pants, then reached for his shirt.

The two of them had a mission, and he wasn't about to let one sexual encounter ruin it.

At least he hoped he wasn't.

CHAPTER FOUR

I knew it! Look at them. Did I not tell you that all that sniping was because they were seriously attracted to each other?"

Joe looked up at Tee's words to see Rhea and Ace through the two-way mirror of his office. Damn, Tee had been right. They were making goo-goo eyes at each other.

"Shit," he said under his breath.

"What?" Tee asked innocently.

"Work and play don't mix."

Tee gave him an arched look. "Since when?"

"Since we have to send her in practically naked to beat information out of an arms dealer. Given the way Ace is eyeballing her, I don't think he's going to approve."

"What has that got to do with anything? Ace is a good enough agent to do what he has to."

"Yeah, right."

Tee gave Joe an angry frown. "You and I are best

friends, and how many times have you sent me into danger?"

"That's because you're the Dragon Lady. You'd take the head off anyone dumb enough to cross you."

She cocked her head at him and said pointedly, "I haven't killed *you* yet."

"Not from lack of trying on your part, and personally, I'd rather you kill me than make me sit down and talk to your mom. That woman hates my guts with an unfounded reasoning."

"You keep talking like that about my mother, Joe Public, and I just might make sure that your automatic car payment gets misrouted." She looked back at Rhea and Ace. "Trust me. This'll be fine."

Now it was Joe's turn to scoff. "The last time I trusted you, I got three bullets in my back."

"No, you got shot because you trusted me and then you didn't listen to what I said and did your own stupid thing."

He mocked her by screwing up his face and repeating her words back at her.

"That's it. I'm e-mailing my mother to come have lunch here tomorrow."

"No!" Joe snapped, immediately contrite. "She makes me crazy. She won't even speak English when I'm around, and I know she speaks it better than I do."

"We will finish this later," Tee snapped before she opened the door to let Ace and Rhea in.

Ace looked a bit sheepish as he came to stand in front of Joe's desk, while Rhea took a seat in the black leather chair in front of it.

"So how was your morning?" Tee asked as she came to lean against the side of the desk. "Did Beullah do her job?"

Ace nodded. "Oh, yeah. They hog-tied me in a manner to make you proud, Tee."

"Good. Pity they let you up."

Ignoring her, Ace looked at Joe. "So what's the new information?"

Joe shuffled through a couple of folders. "Bender's on the move. You two are going to have to head out to Germany tonight."

Both Ace and Rhea gaped.

"What?" Ace asked.

"You heard him," Tee said. "I already have your flight booked."

The news went over Ace like sandpaper. "She can't go in alone. She hasn't had time to prepare herself yet. Hell, she barely knows what she's doing."

"Excuse me?" Rhea asked, her tone extremely offended. "I think I should have beat you harder."

He glared at her.

"Don't worry, Ace." Tee pulled an envelope off Joe's desk. "You're going in as Hermann the towel boy."

"Pardon?"

Joe tossed Ace a passport. "You and Dieter will be right outside the room, listening in case she needs backup. Retter will be on recording detail along with Dagmar. There shouldn't be any trouble you guys can't handle. God knows you've all had worse."

Tee handed the entire file to Ace. "You two are technically on vacation for the next few days while Rhea learns her stuff over in Germany. I've ordered some training DVDs for you to study so that you can learn how to beat him black and blue. Bender that is, not Ace."

Rhea nodded. "Okay."

"We don't know when Bender is going to show up, looking for Ute," Joe said. "But according to Ute, he always gets feisty right before a big coup, and his latest find definitely qualifies. I figure you guys have three days to a week before he shows himself. What do you think, Ace? You know him better than anyone."

"You're right," he said. "He usually books time with Ute the night before he pulls off his shit. We need to get over there and be ready."

"Then you two go ahead. Retter is already in Germany and waiting for your orders. The rest of us will follow you over there on a later flight."

Ace handed Rhea her passport and printout for her plane ticket, then led the way out of Joe's office.

"You don't think they suspect anything, do you?" Rhea asked in a hushed tone as soon as they were out of hearing range.

On the way over here, they had decided that it would be business as usual for them so that no one else in the office would know what had happened.

God help them if any of the losers here ever learned they'd had sex. They would tease them to the point they'd have to kill someone.

Ace glanced back over his shoulder. "Joe's pretty dense. Tee . . . I don't know. I swear sometimes that woman can read minds."

"Oh, don't say that. That makes me nervous."

"Yeah," he agreed. "So how do we handle the next few days?"

"Well, normally we'd do deep, intensive train-ing . . ."

Ace couldn't stop the grin that took over his face. "I was hoping you'd say that."

She shook her head at his enthusiasm. At times he was simply evil.

But she was glad this was one of those times.

———

Once they reached Germany, they spent night and day together. Rhea was stunned at how comfortable she became around Ace while she was completely naked. It was liberating to have no sense of being body-conscious around him.

How could she, when he seemed to prefer her that way?

"I'm supposed to be training with you tied up," she said as Ace secured her hands, which were tied together to her headboard.

"Turnabout is fair play."

She supposed it was.

"What are you doing?" she asked as he took one ankle carefully in his hand.

He kissed the sole of her foot.

Rhea moaned as he moved to lick her toes and to torment them one by one until she was squirming.

"I'm having my way with you, princess." He tied her foot to the bedpost.

After he had the other leg secured, Ace stood back. He'd never thought about tying someone up as being particularly sexy, but he had to admit the sight of her tied and waiting for him turned him on a lot more than he would ever have guessed.

He slid his briefs off, then pouted slightly. "I should have tied you down on your back."

"Too late."

"Not necessarily." Grinning at her, Ace slid himself slowly up under her.

Rhea hissed at the feeling of him there. She was completely open and exposed to his every desire.

She dipped her head down to kiss him while he slid his hands down her back to gently cup her butt and press her hips to his. She could feel him growing hard against her stomach.

"Hmmm," he breathed, rubbing himself against her. "What have I found?"

Rhea sucked her breath in sharply as his rough fingers gently prodded her clit.

"You do know, I'm getting entirely too attached to you, Ace?"

"Yeah," he said as he slid one long, lean finger inside her. "And I know that I should get up, get dressed, and go to my room."

But he didn't move to get up, and that thrilled her most of all.

"Why aren't you leaving?" she asked.

"Honestly?"

She nodded.

"I'm desperate for you, Rhea." He pulled his hand away from her, then brushed the hair back from her face so that he could look at her. "I've been desperate to taste your body since the day you first came into the office, stumbled, and fell, flashing me those little pink panties you had on under your skirt."

Her face flushed with heat. "You saw that?"

"Oh, yeah, and I've dreamed of nothing but peeling those pink panties off you ever since."

"And now that you have?"

"I want the right to keep peeling them off you anytime you make me hot."

She rolled her eyes at him. "That is without a doubt the most unromantic thing I have ever heard, and if I wasn't tied down, I'd leave."

He laughed low in his throat as his hand returned to stroke her between her legs. "Then it's a good thing I tied you down first, huh?"

It was hard to think straight while he touched her like this. While his fingers stroked and circled her.

"Tell me what you want, Rhea."

"I want you inside me."

Ace gave her a fierce kiss, then moved his lips slowly down her body to her breasts, where he took his time teasing her. Then lower and lower while her body burned for him. He licked his way to her thigh, then nipped her hip as he slid completely out from under her.

Rhea tried to look over her shoulder but couldn't see anything.

She felt the bed dip with his weight as he moved to lean over her.

He brushed the hair back from her neck before he nibbled at her earlobe. She shook all over as his tongue teased her ear. His breath scorched her.

He slid his hand around her hip, to sink it deep in her fold before he entered her.

Rhea gasped as pleasure assaulted her.

Ace was blinded by the sensation of her warm, wet heat. He could lose himself inside her forever.

But today was their last day to play. Tomorrow Bender would show himself.

One of them could die. It wasn't something agents gave much thought to, but as he rode her slowly, that fear finally found him.

What if something went wrong?

"Ace? Are you okay?"

He placed a kiss to her cheek. "I'm fine, baby."

Rhea moaned as his fingers stroked her while he thrust deep inside her. Still, she could tell something was different about him in spite of what he said. There was a hesitancy to his touch. A reservation.

But she didn't have long to contemplate that before her orgasm claimed her.

Ace held her tight, his fingers working their magic until the very last tremor had been coaxed out of her.

A few heartbeats later she felt him tense as he too joined her in bliss.

Rhea lay there with his weight pleasantly crushing her while he untied her hands.

"I'm going to miss our 'training' sessions."

"I'll bet you will," she said with a laugh.

He moved to the side of her so that she could roll over and snuggle close.

Tenderly, he brushed the hair back from her face.

Rhea sighed. "I wish we could go back and do the last few days over."

"Yeah, me too. But you know, this doesn't have to end . . . does it?"

Rhea swallowed at his question. "I don't know, Ace. A relationship is hard enough. But between two agents . . ."

"Dagmar and Dieter make it work."

That was true. The two of them were married, and to Rhea's knowledge they'd never had so much as a hiccup in their relationship.

He took her hand in his and moved it to his lips so that he could nibble her palm. "Can we at least try?"

She smiled at him. What woman could say no to that look? "Okay."

Ace returned her smile before he kissed her on the brow. But at the back of his mind, he couldn't shake the sensation that something was going to go seriously wrong tomorrow.

CHAPTER FIVE

Ace was in position, waiting with Dieter while Rhea dressed herself for the arrival of Bender. It had taken some doing to get the PussyCat Club to "hire" Rhea, but after a nice long talk with the German authorities, the owner decided it would be in her best interest to let Rhea do her job.

Now Rhea was in a locker room that the dominatrixes used to garb themselves in their work attire while Ace and Dieter were outside in the blood-red hallway that led to all the "service" rooms.

"Are you all right, Krux?" Dieter asked as they stacked towels onto a cart so that to any passersby, they would look like two regular workers restocking the towels for the clients.

Dieter was a tall, extremely muscular, blond German native. He'd been recruited by Joe a little over a year ago and since then had been quite an asset to their team. Having been born and bred in Europe, Dieter knew every back hole and dive in six countries. Better still, he had questionable associates who often leaked vital information to them.

Ace could feel a tic working in his jaw. "No. I don't like sending her in there alone with a psycho."

"Relax. But I know what you mean. Dagmar never listens to me either. She is"—he paused as if searching for the foreign English word—"stubborn. Many times she goes when she should stay. But Rhea is more cautious. She knows what to do. I don't think we have anything to worry over with that one."

Yeah, but Ace really hated the thought of her tying Bender down. The beating part he could live with. It was the "other" unknown variables that had his stomach knotted.

"Excuse me?" an extremely well-built, leather-clad mistress said in German as she came into the hallway from a room three doors down. "What is it you two do? You need to be working at getting these towels to the room and not dawdling with idle chatter."

"*Ja,* we're working," Dieter responded, knowing that Ace's German was flawless, but accented enough to give him away as a foreigner.

"You," the mistress said, indicating Dieter. "I need you standing by Room Five after Herr Bender leaves."

Ace's heart stopped beating.

"Why?" Dieter asked.

She sighed heavily. "He always leaves his woman a mess. We will need to get Bettie to our doctor as soon as he goes, and you look more than strong enough to carry her."

"Pardon?" Ace asked as his sight turned dim.

"*Ja,* he is not a good man, but he pays us well."

"But I thought he was the one who liked to be tied up," Dieter said.

She laughed as if the very idea amused her. "Who told you such? *Nein,* he would never allow anyone else to tie him up." She cracked the small riding crop in her hand at them. "*Schnell, schnell.* He will be here momentarily."

Neither of them moved until after she'd entered a room on the left.

"We were fed bullshit," Ace said from between clenched teeth.

He grabbed his cell phone from his pocket and buzzed Retter, who was in the building across the street with the recording equipment. "We have a problem, Retter. My informer lied. Bender doesn't get beaten. He does the beating."

"What?"

Ace clenched the phone so hard his hand was shaking. "You heard me. What do we do?"

He could hear Joe in the background telling Retter what to do after Retter had filled him in on what was happening. " It's too late to call this off without blowing our covers. Rhea will just have to go through it."

Ace saw red. "Hell, no."

He hung up while Retter started to yell at him.

"What did he say?" Dieter asked.

"Something I didn't want to hear. I'm pulling Rhea out."

"If Retter said—"

Ace cut Dieter's words off with a staggering punch that rendered him unconscious. Ace grabbed the huge bear of a man and shoved him into the towel closet, covered him with towels, then shut and locked the door.

God help him, Dieter would beat the shit out him later.

But that was later.

Right now he had a damsel who was about to get seriously distressed.

❧

Rhea was checking out her stockings in the mirror when the door to her dressing room opened. She frowned as she saw Ace.

By the look on his face, she could tell something was wrong. "What's up?"

"I'm getting you out of here."

"Why?"

"Bender is a psycho, and he is going to beat you. Not the other way around."

Rhea went pale at this disclosure. "What did Retter say?"

"I don't give a shit what he said. Retter is an idiot, and I'm not going to send you in there so that fat bastard can mangle you. This is my case, and I'm—"

"This is my job, Ace. It's what I do."

Ace cursed in frustration. "Will no one listen to reason?"

Narrowing her gaze at him, she put her hands on her hips to let him know that she thought he was the one being unreasonable. "Ace, we have to nail this bastard. If he confesses—"

"And if the bitch lied about who gets beaten, doesn't it stand to reason that she lied about the confession bit as well?"

"Maybe she didn't. We have to get this guy off the street, and if this is the way, then this is the way."

That didn't make a bit of sense to him. "Fine, I'll kill him, and we—"

"We're not assassins, Ace. We work by law and order."

His fury roiled through him at that. "You don't know Tee very well, do you? I hate to be the messenger, Rhea, but Tee is a cold-blooded killer."

"Oh, please."

Rhea started for the door.

Unable to stand by and watch her be hurt, Ace ran for her. He grabbed her before she could stop him.

"What are you doing?"

He pulled the handcuffs out of his backpocket that he was supposed to reserve for Bender and slapped them over her wrists.

"Ace!" She tried to squirm out from his hold.

He took the scarf from her neck and used it to gag her. "I'm sorry, Rhea. I can't let you do this. You're right. Someone has to go in there. But by God, it won't be you."

Picking her up, he carried her to a locker and set her inside even while she fought against him.

Rhea was furious. Ace could see it plainly in her brown eyes as he shut the door and locked it. But it was better she be pissed than dead.

"All right, Krux," he said to himself under his breath. "It's time to do the nasty."

Personally, he'd rather be dead, but what was a little dignity compared to Rhea's life?

"Well, it worked for Tim Curry." Ace surveyed himself with a critical eye. He definitely wouldn't win a beauty pageant. With any luck, Bender might even be half-blind.

Or half-drunk.

It was dark in the rooms . . . maybe Bender wouldn't notice much.

Maybe.

"I am so fired," he muttered. But it would be worth it.

He hoped.

Pulling his garter belt straight, he headed down the hallway to the room where Bender should be waiting.

Sure enough, the man was there. He had on a long, black PVC coat with buckles and straps that looked strangely close to a straitjacket. At least the man did have on a pair of glasses. Maybe he would be blind as a bat.

"Who are you?" Bender asked in German, curling his lip as he surveyed Ace with a disgusted look.

"Latex . . . Bettie." Ace tried not to cringe at the latter as he kept his voice high and singsongy in an effort to mimic some kind of European accent while he spoke German. Hell, he hadn't been born in Hollywood for nothing.

He would just remember that this was to save Rhea and all the other innocent victims Bender intended to prey upon.

Bender cocked his head. "You don't look like Bettie Page."

Ace put his hands on his hips and feigned indignation. "And you don't look like Brad Pitt, but notice I'm not complaining."

Bender gave him an arched glare. "You are uppity. I like that in a woman. Now show me your tits."

Yeah, right.

"How about first we see yours?"

Before Bender could leave or call for help, Ace seized him, ripped his coat, and pulled it down on his arms so that he was bound and unable to move.

"Ah," Ace said with a tsk in his faked accent. "You have not been working out, Herr Bender. What do you do that you are so weak in the arms?"

"See here, I—"

"Shh," Ace said, cutting him off. "Bettie will take care of you, *Schatz*." Provided "Bettie" didn't toss her cookies in revulsion. "Tell her what you want done to you."

Hopefully it involved a bullwhip and this guy's ass on the floor.

Bender shouted furiously, "Let me go!"

"*Nein, nein.* You have paid for the hour of domination, and an hour you will get. Now tell Bettie what she wants to hear."

❦

Rhea was ready to choke the life out of Ace by the time the door to her locker was opened.

She looked out to see Retter, who whistled low.

"Nice outfit, Rhea."

She glared at him as he removed her gag.

"Where the hell is he?" she snapped.

"Up shit creek."

"Good. Now give me the paddle so I can beat him with it."

Retter laughed as he unlocked the cuffs.

Rhea rubbed her sore wrists as she continued to glare at Retter. At six-four, he was every bit as handsome as Ace, but nowhere near to dying as Ace was at the moment.

Just wait until she got her hands on him.

"He blew it, didn't he?" she asked.

Retter set the cuffs aside. "Yes and no."

"What do you mean yes and no?"

"I think your boyfriend has quite a future as a dominatrix."

Rhea frowned, but Retter didn't elaborate. Instead, he handed her his jacket, then led her out into the hallway, where there were several German agents along with Joe and members of the CIA and Interpol.

"What's going on here?" she asked Joe. "Where's Ace?"

"In custody."

Her stomach clenched. "Custody? Whose? For what?"

"Ours," Retter said. "For being the ugliest transvestite in the history of humanity. I swear, we ought to be allowed to kill Bender for sheer, blind stupidity alone."

Rhea was even more confused. "What?"

"Ace went in as you, or rather as Latex Bettie," Joe explained.

Her heart stopped beating at the thought of Ace trying to pose as a woman. Yeah, right! Ace would never pass as a female. He was far too masculine.

"Oh, no. Did Bender get away?"

"No," Joe said. "We got him, along with a full confession."

Rhea gaped. "How?"

Retter let out a deep, evil laugh. "Latex Bettie wields a mean whip. He had Bender spilling more guts than a kosher butcher."

"So why is Ace in custody then?" Rhea asked.

"Mostly for pissing me off by not following orders," Joe said in a surly tone. " He's lucky I don't let the German authorities keep him."

Retter gave a crooked grin. "I can arrange that, if you want."

"Don't tempt me."

"Can I see him?" Rhea asked.

"Trust me," Retter said. "You don't want to see him. Think Frank-N-Furter gone bad. Real bad."

Why was it every time Retter spoke, he only confused her more? "Frank-N-Furter?"

"Rocky Horror Picture Show." He shuddered.

"C'mon," Joe said, leading her away from Retter. "I have Ace in a room down here."

She followed Joe down the garish hallway to a small room where Dieter sat with a cold pack held to his jaw while Dagmar stroked his hair.

Dieter glared at them. "I'm going to kill him, Joe."

"I know, Dieter, hang around and I might authorize it."

"If you don't," Dagmar snapped, "I will. How dare he hit my Dieter. I want his tenticles cut off."

Rhea had a bad feeling Dagmar meant *testicles*, but in the mood the Czech woman was in, Rhea wasn't about to correct her.

Joe opened another door in the rear of the room, which led to one of the theme rooms. It was a garish red, gauzy place that looked even tackier under the bright fluorescent lights that were only turned on for cleaning.

Ace sat on a bench with his back to her. His hands were cuffed behind him.

And he looked awful.

"Oh, good grief," Rhea said as she surveyed the mess that was Ace, dressed in a PVC teddy and fishnets. The black wig on his head did nothing for his features, which were outlined in grotesque, overdone makeup. He looked like a cross between Gloria

Swanson and Bozo the clown. "If Bender thought for one minute that you were a woman, I am seriously offended on behalf of every member of my gender."

Ace turned around to see her. "You okay?"

"Her?" Joe asked disgustedly. "It's your own ass you should be worried about, Krux."

Still, Ace's concern for her made her strangely weepy.

Ace's intense blue gaze never left hers. "Before you fire me, shoot me, or hand me over to German custody, could you give me a few minutes alone with her, Joe?"

"Sure." He walked out and shut the door.

Part of Rhea wanted to kill Ace for what he'd done. "Why did you do this, Ace?"

He frowned at her. "Don't you know?"

"No. I can appreciate the fact that you didn't want me hurt, but this is what I do. It's what *we* do. You can't just go off half-cocked and pull a stunt like this. What if Bender had gotten away?"

Ace let out a tired breath. "Look, Rhea, I never wanted to feel like this about anyone. But there was no way on earth I could have stood there and let that bastard hit you. I don't care if they lock me up for the rest of eternity, I will never allow another man to hurt the woman I love. So I figured it was either this or I kill him."

Rhea couldn't breathe as she heard those words. It couldn't be true. "You don't love me, Ace. How could you?"

He looked aghast at her. "Look at me, Rhea. Do you think anything other than love would *ever* have me in this godforsaken outfit?"

Tears welled in her eyes as she closed the distance between them. "Really?"

"Yes, baby, really. You're all I've ever wanted."

How could any woman ever hold that against a man? Cupping his face in her hands, Rhea kissed him soundly. She broke off the kiss a few seconds later, laughing.

"What?"

"You have no idea how confusing it is to kiss a man dressed as a woman."

He grimaced at that. "I don't know how you wear this stuff. The hose alone are killing me."

Laughing, she pulled the wig off his head and unlocked the cuffs.

Ace seized her then and held her close as his tongue explored every inch of her mouth. Rhea sighed at the kiss and held him tight.

She laughed again. "You look so ugly as a woman."

He joined her laughter. "Yeah. This stuff definitely looks better on you."

The door to the room swung open.

"Ugh!" Joe snapped. "I'm blind *and* repulsed."

Rhea tried to move away, but Ace held her close.

"What do you want, Joe?" he asked gruffly.

"I only wanted to remind you that this room is wired, and we're still recording everything the two of you are saying."

"Did you hear?" Rhea asked.

"Every word, and I have to say that in all the years I've known Ace, I've never known him to say that to another living woman, except for his mother." He shook his head at them. "Fine, Ace. Since we got Bender, I'm going to let you off this time. But if you ever do this stunt again—"

"I know. You'll cut off my tentacles."

Rhea laughed at Ace's imitation of Dagmar.

"Exactly. Now as you two were. Just don't forget you have a debriefing in an hour and a plane to catch in three." Joe started out of the room.

"Hey, Joe," Ace called.

Joe paused.

"Thanks, bud. I owe you."

Joe nodded, then quietly left.

Ace gave her a devilish grin. "So, we have an hour . . ."

Cocking her head with attitude, Rhea stepped back and seized a whip.

"What are you doing?"

She cracked the whip near him. "I want to make an honest woman of you, Ace."

"Huh?"

"Get on your knees and propose."

Ace laughed. "You're not serious?"

"Are you?"

He sobered. "Yeah. For the first time in my life, I am." Without hesitating, he got down on his knees. "Rhea, will you marry me?"

"I dunno. Now that you're proposing, I really have to think about this. . . . Transvestites really aren't my thing." She walked over to him and brushed his hair back from his forehead. "Do you promise to never again interfere with my job?"

"I can only promise that I will do my best. I know you're capable, I do. But you have to understand that emotions don't always think before they act."

That was true enough. Rhea doubted if she could ever stand by and let him be hurt either. She would have done the same exact thing had their roles been reversed. "Okay, we'll take it on a case-by-case basis."

"Thank you."

Rhea shuddered as one of his false eyelashes came free. "Can you at least promise me that you'll never, ever wear that outfit again?"

"Definitely."

She nodded. "Then fine. I can marry you."

Ace grinned and rose to his feet. He lifted her up in his arms and headed for the door.

Before he could open it, Rhea stopped him. "By

the way, just for the sake of clarification, *I* will be the one in the wedding dress, correct?"

"No doubt about it. Now I have to go get out of this outfit before we hit debriefing."

Rhea gave him a playful look. "So does this mean I get to see you naked?"

"Yes, ma'am, it certainly does."

Pocket Books
proudly presents

BAD ATTITUDE

Sherrilyn Kenyon

Available in hardcover October 2005
from Pocket Books

The following is a preview of *BAD Attitude*. . . .

Satisfied that the Escalade was off of them, at least for the time being, she took the first exit and headed for their rendezvous.

"Don't do it."

She frowned at Steele. "Don't do what?"

"Head for Andre. They'll be watching us."

"There's no way they can be watching us." She glanced at him and felt her heart sink as she saw how badly he was bleeding. He had one hand pressing against his shoulder, but it was doing very little to staunch the blood.

They had to get him help quickly or he was going to die.

"They'll be watching us," he said through clenched teeth. "How many satellites do you think bear down on D.C. every minute of every day? I assure you, they have us on their radar and are tracking our every movement. If they weren't, the Escalade would still be behind us, police be damned. In fact, Andre needs to cut the communication before they pick up on the wire and use it against us too."

"You're so—"

"I was in the Army, Syd. I know what we can do to track a target and that was two years ago. God only knows what they've got now."

"He's right," Andre said in her ear. "Swap out transport and meet up at the hole in two hours. All communication is cut in . . . three . . . two . . . one."

Her earpiece went dead.

Damn.

"Okay," she said, looking over at Steele as they headed west. "We need to get you a doctor."

"Since someone told the authorities that I'm an escaped felon, that's not a wise move now, is it?"

She ignored his sarcasm. "We can get you—"

"No," he snapped. "Find us a hotel and I can field dress it."

She rolled her eyes at his stupidity. "What are you going to do? Dig the bullet out yourself?" she asked, echoing his own sarcasm.

"It won't be the first time."

Syd did a double-take sideways at his words. But more than that was the sincerity she heard in his tone. He wasn't kidding. The thought of him lying out in the field someplace with a gaping wound he was dressing by himself brought a peculiar pain to her chest. For some reason she didn't understand, it actually made her hurt for him.

He sat beside her, still holding his shoulder as even more blood covered his hand. A light sheen of perspiration covered his handsome face, which now held a grayish cast to it.

Unwilling to argue more since time was critical for him, she decided to heed his advice. "You still need a doctor."

"Then you and your friends had better sneak one in, otherwise this mission is totally fubarred."

"Fubarred?"

"Fucked up beyond all recognition."

She headed toward what she hoped would be a safe hotel. "We're not fubarred."

"Yeah, we are. Our friend back there in the Escalade has twenty-four hours to kill me so I have a strong feeling we haven't seen the last of him." He placed her gun on the seat next to him. It was completely covered with blood. "We also need to get me a weapon of some sort so that I can give him a dose of his own medicine. Let him bring it on when we're on equal footing."

"Wait, wait, wait. Go back to the first thing. What's this twenty-four hour thing? Andre didn't tell me anything about that."

Steele gave her a mean glare. "You wanted me to get a job. Well, lady, that's their job screening. I kill him or he kills me. Winner gets the job."

"You're kidding."

"Absolutely. I'm not the least bit serious. All of this is one big hallucination. And I'm not sitting over here bleeding to death. But hey, since it's a hallucination, could you please make my arm stop throbbing because right now it hurts like hell." He practically snarled the last bit at her.

"You don't have to be so nasty."

He growled at her like a wounded bear—which she supposed he was. That growling only increased as she pulled up to the Henley Park Hotel and parked off to the side so that their beat-up car wouldn't be quite so obvious.

"What the hell are we doing here?"

She gave him a menacing glare as she put the car in park. "Getting a room."

"In a swanky hotel? Sure. Why not?"

"The assassin won't be looking for us here."

He rolled his eyes at her. "You can't outrun the satellites, Syd. Not to mention the fact that I'm just a little hard to hide right now. How do you propose we get me in there? I think they might get upset if I bleed all over their polished floors."

"Don't worry, Steele. This is one hotel where they have plenty of security. If someone comes into this place who isn't a registered guest, they *will* be stopped. There's a French politician and his family who are here on vacation and they have elevated their procedures to accommodate him. It's the safest place I know of."

She balanced her weapon on his thigh. "Here. Protect yourself while I sign us in." She hesitated as she saw the agony of his expression. "Hang in there for me, okay?"

He took her weapon grudgingly. "What? You going soft, Syd Vicious?"

She gave him her own growl before she got out

and rushed across the sidewalk, toward the entrance.

Steele forced himself not to say anything while she left him out in the open like a neon sign begging the independent contractor to come finish him off.

As he looked around the car with all the obvious bullet holes and shattered glass, he started laughing at the thought of what it must look like outside with the fender damage too. Yeah. They looked like they belonged at a fine hotel, huh? It was a wonder management wasn't calling the police to escort the riff-raff off the premises.

He didn't know what would be worse.

Steele's eyes narrowed as a black unmarked sedan entered the lot, then slowed down as it came into view of his car. It crept along, slowing even more as it came alongside him.

He gripped the weapon, ready to fire.

It parked two spaces down. Grinding his teeth against the pain, he pulled the slide back to lock a bullet in the chamber as he held his breath and prepared to shoot.

Until he saw two young women get out of the car. They were chatting together as they put their designer purses on their shoulders and grabbed several shopping bags from the backseat. Completely oblivious to him, they chatted away as they headed for the hotel.

Steele drew a long breath as he switched the safety on and relaxed even though the pain of his shoulder was a throbbing nightmare. He'd learned a long time ago to deal with physical discomfort. The wound would either stop throbbing eventually or kill him.

At the moment, he had no preference for either one. *Just make the damn pain stop.*

Grinding his teeth, he tilted his head back and took long, deep breaths. He wasn't sure how much time had passed before he saw Sydney headed back toward the car.

She ran to his side.

"Stay there a second," she mouthed through the only piece of glass that wasn't shattered.

"You know, I can hear you just fine since most of the windows are gone," Steele said sarcastically, frowning as he watched her go to the trunk. A few seconds later, she returned with a long coat. She opened the door and made a face of sympathetic pain as she saw the blood that had soaked the faux leather interior of the car.

"Sorry, hon," he said, wiping the sweat from his brow. "I made a mess."

She didn't look amused. "Are you okay?"

"For a guy who's bleeding to death, I'm doing pretty good. You?"

She shook her head at him as she wiped her hand over his face. He closed his eyes at the tenderness of her unexpected actions. He didn't know how her touch could make him feel anything other than the pain of his injury, but it did. Hell, it even made him hard again.

She brushed his hair back from his brow. "We need to get you inside."

"What about the car?"

"It'll be taken care of."

Deciding not to argue, Steele got out slowly and pulled the coat on. He let out a groan as his shoulder flamed even more. He heard Syd hiss in sympathetic pain. She helped him put it on gently, then buttoned it.

It was a bit warm for a coat and no doubt it would gain them too much attention, but Steele went with it anyway. The coat would be less conspicuous than the blood.

"We need to get to the room, before I bleed through this," he mumbled.

She nodded as she tried to help him away from the car.

"I got it, Syd. It'll be too obvious if you help me."

"Okay," she said as she led him toward the hotel.

"I still think it's a mistake to stay here."

"Don't worry. This place is crawling with security."

Was that supposed to make him feel better? The last thing he needed was for any of them to be TV watchers who'd seen his supposed jailbreak.

"We're on the third floor," she said as they entered the lobby and she led him toward the elevators.

He would have put the sunglasses back on, but seeing how dark the lobby was, that would make him look even more suspicious than he already did. So Steele kept his head down, but he was well aware of everyone in the place. Luckily the two desk clerks were busy chatting and the only man who was obvious in the lobby was sitting with his laptop, working.

Syd pulled out her cell phone and pressed a button. She started speaking in spook talk, which meant she was saying nothing while updating someone on their situation. Steele had no idea who she was talking to and frankly he didn't care. His head was starting to buzz and the last thing he could afford was to pass out.

He leaned against the back wall of the elevator car while she pressed the button for their floor. It seemed to take forever before they went up and the doors opened onto an elegant hallway. Syd led him out to a room that was halfway down, between the elevator and the stairwell.

"Let me guess," he said as she fumbled with the lock, "not a coincidence?"

She shook her head as she hung up the phone. "We need an escape route."

"Good woman."

As soon as she had the door open, Steele headed for the bed so that he could finally lie down. But what he really wanted to do was pass out.

If only . . .

Syd bit her lip as she headed for Steele and helped him remove the coat, which was now completely soaked with blood. She sucked her breath in sharply at the sight of his wound. "I'm sorry. I didn't realize how bad it was."

"It's just a flesh wound," he said in a bad rendition of the old Monty Python movie, Holy Grail.

"What are you a loon?" she asked, using another quote from that scene.

He laughed, then groaned. "You like Python?"

She nodded as she dropped the coat to the floor. "See the violence inherent in the system. Help, help, I'm being oppressed."

His eyes were light even though his brow was creased with pain. "I need some towels, a knife, and a sewing kit with some kind of alcohol to soak it in."

Syd scowled at him. "Oh, you are not seriously going to tend this on your own, are you?"

"The only other way is to cauterize it. In which case I need towels, a knife, and a lighter."

She stared aghast at his calmness. "You're just going to dig it right out of your shoulder all by your lonesome, huh?"

"It would be nice for you to do it, but since I don't trust you not to nick an artery and kill me, I think I should handle it."

"Do this a lot, do you?" she asked as she went for the towels.

"Only when I have to."

And that made her stomach clench. She grabbed two towels and headed back to him. In all honesty, she was worried about him. He didn't look good, but then given his current state there was little wonder about that.

"Lie back," she said as she pressed the towels to the wound. "Andre will be here momentarily with help."

"No!"

She glared at him. "Yes, Steele. We can't afford to have you die on us. We're compromised enough."

She could tell he wanted to argue, but he merely laid his head back and kept his jaw clenched.

Someone knocked on the door. "Housekeeping."

Steele had the gun up and angled at the door before she could even reach for it. She motioned to him to stay down while she approached the door, half expecting it to be the hired killer.

She lifted herself up so that she could see out of the peephole. "Yes?"

"You need extra towels and alcohol?"

She relaxed only a hair at the code words. Still, she wasn't foolish enough to trust them completely. She glanced back at Steele who still had the gun up before she unbolted the door and slowly opened it.

The maid came in slowly with Andre one step behind.

Steele frowned at the small Hispanic woman in a cleaning lady's uniform as he let his arm with the gun fall to the side. Andre closed and locked the door.

The "maid" had an armload of towels, but instead of heading to the bathroom, she moved toward the bed. He watched as she set them down at his feet and unwrapped a doctor's bag.

"It's all right," she said to him as she moved to cut his shirt from him. "I'm Doctor Vasquez."

"I hope so," he said quietly. "I'd hate to have Alice dig a bullet out of my body. Call me crazy, but I don't think they teach that in cooking school, huh? Not to mention I don't ever recall the episode with Marcia, Greg, or Cindy getting a bullet wound."

She patted his arm before she unwrapped alcohol swabs, then set about cleaning his injury. "I know the pain makes everyone snappish."

"He's always like this," Syd said dryly.

He snorted at her. "Oh, I'm barely getting started. Just wait until the pain really gets bad."

Syd didn't say anything as she moved out of the way while the doctor prepared to give him a local.

"Any word on our friend?" she asked Andre.

Andre shook his head. "He lost the cops and vanished on the interstate. He was last headed north of here."

Syd sighed as if that information irritated her. "That tells us nothing."

"I know."

Syd looked back to where Steele was watching the doctor dig the bullet out of his shoulder. Her stomach shrank again. The man definitely had guts. She'd give him credit there. There was no way she could watch a doctor work on her without losing her lunch.

She turned back to Andre. "We're going to need a few supplies . . ."

"An M21 rifle," Steele said from the bed. "I also want a handgun, butterfly knife, and a few smoke bombs. A coded, secure cell phone and a gym bag. I need a Swiss Army knife, clay, wire, and electronic lock picks."

Syd frowned at him. He was really starting to sweat. "How on earth can you concentrate while she's digging a bullet out of your shoulder?"

He gave her a droll stare. "Mind over matter. Not to mention the fact that I don't want to die right now. I've still got a few things I want to do like shove my foot so far up the assassin's ass that he tastes leather for eternity . . . ow!" he snapped as the doctor twisted the unnumbed part of his arm.

Andre shook his head. "Okay I have his list. I'll procure a new car, dump the old one, and get started on everything—"

"Let us procure the car," Steele said. "It'll look more authentic that way."

Andre nodded. "All right, refresh. I'll get a car and park it on the street. I'll put everything in the backseat and lock it tight so that it'll look like you stole it. I'm going to assume you know how to hot wire?"

Steele nodded.

Andre looked at Syd. "You two be careful."

"We will."

At least she hoped. But it was hard to be certain since neither of them knew who they were up against.

Syd let Andre out of the room, then didn't speak while the doctor stitched Steele's wound. His strength was absolutely amazing and she had to admit that she was learning to respect this man. How had someone like him lost his temper to the point he took a shot at his C.O.?

It didn't make sense.

Which made her wonder what else had happened between them. What had the C.O. failed to mention and what secrets was Steele keeping? She had to admit she was a lot more attracted to him than she wanted to be. But how could a woman not be intrigued by someone who was so calm and capable in such an extreme situation?

She cocked her head as the doctor finished.

"He'll need someone to help him keep the wound clean," Dr. Vasquez said as she wiped the blood from his stitches. "I'm leaving an antibiotic, swabs, and dressing for the wound. Just make sure it doesn't get angry looking. We need to keep as much infection out of it as we can."

"Got it."

Dr. Vasquez handed her a small bottle. "I also have some Oxycoden for the pain, but I somehow think he might not want to use it since it'll make him drowsy. But just in case . . ."

"Thanks."

"You know, I'm right here, Doc," Steele said. "And I'm not stupid or deaf. I can hear you."

The doctor didn't say anything as she finished packing up. By the time she left the room, the good doctor again looked just like any other hotel maid.

Neither of them spoke as the doctor left with what appeared to be dirty towels.

Syd bolted the door before she returned to Steele, who looked like he was only one step away from passing out. "How you doing?"

"I've been better."

She could imagine. Syd went into the bathroom to get a cool compress.

After wringing it out in the sink, she returned to place it on his damp brow. "I'm sorry, Steele. I didn't know they'd do this to you."

His features relaxed as he closed his eyes. "It's okay, Syd. Who could have imagined that a man who heads up a company of paid assassins and mercenaries would be psychotic?"

She let out a disgusted breath. "Could you please lay off the sarcasm?"

"I can try, but I make no promises. I tend to excel at it."

Yes, he did. "Well, I guess if anyone is entitled to it . . . you are."

He opened one devilish eye to look up at her. "What a day, huh?" To her complete shock, he pushed himself up.

"What are you doing?"

"We can't afford to stay down."

Syd pushed him back. "I have your back, Steele. You need to rest."

Steele started to fight, but the sensation of her hands on his bare chest did something odd to him. It wasn't in him to trust anyone. It really wasn't and yet some part of him was betraying that code even as he tensed.

He lay back down.

Syd smiled at him and his groin jerked in reaction to the way her face softened. She put the cool compress back on his brow before she lightly stroked his hair. It was all he could do not to moan at how good she felt.

He hadn't had a woman take care of him like this since . . .

Ever.

It was true, he realized. Not even his mother had been allowed to coddle him. His father had been adamant that a boy didn't need any kind of sympathy. He'd been afraid of making his son weak. And most of the women he'd dated had been more into their own comforts than his.

"Other than you sister, you got any other siblings, Syd?"

"A younger brother."

He wondered if she'd ever done this for him. "Does your family know what you do for a living?"

"Not a clue. They think I'm an insurance agent."

"Are they proud of you?" He wasn't even sure why he asked that, but some part of him was curious. His father had never been proud of him. There were times when he suspected that the man couldn't even stand being in the same room with him and that was even before his arrest. Not that he cared. He'd come to terms with his father's emotionless state years ago.

"They are, but I wonder what they'd think if they ever knew what I really did for a living."

"I'm sure they'd be concerned for your safety."

She nodded. "What about you? Weren't your parents afraid of having a son in the military?"

"Hardly. My dad couldn't wait for the day I turned old enough to join so that he could kick me out of the house. My mom's the kind who would gladly hand me a rifle and tell me not to embarrass her as I head off to war. I think she must have been a Spartan mother in a former life."

She pulled the cloth from his brow.

Steele opened his eyes to find her staring at him with a strange, almost weepy look. "Is that why you don't go by your name?"

"Not really. No one ever really used it. My dad always called me boy, or son. My mom and sister used J.D. and all my friends used my last name just to jerk on me, so Steele stuck long ago."

She cocked her head as she wrinkled her nose at him. "You don't look like a J.D."

"No?"

She shook her head. "Besides, that has too many derogatory meanings."

"Such as?"

"Jury duty. Justice Department. Juris Doctorate. Juvenile delinquent."

He gave her a lopsided grin. "Rather appropriate. I am a felon."

She lightly stroked his cheek. "Maybe, but you look more like a Josh to me."

Steele reached up to cup the softness of her cheek. He focused on those lips of hers that always seemed to beg him for a hot kiss. "If I let you call me Josh, will you kiss me?"

"Steele . . . I already told you—"

He pulled her to him and cut her words off with a kiss. Steele sighed as he tasted the sweet warmth of her mouth. For a woman who wanted to put this morning behind them, she had a funny way of responding to his touch. She buried her hand in his hair as she tugged lightly on his bottom lip with her teeth.

And even though his arm hurt like hell, he knew that underneath that little skirt, she was still naked and he couldn't help wondering if this kiss was making her wet for him.

Syd found it hard to think with him kissing her like this. What was it about him that was so addictive?

He deepened his kiss as he took her hand into his and led it to his cock so that she could feel just how swollen he was. She cupped him through the denim, taking care not to hurt him. She moaned at the size of him, as an image of him in her arms tore through her. More than that, she remembered exactly how good he'd felt earlier.

He was right, she couldn't really put it out of her mind.

But she had no choice. Pulling her hand away, she withdrew from his lips.

She saw the look of disappointment in his eyes.

"I know," he said gruffly. "Not the time or place."

"Not to mention you're wounded."

"Yeah, but you know what they say."

She frowned. "About what?"

"You can't feel both pain and pleasure at the same time. Since I can't take the meds, you wouldn't want to ease my ache would you?"

She made a disgusted face at him. "You have to be

the king of bad come-on lines. Have you *ever* had a woman take you up on one of them?"

His look turned devilish. "All the time. Women love my debonnaire wit. Besides, it was worth a shot."

"You keep talking like that and you'll have another 'shot' to deal with."

"Yeah, yeah." He reached into his pocket.

Syd frowned as she saw him pull out a wad of dark green fabric. Her face flamed as she realized it was her underwear. "Give me that!"

He held it away from her. "Let me put them on you and I will."

"You've got to be kidding me."

He shook his head.

Syd glared at him. Honestly, it would be easy to take them back, but to do that would hurt his injury even more. It could even reopen it.

Just do it. Get it over with and get your underwear back.

It wasn't like he hadn't already touched her. That thought seriously backfired as she remembered exactly how good he'd felt this morning.

"Fine," she said angrily.

His dark eyes were taunting as he unwadded them and got up slowly. In all honesty, she couldn't breathe as she watched him kneel on the floor in front of her. With one hand on the wall to steady herself, she lifted one leg and inserted it into the panties.

She knew from his position that he had a perfect view of her underneath her skirt. It was strangely erotic, especially given the heated look on his face. She knew he was thinking of how she'd tasted earlier and the truth was, she wanted to feel his mouth on her again. Her body was already on fire as she felt the moisture pooling for him. Licking her lips, she lifted the other leg.

Steele pulled the panties up slowly, rising with them until he stood before her. He pulled the hem of her skirt up all the way to her waist before he slid his hand down between their bodies.

"Look me in the eyes, Syd, and tell me you're not wet for me. Tell me right now that you're not aching to feel me touch you."

She couldn't speak. He was right. Her body was absolutely throbbing with bittersweet pain.

As he tugged at her panties, his knuckles grazed against her sensitive cleft. She moaned in spite of herself.

One corner of his mouth quirked up as he released her underwear and ran one long, hard finger against her. She shivered as he wiggled it against the part of her that was swollen for him.

Steele wanted to shout in triumph at how wet she really was and at the fact that she wasn't pulling away from him. Dipping his head down, he kissed those plump, taunting lips. She clutched him to her as he slid his finger deep inside her.

So much for forgetting about this morning, huh? But he would never tease her with that. The truth was he didn't want her to forget anymore than he wanted her to pull away from him. Pain or no pain, he wanted another taste of her.

More than that, he wanted her to ride his cock the way she rode his fingers.

His body burning, he'd started to reach for his fly when he happened to see a strange shadow flash on the wall beside her.

Syd whimpered slightly as Steele pulled back from her white-hot body. He was now looking at the window and not her. Scowling, she turned to see what had him distracted.

But before she could do anything more than twist at the waist, Steele sank to his knees and pulled her to the floor with him.

Three seconds later, she heard a pop in the wall. She looked up and went pale.

There was a bullet hole in the vicinity of where her head had been just a second before.

Carnival Pride™

April 2-9, 2006
7-Day Exotic Mexican Riviera Itinerary

DAY	PORT	ARRIVE	DEPART
Sun	Los Angeles/Long Beach, CA		4:00 P.M.
Mon	"Book Lover's Day" at Sea		
Tue	"Book Lover's Day" at Sea		
Wed	Puerto Vallarta, Mexico	8:00 A.M.	10:00 P.M.
Thu	Mazatlan, Mexico	9:00 A.M.	6:00 P.M.
Fri	Cabo San Lucas, Mexico	7:00 A.M.	4:00 P.M.
Sat	"Book Lover's Day" at Sea		
Sun	Los Angeles/Long Beach, CA	9:00 A.M.	

Ports of call subject to weather conditions.

TERMS AND CONDITIONS

Payment Schedule:
50% due upon booking
Full and final payment due by February 10, 2006
Acceptable forms of payment are Visa, MasterCard, American Express, Discover, and checks. The cardholder must be one of the passengers traveling. A fee of $25 will apply for all returned checks. Check payments must be made payable to Advantage International, LLC and sent to: Advantage International, LLC, 195 North Harbor Drive, Suite 4206, Chicago, IL 60601

CHANGE/CANCELLATION:
Notice of change/cancellation must be made in writing to Advantage International, LLC.

Change:
Changes in cabin category may be requested and can result in increased rate and penalties. A name change is permitted 60 days or more prior to departure and will incur a penalty of $50 per name change. Deviation from the group schedule and package is a cancellation.

Cancellation:

181 days or more prior to departure	$250 per person
180–121 days or more prior to departure	50% of the package price
120–61 days prior to departure	75% of the package price
60 days or less prior to departure	100% of the package price (nonrefundable)

U.S. and Canadian citizens are required to present a valid passport or original birth certificate and state issued photo ID (driver's license). All other nationalities must contact the consulate of the various ports that are visited for verification of documentation.

We strongly recommend trip cancellation insurance!

ADDITIONAL TERMS
This offer is only good on purchases made from August 30, 2005, through April 1, 2006. This offer cannot be combined with other offers or discounts. The discount can only be used for the Authors at Sea cruise and is not valid for any other Carnival cruises. You must submit an original purchase receipt as proof of purchase in order to be eligible for the discount. Void outside of the U.S. and where prohibited, taxed, or restricted by law. Coupons may not be reproduced, copied purchased or sold. Incomplete submissions or submissions in violation of these terms will not be honored. Not responsible for late, lost, incomplete, illegible, postage due or misdirected mail. Submissions will not be returned. Improper use or redemption constitutes fraud. Any fraudulent submission (including duplicate requests) will be prosecuted to the fullest extend of the law. Theft, diversion, reproduction, transfer, sale or purchase of this offer form and/or cash register receipts is prohibited and constitutes fraud. Consumer must pay sales taxes on the price of the cruise.

For further details call 1-877-ADV-NTGE or visit www.AuthorsatSea.com.

For booking form and complete information,
go to www.AuthorsatSea.com or call 1-877-ADV-NTGE.

Complete coupon and booking form and mail both to:
Advantage International, LLC
195 North Harbor Drive, Suite 4206, Chicago, IL 60601

12935